AN ENEMY OF THE PEOPLE . . .

Granddad told me about Amanda Green, a teacher in a small town near San Francisco. When she didn't show up at school one morning, someone went to see if she was hurt—and found her house trashed, all her files and computer gone, but no sign of her.

And her valuables untouched. No ordinary burglars.

Her neighbors knew nothing. But they'd heard the familiar sounds of the sirens and car doors slamming and thumping feet in the middle of the night . . . and they'd closed their houses up tight.

A terrorist, claimed the HSS, inciting her students to rebel against the state.

A homely grandmother, a dedicated teacher, loved by her students, and respected by the community, a terrorist? For teaching her students the meaning of life, liberty and the pursuit of happiness?

Amanda Green was the spark that lit the fire. It started quietly, like a burning ember, as groups held sporadic protests here and there. Only to be brutally repressed by the HSS police.

The TV coverage inflamed the nation. Within days millions of people across the country were parading with signs saying "Liberty or Death," "Don't Tread on Me," and even "Taxation is Theft."

—from "Renegade" by Mark Tier

Baen Books also edited by
Mark Tier & Martin H. Greenberg

Give Me Liberty

VISIONS OF LIBERTY

edited by
Mark Tier and
Martin H. Greenberg

Visions of Liberty

This is a work of fiction. All the characters and events portrayed in this book are fictional, and any resemblance to real people or incidents is purely coincidental.

A Baen Books Original

Baen Publishing Enterprises
P.O. Box 1403
Riverdale, NY 10471
www.baen.com

ISBN: 0-7434-8838-5

Cover art by Carol Heyer

First printing, July 2004

Distributed by Simon & Schuster
1230 Avenue of the Americas
New York, NY 10020

Production by Windhaven Press, Auburn, NH
Printed in the United States of America

Contents

Introduction: Visions of Liberty

by Mark Tier

Imagine we're on a plane; we've crossed an ocean, we've landed; we're taxiing up to the gate. As we file off the plane we have our passports ready.

But something rather strange happens: no one wants to look at them. We see no official-looking types of any kind.

Perhaps we have to get our luggage first. But as we come down to the baggage carousels we don't see any customs or immigration officials; nor do we see any barrier between us and the outside world. We can pick up our bags and walk straight out of the terminal off an international flight into a taxi. Which is exactly what we do.

Welcome to Freelandia, a country—perhaps it's better to call it a place—which is truly free: there's no government to invade and restrict our liberties. Of course, Freelandia doesn't exist (yet) except in my imagination.

And in science fiction, the literature of the imagination. Where else can we skim across the surface of black holes, dive into the sun, and journey to the beginning, the end, and the edge of the universe? And visit a society without government that works.

Could that be possible in reality, not just in science fiction? After all, if you counted the number of societies without government on the fingers of one hand, you wouldn't even open your fist. And if government disappeared, wouldn't the result be anarchy? Chaos? Isn't government an essential prerequisite of peace and order?

If we were to travel back in time, some ten or twenty thousand years, before the development of agriculture and the beginnings of civilization, we wouldn't find any governments as we know them today. *Homo sapiens* were hunter-gatherers, living in tribes of some hundred or so people. Yes, tribes have rulers too. Chiefs and shamans. But tribal chieftains rarely have the power to *force* their decisions on the members of their tribe. They are more like leading citizens who rule by moral suasion and consensus rather than police power.

That all changed with the development of agriculture some ten thousand years ago. For the first time, a few dozen square miles of land could support human populations much larger than a hundred-odd hunter-gatherers. For the first time, our ancestors stayed fixed in one place.

For the first time, there was something to loot.

Pick up any history book and you'll find a record of kings, princes, shahs, chiefs, emperors, czars and their battles. What were they fighting over? Today, governments will tell you they're fighting for freedom. But freedom is a very recent phenomenon. The concept of freedom originated with the Greeks and Romans, but did not become a part of the political landscape until the Renaissance just a few hundred years ago.

Even today, words that we take for granted like "freedom," "rights," "liberty," and "free will" simply have no counterparts in most of the world's languages. For most of the world's people, these concepts just don't exist.

No medieval king or Indian maharajah ever fought for freedom. They fought to keep their power or to expand it. Their prize: the surplus they could extract from the peasantry that financed the building of their glittering palaces and ornate churches and temples. Today's major tourist attractions—the pyramids of Egypt, the Taj Mahal, the Angkor Wat, Notre Dame— were all built by forced or slave labor for the pure benefit of the rulers. There was no pretense that "we're doing this for your own good."

Many times, kingdoms and empires were overrun by latter-day hunter-gatherers. The Greeks and Romans called them barbarians; the Europeans called them Huns; the Chinese called them Mongols. They came with only one objective: to loot as much as they could.

And sometimes they stayed; after all, a steady stream of loot in the form of taxes can be more attractive than the spoils of hit-and-run raiding.

The greatest of these was Genghis Khan. His empire collapsed upon his death but his grandson, Kublai Khan, established the first alien dynasty to rule all China—the Yuan (1279–1368). History, of course, is written by the victors, so Genghis Khan and Kublai Khan were transformed from bandit leaders into great princes. After all, only *losers* remain barbarians.

From the agricultural revolution until the Renaissance, mankind had the choice of rule or be ruled; to be the oppressed or the oppressor. The idea of freedom—that you should neither rule nor be ruled, but be left alone to pursue your own happiness in your own way, and grant others the same right—did not exist, just as it still doesn't exist in most parts of the world.

When you are ruled you have no rights. You are property. Such is the meaning of "the divine right of kings," the ideology which flowered in Europe in the Middle Ages. Kingdoms did not have citizens; they had vassals. Under "the divine right of kings," everything *and everybody* in the kingdom belonged to the monarch. Kings fought each other for territory and to the victor went the divine right to rule. In China, when a new dynasty was established they said that the old one had lost "the mandate of heaven." In Japan, as in Thailand, the ruler was thought to be the representative of God on earth. All these names are no more than Orwellian double-speak to dress up and legitimize the reality that might was right.

We can trace the origin of government back to the

first thug who spied the opportunity to live a life of ease on the backs of the peasants. His spiritual successors are still in our midst today, with names like Lenin, Stalin, Mao Zedong, Pol Pot, and Idi Amin—and those petty bureaucrats who love to flaunt their power over you whenever you have some dealing with a government agency.

A revolution in the idea of government began with the Renaissance, was crystallized by John Locke among others, and came into being for the first time in human history with the American Revolution. The idea: that government should serve man instead of man serving government; that rulers should be the people's *servants*, not their masters. That people have the *innate* right to life, liberty, and the pursuit of happiness, and that the purpose of government is to defend those rights, not to invade them for the benefit of the few at the top.

But how to create such a government? Because what sets government apart from every other organization is that it is the legal instrument of force within a society. No other group has the right to use force except in self-defense, and the people who do we call criminals.

When so much force is concentrated in one organization's hands, how can you limit its use? And you *must*, if you want to live in a free society; only the initiation of force can divert you from the pursuit of your own happiness. Only the initiation of force can threaten your life. The greatest danger to your freedom is not some foreign power—it is your own government. When Thomas Jefferson said "the price of liberty is eternal vigilance," it was the government of the United States that he was warning his fellow citizens to be vigilant against.

The solution of America's founding fathers was to delineate and restrict the role of government. Via the Constitution and the Bill of Rights they clearly (they thought) laid down what government could do, saying that everything else was reserved to the people.

Unfortunately, the imperative of every human organization is to grow. Businesses grow by making more sales and gaining market share; associations grow by signing up more members; governments grow by expanding their power.

This never happens overnight; government grows by salami tactics, slice by slice. For example, when the income tax was introduced in 1913 no one in his right mind would have suggested a top rate of 90 percent. In fact, there was considerable support for capping the income tax at 4 percent. This was shot down by those who argued that specifying such a maximum rate would mean the income tax would rapidly rise to that (then) horrific level. Can you imagine living in a world where an income tax of 4 percent is unthinkable!?

So the government of the United States has grown, slice by unnoticeable slice, till it bears scant resemblance to the government at the country's birth.

Perhaps there is some other way to put a government's use of force into a straitjacket from which it cannot escape. To the best of my knowledge, no one has ever come up with a convincing, workable proposal along these lines.

As Ayn Rand put it in *The Fountainhead*: "The only

way in which we can have any law at all is to have as little of it as possible. I see no ethical standard by which to measure the whole unethical concept of a State, except in the amount of time, of thought, of money, of effort and obedience, which a society extorts from its every member."[1]

If the initiation of force is unethical, then it logically follows that government, as we know it, is also unethical. But that, of course, does not answer the question: Could a society without government actually work? If it's hard to imagine a world in which a 4 percent income tax is unthinkable, it's much harder to imagine how a governmentless society could avoid breaking out into a civil war, or simply degenerating into chaos.

That's a common view; after all, the word "anarchy" is generally used to mean "chaos in the absence of government." But that's to assume, mistakenly, that government is the source of law and order.

On January 24, 1848, the California gold rush began. But it took eighteen years for the U.S. Congress to enact a mining law to regulate such discoveries. Meanwhile, gold production in California boomed. How could that have happened without a governmental framework to recognize mining claims, register titles, and regulate disputes?

The miners created their own. They established districts, registries, procedures for establishing and registering a claim and buying and selling claim titles, and a system for resolving disputes. Officers were usually elected, including the recorder of claims. Their private arrangements were recognized in California state courts; and Congress's 1866 statute "explicitly noted that all explorations for minerals would be subject to those 'local customs or rules of miners in the several mining districts' that were not in conflict with the laws of the United States."[2]

This is just one of many historical examples of what Friedrich Hayek calls "spontaneous order," demonstrating that neither government nor even leaders are needed for order to appear.

So perhaps Freelandia is possible after all. And thanks to the rich imagination of science fiction authors, we can visit a plethora of Freelandias.

Although there's a strong individualistic streak within science fiction, until recently very few stories were set in a completely free society. One reason, perhaps, is that all fiction thrives on conflict and a truly free society is so peaceful that there's not very much to write about. So in stories like Eric Frank Russell's classic " . . . And Then There Were None," the conflict comes from outside, in the form of invaders from an authoritarian empire. (You'll find this story—and some other classics of this genre—in this book's companion volume, *Give Me Liberty*, also published by Baen Books.)

Another example is James Hogan's (in my opinion) sadly neglected *Voyage From Yesteryear*. L. Neil Smith has been very prolific in this area, two of his novels, *The Probability Broach* and *Pallas*, winning the Prometheus Award for Best Libertarian Fiction. In his most recent book, *Forge of Elders*, humans meet aliens who are, horror of horrors, capitalists!

Here in this volume are nine more visions of liberty, all set in societies without governments that work.

As you'd expect from the fertile minds of science fiction authors, each is very different from the others.

They are not Utopias. Like real life, there's pain and suffering, as one story here (I won't tell you which one) tragically shows us.

And there are visions of how, in the words of Aristotle, life could and should be. A cornucopia of Freelandias that I hope inspire and entertain you as they have me.

---

[1] Ayn Rand, *The Fountainhead* (Plume, New York, 1994), pp. 101-102
[2] Hernando de Soto, *The Mystery of Capital* (Basic Books: New York, 2000), pp. 146–147

The Unnullified World

by Lloyd Biggle, Jr.

The world was named Llayless. Its principal community—in fact, its only community of any size—was a desert mining center named Pummery. A number of narrow-gauge electric railway lines left Pummery through tubes built to protect their tracks from the swirling sands. When they reached the steep slopes of the surrounding mountains, they emerged to become cog railways.

At one of the railheads, swinging down from the single passenger car that was attached to an interminable string of empty ore cars, Birk Dantler encountered a sign that announced LAUGHINGSTOCK MINES. A short distance beyond it, he found a tiny town nestled amidst the clutter of the mining operation. There were machines to load ore into the railway cars. Farther up the slope, there were machines extracting ore from the mountain. Other machines were bringing ore to the railhead. The town was little more than a spread of small worker's cottages except for a neat, prefab building that housed the mining offices, and, standing next to it, another prefab building that was, unmistakably, a school.

All of this represented a substantial capital outlay for a mining claim on a remote world, which meant that the mines collectively known as Laughingstock were productive enough to provide that capital.

Dantler went directly to the mining office and asked a clerk for information. The clerk looked at him narrowly. "You got a reason for being here, fellow?"

Dantler presented his credentials. The clerk glanced at them and winced. "GBI? You're a Galactic Bureau of Investigation Officer? What's the Inter-World Council want with us?" When Dantler did not answer, he shrugged and grinned. "Your credentials say anyone who doesn't cooperate with you will be deported instantly, and that's reason enough to cooperate. You must know personally all of the many skeletons in the Llayless Mining Corporation's closets to be able to pry a document like that out of it." He returned the credentials. "What is it you want to know?"

"Nothing complicated, I'm sure. Where is the mine called Last Hope?"

"That's fairly complicated until you get through the Laughingstock diggings. After that there's a path. I'd better draw you a map." He went over it with Dantler, and when he was satisfied that his directions were clear, he leaned back and scrutinized Dantler's energy-charged form, taut face—no one had ever called him handsome—and neat, conservative dress. "You prepared for a long walk?" he asked.

"Isn't there any transportation?"

"There are a couple of pack mules, but they're kept on the other side of the mountain. Figure on a long walk."

"How do they bring the ore out?"

"Slowly and with great difficulty. When they've accumulated enough, they load the two pack mules and fill two or three handcarts. All the men they have take the day off and haul ore. The Llayless Mining Corporation built them a short siding off our railway line, and it keeps an ore car parked there. When they get it filled, the Corporation hauls it away and leaves an empty for them. That's as much as it's willing to do for a marginal operation. The men at Last Hope confidently expect the vein they are working to get richer instead of playing out as most marginal mines do. All miners are optimists."

Then he leaned over his desk to look at Dantler's feet. "At least you've got sturdy shoes. As I told you, it's a long walk. I've never tackled it myself, no reason to, but those who have say it's a good ten miles, and half of that is a steep climb up to the pass. It's best to make a two-day trip of it, and you have to figure on an uncomfortable night. There's no hotel or bed and breakfast place—no houses at all, in fact. And you'll be lucky if they can provide you with a sleeping bag, but you'd be an idiot to try to find your way back here in the dark. You got urgent business with the Last Hope?"

"I think it's urgent," Dantler said. "I'm investigating a murder."

The clerk nodded thoughtfully. "I did hear something about that, but it must have been two or three years ago. You just getting around to investigate now?"

"God's mill grinds slow but sure," Dantler said and left the clerk staring after him perplexedly.

Dantler found the path without too much difficulty and began to climb. It led steeply upward through a dense forest of native trees with large, ovate, yellowish leaves and shaggy green bark with strips of red in it. They seemed to exude fresh-smelling oxygen. Without them, the climb into thinner air would have been far more difficult.

When he reached the top, he discovered that the steep descent was almost as difficult as the climb. It was late in the day when he finally reached the Last Hope diggings. There was a scattering of holes with heaps of dirt around them. He walked on, past several small tents, past a makeshift corral from which the two mules eyed him suspiciously, past a more ambitious digging that had produced a tunnel burrowed into the mountain.

Suddenly he received a sharp blow on the head that nearly knocked him senseless. He reacted instinctively, twisting as he fell, somersaulting into a thick growth of shrubbery, and coming to his feet ready for action.

There were three bearded, shabby-looking men facing him. All of them were armed with whatever they had been able to grab when they saw him coming. One brandished the handle of some kind of hand-operated machine. Another had a piece of firewood. The third had an ax raised high over his head. They began to edge forward.

Dantler's head ached, and when he brushed his hand across a swelling lump, it came away bloody. He sensed that the men were about to rush him, so he decided to act before they did and talk afterward. He drew a small electronic pistol from an inner pocket and sprayed them.

They were halted in their tracks. One at a time they toppled forward and lay twitching on the ground. Dantler noticed a spring nearby, and he went to it, drank deeply, and washed the blood from his head. Then he seated himself on a convenient boulder and waited. He felt exhausted, and his head throbbed fiercely. He wanted to lie down with the three men and twitch for a few minutes, but he couldn't spare himself that luxury.

As the charge began to wear off, his victims displayed the usual reactions. They rolled over onto their backs. They flexed arms and legs. They touched their faces and wriggled tingling fingers. None of them had come through his ordeal unscathed. One, a man with a long gray beard and a fierce-looking mustache, had a bloody nose from his fall. Another, with a blond beard, had smacked his forehead on a stone. It was already a black and blue swollen lump. The third, with a neatly trimmed black beard and newish-looking clothing, was going to have a splendid black eye.

Finally the man with the mustache, sat up. He stared at Dantler.

"Bashing a visiting stranger over the head is a perverted kind of hospitality," Dantler observed pleasantly. "Or were you expecting someone else?"

The other two men struggled to sitting positions. "What'd you do to us?" the man with a blond beard asked.

"Something a trifle more civilized than the bashing you had in mind," Dantler said. "I trust that one dose will be sufficient."

"Hell, yes," the man with the mustache said. "Who are you?"

"As I said, a visiting stranger. I walked ten miles over the mountain to ask the favor of some information. I wasn't expecting this kind of welcome. I have credentials issued by this world's factor. Perhaps you would like to examine them." He held one of them under the man's nose. "As you see, a word from me, and the Last Hope mine will have exhausted its last hope. All of its employees will leave Llayless on the next ship. I was hoping I wouldn't have to use it. Are you ready to talk?"

"No reason not to. We thought you were a whacker."

"What's a whacker that makes him deserve that kind of reception?"

"Whackers kill miners and take over their claims."

"Really. Are there whackers on Llayless?"

"Don't know of any, but we've encountered them elsewhere. Better to act first and then ask questions."

"Only yesterday I talked with Jeffrey Wallingford Pummery, who is the esteemed—I hope—factor of the world of Llayless and he told me Llayless was the most law-abiding world in the galaxy."

The man laughed derisively. "That's a good one. Llayless has got no government. It's got no laws—just a few regulations about mining. If it had laws, there would be no one to enforce them. It's got no law officers. It's got no judges and courts. On my mining claim, I'm the law—that's what my contract says. The only law on Llayless is what the person who controls a bit of ground can enforce at the end of a stick."

The man with the black beard had recovered enough to get to his feet and hobble around. "Never expected to get stunned out here in the mountains," he said resentfully. "What's this information you want?"

"I want to hear all about the murder of Douglas Vaisey by Roger Lefory."

"Never heard of either of them," the man with the black beard said. "What's that got to do with us?"

"Walt is a newcomer," the man with the drooping mustache explained to Dantler. "The murder happened before his time. I thought all that was dead history."

"Murders are never dead history."

"What do you want to know?"

"Everything," Dantler said. "By the way, who are you?"

"Kit Grumery. I'm the claim owner here. Everything I know about that murder won't take long to tell. My men work on shares, see. They get fed but nothing fancy. They make their own sleeping arrangements. Beyond that, whatever the ore smelts down to is divided into shares. It's hard work and poor pay, but we all hope to hit a mother lode and get rich. Lefory and Vaisey were working for the Laughingstock, and they came here taking a gamble on sharing in something big. Dougie was a nice kid, a good worker. Lefory was a loafer. He took so many breaks it sometimes was hard to say whether he was working or not, and he had a hell of a temper. He and Dougie got in an argument over Lefory not doing his fair share, and Lefory charged at him and brained him with a hand ax. Killed him instantly. That's all there was to it."

"Not quite all," Dantler said. "What did you do then?"

"Did what I always do when a worker is killed. Mining is dangerous work. Death doesn't happen often, but it does happen, and there's a procedure to follow. We buried Dougie—I can show you his grave if you like. Regulations don't call for it, but we held a bit of a ceremony for him. Shorty Klein—he's working further up the mountain today—has an old Bible, and he read a couple of passages and did a prayer, and I carved a marker for Dougie's grave myself. As I said, he was a nice kid, and I liked him. That's all, except that I also took care of the paperwork."

"What sort of paperwork?"

"Every death has to be reported to the Llayless Record Section. It insists on knowing who's still on the planet. I also figured what Dougie had coming from his work share, and I filled out the form the Record Section requires and sent it down to Pummery along with a voucher for the money due Dougie and the few trifles of personal effects he owned. The Record Section is supposed to cash in a dead man's return ticket and put the amount received with the other assets the man had. Everyone arriving here has to place on file a fully paid return ticket to the world he came from or they won't let him off the ship."

"I know about that," Dantler said. "I suppose it's sort of a guarantee he won't become a public charge."

"Right. Records is supposed to cash the return ticket and send the money along with all of his other assets to his designated beneficiary. Whether it actually does this I couldn't say. And that's the whole story."

"You didn't report the murder to the police authorities?"

"What police authorities? I just told you—Llayless has got no government. It's got no authorities, police or any other kind. Who would I report it to?"

"Then a murderer can't be arrested and brought to trial?"

"Who would arrest him, and who would hold his trial? There's no police. There's no court. There's no judge. There's no jail for wrongdoers. Actually, it was a dirty shame. Dougie was well liked, and Lefory was a jerk. Everyone was angry about what happened."

"But you let him carry on scot-free as though he hadn't done anything?"

"I wouldn't say that. We shouldered him right out of camp."

"How did you do that?"

"No one would talk with him. No one would work with him. No one would eat with him—we form teams and take turns cooking. No team would have him. No one would kip with him. After a couple of days of that, he left. Sneaked out of camp early one morning and walked over the mountain to the Laughingstock. It was almost a day before anyone missed him."

"That seems like a rather mild punishment for a murderer," Dantler observed dryly. "What happened to him after that?"

"He got a job at the Laughingstock. Llayless's mines are always short of labor. But we let the Laughingstock workers know about him, and he didn't stay there long. Probably they shouldered him, too."

"But you don't know that for certain."

"No, I don't know it for certain. But I know he didn't stay there long."

"Do you know where he went from there?"

"I never heard him mentioned again after he left the Laughingstock, but you can bet that the workers there passed the information about him along to workers at the next place he caught on."

Dantler stayed overnight. The men gave him what was, for the Last Hope, a fabulous luxury—a tent all to himself. The food was rough but filling. The other amenities were just a shade above zero. There was barely enough hot water—heated over a campfire—to go around. There was plenty of ore soup, though—a hot, stimulating drink made with local herbs—and it was obvious that no one at the camp went hungry. Early the next morning he walked back over the mountain to the Laughingstock. All of the camp's men came along to make certain he didn't get lost. The loaded mules came, too, and the men took turns pushing cartloads of ore.

"Paths look different going the other way," Kit Grumery explained.

At the Laughingstock settlement, he took his leave of his Last Hope companions and went directly to the office and asked to see the manager. A different clerk was on duty, and for a second time Dantler presented his credentials. He was admitted to the manager's office at once and greeted by Ed Mullard, a grizzled oldster who had spent his life scratching for pay dirt and finally rode to riches on the coattails of someone luckier than he who found the Laughingstock claim.

He scowled at Dantler's credentials, then scowled more fiercely at Dantler. "I hope you're not about to interfere with our operations. There's nothing for the GBI to investigate here."

"My information is that you harbored a murderer. That's what I want to know about."

Mullard leaned back and stared at Dantler. "If there's ever been a murderer on this claim, it's news to me."

"A man named Roger Lefory came to work for you immediately after murdering a fellow worker at Last Hope."

"Lefory," Mullard mused. "Yes, I do remember him because he was always complaining about something. But I had no idea he was a murderer."

"Tell me about him," Dantler said.

Mullard leaned back and meditated. "For one thing, he was the most accident-prone man I've ever met. Mining is a dangerous business, and things do happen, but with Lefory it got to be ridiculous. Tunnels only seemed to collapse while he was in them. Scaffolding gave way only when he was passing it. Machinery failed dangerously only when he was tending it. Hot water spilled only when he was there to get burned. He kept complaining that his fellow workers arranged these accidents, which of course was nonsense. No one could have arranged all that. They were the sort of things that are bound to occur from time to time, and he happened to be unlucky. Finally a gear broke on a tipcart loaded with ore, and he was buried up to his neck and had to be dug out. He just missed being buried alive. The next day he turned up missing. There's a passenger car on every ore train, so it's easy for men to desert if for any reason they don't like their work here."

"Do you know where he went?"

"To Pummery. That's where all the ore trains go. He found a job at one of the smelters. I received a notice with the usual request for his work history."

"Did you send down his personal effects and any wages he had due him?"

"By quitting without notice, he forfeited any wages owed to him. I know nothing about his personal effects. Probably he took with him anything he wanted to keep. He hadn't been here long enough to have accumulated much."

Obviously Mullard had nothing more to tell him, so Dantler boarded the passenger car on the next departing ore train and rode down to Pummery in a totally frustrated mood.

The world of Llayless had been named after an early explorer, but through eight sectors of space it was known as "Lawless." Among worlds, it was a genuine oddity—a single-owner world. Old Albert Nicols, the original owner, who had managed, by dint of rigged poker games, loans foreclosed with indecent haste, and questionable wills to consolidate several hundred claims into one title deed, had taken a young wife just before he died. By that time Llayless was an extremely wealthy mining world with only a tiny fraction of its potential being exploited, and the widow inherited everything. She immediately established her residence several sectors away on a world that offered far more comfort than the world of Llayless could have provided for her, and from that vantage point she kept close tabs on her accumulating mining royalties and gave generously to charities.

Single ownership was not the world's only peculiarity. It had no government. Those who leased land and mineral rights were responsible, by contract, for their holdings and everyone they permitted on them. Some administered them in a stern, paternal fashion; some were tyrannical dictators; a few ran their holdings congenially as partnerships. Occasionally one let things degenerate into rowdyism but only until the world's factor heard about it.

Finally, the world of Llayless was "Unnullified." This was a form of probation inflicted on all recently discovered and newly settled worlds. The sacred constitution of the Inter-World Federation guaranteed certain human rights and considerations throughout its territory, and a world that failed in this respect was nullified, which meant that it was totally embargoed. A world without government was placed in limbo with the label "Unnullified" until it got its act together. After a reasonable time the world would either be normalized or changed to Nullified status.

Birk Dantler had looked into the Llayless's history before he left on his assignment. He was startled to find that there had been no updating of its status since it was, as a newly settled world, marked "Unnullified." He took the matter to his superiors, who took it to their superiors. Someone had goofed. As a result, Dantler was given an important subsidiary mission. In addition to tracking down a murderer, he was to give the world a long-overdue evaluation of its status. If the unusual nature of the world posed any complications for him, he had the authority to recommend immediate reclassification to "Nullified."

Arriving on Llayless, Dantler discovered that custom and immigration procedures were both informal and simple. There almost weren't any. Each new arrival had to place on file a fully paid return ticket to the world he came from. His fingerprints and the name of his next-of-kin were recorded, but that was only so the Llayless Mining Corporation would know who was on the world just in case some other world's investigative branch should come looking, and so there would be someone to notify and send his property to in case he died. These formalities taken care of, a wave of the hand conferred the freedom of the planet.

One thing about this process puzzled Dantler. As the new arrival passed through the gate that opened on the world of Llayless, he was immediately swarmed upon by a dozen or so lean and voracious-looking men who reminded Dantler of a flock of vultures. He asked the man ahead of him in line who the vultures were.

"Labor brokers," the other replied. "Didn't anyone warn you? You have to watch yourself, or you may suddenly find you've signed away your life for the next seven years. If you catch so much as a glimpse of a piece of paper coming your way, put your hands in your pockets. If you find a stylus in your fingers that you don't remember picking up, throw it as far as you can. Be careful who you drink with. They have to get your signature and also your fingerprints on the contract, but no contract has ever been voided because the man who signed it claimed he was drunk."

When Dantler's turn came, he brushed the finger-printing pad aside along with the rest of the formalities and passed his credentials across the counter: passport with several pages bearing arrival and departure stamps from various worlds, an embossed identification card, and a letter. The clerk scrutinized them in turn and, after giving Dantler a startled glance, turned to a computer, typed briefly, and accepted the result from a printer. He added one more stamp to Dantler's passport. Then, as an afterthought, he carefully printed a number beside it.

He handed Dantler the form the computer had produced. "You should keep this with your passport," he said. "You'll be asked for it when you leave Llayless. Just in case you lose it, which has happened, I've recorded your arrival number in your passport. If you lose that, there'll have to be a tedious investigation, so don't lose it. The town is only half a kilometer from the port, but don't try to walk there unless you're equipped with sand shoes. There's a conveyor you can ride, or there's a 'bus that's a little faster and a lot less comfortable."

He added, "Welcome to Llayless. I hope you enjoy your stay," and turned to the next new arrival. Towing his space trunk, Dantler passed through the gate and was surprised to be totally ignored by the labor brokers. The clerk must have given them some sort of signal.

Dantler headed directly for the exit and opted for the 'bus. When he arrived on a new world, he wanted to see as much as possible as quickly as possible, and he knew he wouldn't be seeing anything at all while riding in a conveyor tube. The 'bus was a sturdy, tracked conveyance, and a glance at it told a traveler all he needed to know about travel in the deserts of Llayless. Mountains loomed on all sides, providing a distant haze of superb beauty. The desert was a disaster of sand dunes and slag heaps. Crossing the former, the 'bus left a cloud of sand behind. With slag heaps, it was a cloud of dust.

Pummery, the principal commercial city of the world of Llayless, had been almost invisible when the spaceship was settling in for a landing. It was a complex of massive domes enclosing business buildings, residences, smelters, and the immense nuclear power plant, with tubes for the network of railway lines that extended in all directions like spreading tentacles. Domes and tubes were more than half buried in the shifting sands of a narrow, elongated desert. The spaceport, unfortunately, had to be kept cleared of sand, and a platoon of dozers worked full time at the task.

The domes and tubes were an afterthought engendered by necessity. In its remote past, which could have been as long ago as three or four decades, the municipality of Pummery had been a struggling desert mining town calling itself Struth. Then someone struck it rich, and the manipulators took over. After the usual period of underhanded contrivance and downright chicanery, Old Albert emerged triumphant.

When he died, his widow hired a factor, one Jeffrey Wallingford Pummery, to manage the world for her, after which she shook the sands of Llayless from her heels forever. One of the factor's first acts was to manipulate a name change. Llayless's principal commercial center, Struth, became Pummery, thus splashing the factor's own name prominently on the world's map. No one objected. As long as Pummery operated efficiently and honestly and kept her royalties coming, the widow didn't bother herself with minor things like name changes. The factor was, for all that Dantler had heard, a shrewd and honest operator who built for the future.

The Llayless desert was a terrible place for a world's commercial center, but Pummery was perfectly situated to serve mining operations in the mountains on all sides. The narrow-gauge electric railway lines bringing ore to the smelters from the mines were able to coast down the mountain slopes, thus hauling their loads at a profit because they generated electricity in the process. The only cost was for replacing their frequently worn-out brakes.

Those mines were rich enough to occupy the Llayless Mining Corporation for years to come. Until they played out, the remainder of the world would remain untouched.

The 'bus stopped in front of the Llayless Mining Corporation's world headquarters. Dantler climbed out along with several others who had come to Llayless on business, left his space trunk to be delivered to a sprawling, dilapidated, one-story building farther along the town's central street—its faded sign bore the message " . . . OTEL" —and stood regarding the headquarters building with puzzled scrutiny. Apparently Jeffrey Wallingford Pummery did not go in for luxury, as he was using the same ramshackle three-story building that had been Old Albert's headquarters. It hadn't even been treated to a new coat of paint for years.

Dantler's fellow passengers entered the building ahead of him. Either they were directed at once to the departments that concerned them or they already knew the way because they had vanished by the time Dantler entered. He approached the receptionist, a pert, overalled young lady with bluish blond hair. She eyed him disdainfully. The lobby proctor took in Dantler's appearance with a snort and decided not to like his looks. He took a step forward.

Dantler proffered a letter to the young lady—the same he had shown the clerk at the port. She glanced at it, glanced at Dantler again, and suddenly decided to read it slowly and with care. The proctor came forward and read over her shoulder. When the young lady had finished her reading and made a copy of the letter, the proctor took it and read it a second time.

His attitude had flip-flopped. "Mr. Pummery's personal offices occupy the third floor," he said politely. "If you will follow me, please, I'll show you to the tubes." The levitation tubes were J. Wallingford Pummery's one concession to modern comfort. Probably he became tired of negotiating three flights of stairs to and from his office several times a day.

The receptionist must have warned everyone that

Dantler was coming. He moved as if by magic through the various barricades that Pummery had erected to protect himself from unwanted intruders. Five minutes later, having been shown into a cramped office that was as spartan as Dantler expected, Dantler was settled comfortably in a guest chair and scrutinizing the great man himself while a scowling Pummery scrutinized him. He might have been a retired university professor—tall, slender, neatly bearded, scholarly. The beard was gray, but Pummery looked young and energetic.

Dantler passed a letter across the desk. It was not the letter he had shown the receptionist—that one had functioned merely to get him into Pummery's presence. This one was highly confidential. Pummery read it with obvious astonishment.

"You're a Galactic Bureau of Investigation Officer?" he asked.

"Officer Dantler, at your service," Dantler murmured politely.

"Nonsense. The GBI doesn't serve anyone unless by doing so it forwards it's own interests. You're here on a special inspection trip to reevaluate the world's status?"

Dantler nodded diffidently.

"The letter says you are also here to conduct an investigation. The Inter-World Council has something it wants investigated on Llayless?"

"It does."

Pummery tilted back in his chair and regarded him with puzzled interest. "This is a world without a government. For that reason, people call it a totally lawless world, and they couldn't be more wrong. The fact that a world has no government doesn't mean it has no laws. Humankind brings its own laws with it wherever it goes—sometimes like unwanted baggage it can't get rid of, but it always has them. They are an expression of the deep-seated customs and attitudes it must live by. Is the Inter-World Council trying to introduce its own brand of law and order here?"

"Surely you have read the Federation's constitution," Dantler murmured. "I'm here to evaluate the world's status as the constitution provides and to conduct an investigation of something that has already occurred. If my investigation confirms information the Bureau has received, then I will see that proper action is taken."

"What is it that they want investigated?"

"A murder."

"There has been a murder on Llayless?"

"There has. After I have confirmed that the murder has taken place and that the identity of the murderer has been reported to the GBI correctly, I intend to apprehend the murderer and bring him to justice."

Pummery took the time to read the letter through again, slowly. Then he touched a button and spoke in a normal tone of voice. "Mr. Jabek, please."

While they waited, Dantler amusedly counted the seconds. He had reached six when the door opened. As he expected, Pummery kept everyone who worked for him on his toes.

Pummery did not bother to introduce Jabek. Instead, he introduced Dantler. He said, "This is Birk Dantler, an officer of the GBI, the Galactic Bureau of Investigation. The GBI is the investigative arm of the Inter-World

Council. He has been sent here on a confidential mission of inspection and investigation. Do you know what that means?"

"No, sir," Jabek answered apologetically.

"The Inter-World Council has a stranglehold on every world in the galaxy—if it chooses to apply it. At this moment, Officer Dantler is the most powerful man on the world of Llayless. If he finds this organization or any organization or individual on the world less than completely cooperative, he can express his dissatisfaction, and an absolute embargo will be placed on us. No ship will arrive; no ship will leave.

"You will prepare the necessary credentials for him. He can go wherever he likes, and transportation is to be arranged for him whenever he needs it; he is to see whatever he wants to see; he is to talk with whomever he wants to talk with. Any person who fails to cooperate fully will find him or herself on the next outbound spaceship. The credentials you give him should make that clear."

Pummery turned to Dantler. "I can order everyone on the world of Llayless to cooperate with you, but I have no control over what they say, and I can't make them tell the truth. Neither can I tell you anything about this murder myself because I have no knowledge about it.

"I want to make one thing clear. We may have no government here, but as I already mentioned, we are not without laws—though we don't call them that. We have rules of conduct that we impose on ourselves, and they make human society possible. Until you arrived I would have said lawless Llayless is the most law-abiding world in the galaxy. If there has been a murder on this world, the fact that I never heard of it doesn't mean that the crime hasn't been noticed and the murderer hasn't already been punished—under our form of law, not yours. If I can assist you further, come and see me."

He got to his feet and touched Dantler's hand briefly. Mr. Jabek murmured, "Come with me, please," and led him into the adjoining office.

Half an hour later, armed with every credential Mr. Jabek could provide for him, Dantler returned to the ground floor and nodded perfunctorily at the blue-blond receptionist as he passed her on his way to the exit.

Hunting for a murderer on a world without government was an entirely new experience for Dantler. Regardless of what Pummery had said, there was a principle that held true everywhere in the galaxy: No government meant no laws. As he left for the Last Hope mine, the reported scene of the murder, he wondered again what he would charge the murderer with when he caught him, and what court of justice he would bring him before on a world that had no courts.

Probably it would have to be an intergalactic court on some other world, but on strictly local issues, such courts usually applied the laws of the world on which the lawbreaking occurred. There would have to be some roundabout charge—perhaps based on the fact that by murdering Douglas Vaisey, Roger Lefory had summarily terminated his right to that nebulous old saw of life, liberty, and the pursuit of happiness. The attorneys would have the time of their lives with it, but Dantler was confident of a conviction. Murder was the most serious charge in the legal arsenal, and courts would lean over backward to properly punish a murderer—especially when the murder had occurred on an Unnullified world that had neither government, law, nor courts.

Now Dantler was back in Pummery again, having tracked his murderer to Pummery's huge Smelter No. 2. It was an all-electric operation—clean, quiet, and effectively temperature controlled. Dantler's credentials gave him direct and immediate access to its superintendent, a youngish-looking black man named Edwin Sharle, who seemed as quietly competent and efficient as his smelter.

He was completely unaware that he had harbored a murderer among his employees, but the name "Roger Lefory" was familiar to him. "The man was always complaining about something," he said. "He kept claiming that the other employees were making him the victim of all their pranks. They smeared glue on his chair, and when he sat in it, he couldn't get up. He had to cut his trousers off, and they were ruined. His fellow workers had a way of timing their breaks so he was left with all the work to do. They filled his locker with trash, and another time they balanced a can of paint so it dumped on him when he opened the locker's door. That's only the beginning of a list. I'm sure a record was made. Do you want to see it?"

Dantler shook his head. "What did you make of all that?"

"I checked his work record from the Last Hope

mine and, before and after that, the Laughingstock. Everywhere he worked, he found excuses for not working. Many of the pranks he described sounded like fellow workers being fed up with his constantly shifting his workload to them. So I told him to try to be more friendly and cooperative with the people who worked with him and to do a little work himself."

"With what result?"

"He quit without notice. Went to one of the more distant mines, the Shangri-la, and got a job there. I know that because they asked me for his work record. I never heard him mentioned again."

Dantler's next stop was the Llayless Record Section, where he was given a computer station and access to the complete record of Roger Lefory—to the extent that the world kept records on one of its lesser residents. Lefory's entire employment history was there as far as the Shangri-la. Every employer, including the last one, remarked that the man was lazy and avoided work whenever he could. The file ended with a terse note from the Shangri-la manager, dated almost a year before. Employee Roger Lefory was missing from his job. There was nothing unusual about that—he had left every job he had held without notice—but this time there was no record that he had gone anywhere else. He had simply vanished.

Dantler made inquiries. There were a few solitary prospectors searching for paydirt on the far side of the mountains surrounding Pummery. Some of them had developed a knack for living off the country. There were edible plants, berries, and fruits. There were game birds and animals for those who had the skill to catch them. Most Llayless residents had no time for that sort of thing, but prospectors usually had little money and in any case didn't want to take the time for a long trip back to a commissary. There was nothing unusual about a man being missing for almost a year.

Before leaving for the Shangri-la mine, Dantler paid another call on Jeffrey Wallingford Pummery. The factor greeted him courteously and asked how he could be of service.

Dantler described his investigation to date. "A man was murdered," he said. "There are witnesses who saw it done. No report was made to anyone on the management level of the mines where Lefory worked, or to the smelter where he worked, or to world management because no report was required. The murderer was left free to drift from job to job. Now he has gone prospecting and may be difficult to find. This represents a flagrant violation of the Inter-World Federation's constitution—failing to protect the lives of your citizens by providing no mechanism for taking action against a murderer. I'm going to recommend that your world's status be changed immediately from 'Unnullified' to 'Nullified.' I'll get a spacegram off today. As the law requires, I am giving you written notice of that fact so you can prepare your defense. There will be a hearing, of course."

Pummery glanced at the paper Dantler handed to him and then handed it back. There was a faint smile on his face. "I suggest that you hold off with your report—and with your notification—until you have completed your investigation. You haven't visited the Shangri-la mine, yet. Surely your investigation will be incomplete without evidence from the last place Lefory is known to have worked."

Dantler studied him warily. He scented a trap. After a moment's thought, he said, "Certainly, if you prefer it. It probably won't delay things more than a day."

The Shangri-la was just as promising a mine as the Laughingstock, its manager—one Pierre Somler—told Dantler, but it was still in an early stage of development. Thus far its profits had been invested in machinery; the dwellings were shacks, and so was the office.

The manager vividly remembered Lefory. "The record said he was lazy. He was spectacularly lazy. On my visits to the diggings, I rarely found him working. He was always taking a break."

"But you kept him on because of the labor shortage," Dantler said wearily.

Somler nodded. "That, and because we always hope that a poor employee will change his habits. Usually that happens when dividends are paid and everyone else receives a tidy bonus. A poor employee's long list of demerits results in his receiving nothing. He immediately decides to be at the top of the list when the next dividends are declared. But it didn't happen that way with Lefory. Shiftless he was; shiftless he remained.

"Then there were his complaints about his fellow workers. He kept saying they were trying to 'get' him. He had the darndest accidents, some of them almost unbelievable. He wanted to be a heavy machine operator, but on his first try, a freak short circuit nearly electrocuted him. After that he wouldn't go near one of the machines. The head flew off a fellow worker's pickax and put him in the hospital for a few days. If it'd hit him in the head instead of the back, it would have killed him. That sort of thing. Finally he vanished."

"Was it a planned disappearance? I mean—did he accumulate supplies for a stay in the wilderness and take prospecting equipment with him?"

"I think he did. He had mentioned to one of the workers that he was going back to Pummery the next morning and leave Llayless on the first ship out. He thought this was an unlucky world for him, and he could do better starting fresh somewhere else. But that night someone broke into the commissary and took the sort of supplies a prospector would want, and a worker saw Lefory sneaking away on a mountain path with a pack on his back."

"Is there any other evidence that he is out there in the wilderness?"

"No. But it's the ideal place for him. No fellow workers he has to get along with, he can work whatever hours he sets for himself, and take a day off when he wants to. All he has to do is figure out how to eat regularly."

"And all I have to do," Dantler said, "is figure out how to catch him. A world without a government, and without any police force, is a poor place for a manhunt."

Jeffrey Wallingford Pummery said with interest, "Do you mean you've abandoned your search?"

"Right. Lefory is bound to show up sometime. I'll leave a warrant for him. You'll have to apprehend him the moment he appears."

"Solitary prospectors who go off into the blue are

usually looking for gold. They show up only at long intervals to cash in their accumulation, and if they've been lucky, they may buy supplies that will last for years."

"If he shows up at all, the warrant will see that he is detained for galactic police authorities."

"Have you considered the possibility that he might live the rest of his life out without being seen again?" Pummery asked. "He might be able to cash in his gold without being seen if he has a confederate. Are you still intent on changing the status of this world to 'Nullified?'"

"I am."

"We'll contest the petition, of course. And we'll win."

"How can you possibly win? There is no doubt at all that organizations on Llayless harbored a murderer. Not only did they fail to punish him, but they helped him avoid punishment."

Pummery smiled. "I told you when you arrived— an Unnullified world, a world without government, can be far more law-abiding than your so-called normal worlds. According to the results of your own investigation, Lefory is one of the most severely punished men in galactic history."

"How do you figure that? No one punished him at all."

"Study your notes again. At the Last Hope mine, he was shouldered. At the Laughingstock, he was much more emphatically shouldered. Once he was almost killed. At Smelter No. 2, more of the same thing. The danger to his life was increasing. Finally, at the Shangri-la, he was escaping death by narrower and narrower margins.

"It isn't necessary for management to take a hand in the punishment of a murderer, you see. Every person on Llayless knows that if a Roger Lefory can murder in a fit of temper and escape the consequences, no person is safe. So the people of Llayless set about making an example of him. They put him through living hell, one place after another. And when he finally announced to a fellow worker that he was leaving Llayless, they gave his punishment the final twist."

"And what was that?" Dantler demanded.

"You've already answered your question: He disappeared. His fellow workers so frightened him that he gave up his plan to return to Pummery and leave the planet. He was afraid he wouldn't live long enough to get there. Instead, he went to hide out beyond the mountains, thus condemning himself to perpetual hell. Don't you believe for a moment that he is gleefully basking in the wilderness and chuckling about how he got away with murder. He is eating plants that make him sick and half starving because he hasn't the knack for catching birds or animals. He simply isn't the type for solitary prospecting. He wouldn't recognize paydirt if he fell in it. He desperately needs fellow workers he can shift his own share of work onto. Running back to Pummery and using the return ticket he has on file to get off the world is his kind of gambit, but he was too terrified to try it.

"The sanctity of life is a basic law among humans everywhere. An Unnullified world doesn't need the apparatus of government and courts to punish murderers. Word of a murder circulates among workers almost instantly. The murderer's deed dogs his tracks forever after. It followed Lefory everywhere, and his fellow workers reacted accordingly. If he shows up again, Llayless's community of workers will resume where it left off. His punishment is already a legend that will deter people from murder far into the future. Do you know how many murders there have been on Llayless in its history?"

Dantler shook his head.

"Two," Pummery said. "One happened twenty-eight years ago. That murderer's punishment is still remembered and still a deterrent—as Lefory's punishment will be for decades to come. How many murderers do you know of on normal worlds who have been released through lack of evidence or through legal manipulations? So many you couldn't answer, I'm sure. On an Unnullified world, where the people are the law, punishment is certain—and it is perpetual. It will dog Lefory again if he ever emerges from the wilderness. He can't escape it—can't escape the planet—because no one will let him."

"It sounds suspiciously like mob rule, which the Inter-World Federation outlaws. That simply won't do."

"Ah, but mob rule—thoughtless mob punishment without proper evidence—is an entirely different thing. It wouldn't have popular support. Further, it would bring every management on Llayless down on it. We simply couldn't permit that. Punishment of the mob would be official, immediate, and severe."

He got to his feet. "I'm pleased to be able to introduce you to the way the law works on a world without government—a lawless world. I'm sorry you can't stay longer. We are very strong on law but unfortunately weak in amenities, and I apologize for that."

He nodded politely. Dantler, feeling himself dismissed, left. He had reached the street before he remembered that he had failed to serve on Pummery the notice of his intention to recommend an immediate change in Llayless's status.

He took the paper from his pocket, hesitated, and then tore it into very small pieces. The pieces dropped almost at his feet, and he kicked at them as he walked away.

The Right's Tough

by Robert J. Sawyer

"The funny thing about this place," said Hauptmann, pointing at the White House as he and Chin walked west on the Mall, "is that the food is actually good."

"What's funny about that?" asked Chin.

"Well, it's a tourist attraction, right? A historic site. People come from all over the world to see where the American government was headquartered, back when there *were* governments. The guys who own it now could serve absolute crap, charge exorbitant prices, and the place would still be packed. But the food really is great. Besides, tomorrow the crowds will arrive; we might as well eat here while we can."

Chin nodded. "All right," he said. "Let's give it a try."

The room Hauptmann and Chin were seated in had been the State Dining Room. Its oak-paneled walls sported framed portraits of all sixty-one men and seven women who had served as presidents before the office had been abolished.

"What do you suppose they'll be like?" asked Chin, after they'd placed their orders.

"Who?" said Hauptmann.

"The spacers. The astronauts."

Hauptmann frowned, considering this. "That's a good question. They left on their voyage—what?" He glanced down at his weblink, strapped to his forearm. The device had been following the conversation, of course, and had immediately submitted Hauptmann's query to the web. "Two hundred and ten years ago," Hauptmann said, reading the figure off the ten-by-five-centimeter display. He looked up. "Well, what was the *world* like back then? Bureaucracy. Government. Freedoms curtailed." He shook his head. "Our world is going to be like a breath of fresh air for them."

Chin smiled. "After more than a century aboard a starship, fresh air is exactly what they're going to want."

Neither Hauptmann nor his weblink pointed out the obvious: that although a century had passed on Earth since the *Olduvai* started its return voyage from Franklin's World, only a couple of years had passed aboard the ship and, for almost all of that, the crew had been in cryosleep.

The waiter brought their food, a Clinton (pork ribs

and mashed potatoes with gravy) for Hauptmann, and a Nosworthy (tofu and eggplant) for Chin. They continued chatting as they ate.

When the bill came, it sat between them for a few moments. Finally, Chin said, "Can you get it? I'll pay you back tomorrow."

Hauptmann's weblink automatically sent out a query when Chin made his request, seeking documents containing Chin's name and phrases such as "overdue personal debt." Hauptmann glanced down at the weblink's screen; it was displaying seven hits. "Actually, old boy," said Hauptmann, "your track record isn't so hot in that area. Why don't *you* pick up the check for both of us, and *I'll* pay you back tomorrow? I'm good for it."

Chin glanced at his own weblink. "So you are," he said, reaching for the bill.

"And don't be stingy with the tip," said Hauptmann, consulting his own display again. "Dave Preston from Peoria posted that you only left five percent when he went out to dinner with you last year."

Chin smiled good-naturedly and reached for his debit card. "You can't get away with anything these days, can you?"

The owners of the White House had been brilliant, absolutely brilliant.

The message, received by people all over Earth, had been simple: "This is Captain Joseph Plato of the UNSA *Olduvai* to Mission Control. Hello, Earth! Long time no see. Our entire crew has been revived from suspended animation, and we will arrive home in twelve days. It's our intention to bring our landing module down at the point from which it was originally launched, the Kennedy Space Center. Please advise if this is acceptable."

And while the rest of the world reacted with surprise—who even remembered that an old space-survey vessel was due to return this year?—the owners of the White House sent a reply. "Hello, *Olduvai*! Glad to hear you're safe and sound. The Kennedy Space Center was shut down over a hundred and fifty years ago. But, tell you what, why don't you land on the White House lawn?"

Of course, that signal was beamed up into space; at the time, no one on Earth knew what had been said. But everyone heard the reply Plato sent back. "We'd be delighted to land at the White House! Expect us to touch down at noon Eastern time on August 14."

When people figured out exactly what had happened, it was generally agreed that the owners of the White House had pulled off one of the greatest publicity coups in post-governmental history.

No one had ever managed to rally a million people onto the Mall before. Three centuries previously, Martin Luther King had only drawn 250,000; the four separate events that had called themselves "Million-Man Marches" had attracted maybe 400,000 apiece. And, of course, since there was no longer any government at which to aim protests, these days the Mall normally only drew history buffs. They would stare at the slick blackness of the Vietnam Wall, at the nineteen haunted soldiers of the Korean memorial, at the blood-red spire of the Colombian tower—at the stark reminders of why governments were not good things.

But today, Hauptmann thought, it looked like that magic figure might indeed have been reached: although billions were doubtless watching from their homes through virtual-reality hookups, it did seem as if a million people had come in the flesh to watch the return of the only astronauts Earth had ever sent outside the solar system.

Hauptmann felt perfectly safe standing in the massive crowd. His weblink would notify him if anyone with a trustworthiness rating below 85 percent got within a dozen meters of him; even those who chose not to wear weblinks could be identified at a distance by their distinctive biometrics. Hauptmann had once seen aerial footage of a would-be pickpocket moving through a crowd. A bubble opened up around the woman as she walked along, people hustling away from her as their weblinks sounded warnings.

"There it is!" shouted Chin, standing next to Hauptmann, pointing up. Breaking through the bottom of the cloud layer was the *Olduvai*'s lander, a silver hemisphere with black legs underneath. The exhaust from its central engine was no worse than that of any VTOL aircraft.

The lander grew ever bigger in Hauptmann's view as it came closer and closer to the ground. Hauptmann applauded along with everyone else as the craft settled onto the lawn of what had in days of yore been the president's residence.

It was an attractive ship—no question—but the technology was clearly old-fashioned: engine cones and parabolic antennas, articulated legs and hinged hatches. And, of course, it was marked with the symbols of the pre-freedom era: five national flags plus logos for various governmental space agencies.

After a short time, a door on the side of the craft swung open and a figure appeared, standing on a platform within. Hauptmann was close enough to see the huge grin on the man's face as he waved wildly at the crowd.

Many of those around Hauptmann waved back, and the man turned around and began descending the ladder. The mothership's entire return voyage had been spent accelerating or decelerating at one g, and Franklin's World had a surface gravity 20 percent greater than Earth's. So the man—a glance at Hauptmann's weblink confirmed it was indeed Captain Plato—was perfectly steady on his feet as he stepped off the ladder onto the White House lawn.

Hauptmann hadn't been crazy enough to camp overnight on the Mall in order to be right up by the landing area, but he and Chin did arrive at the crack of dawn, and so were reasonably close to the front. Hauptmann could clearly hear Plato saying, "Hello, everyone! It's nice to be home!"

"Welcome back," shouted some people in the crowd, and "Good to have you home," shouted others. Hauptmann just smiled, but Chin was joining in the hollering.

Of course, Plato wasn't alone. One by one, his two dozen fellow explorers backed down the ladder into the summer heat. The members of the crowd—some of who, Hauptmann gathered, were actually descendants of these men and women—were shaking the spacers' hands, thumping them on the back, hugging them, and generally having a great time.

At last, though, Captain Plato turned toward the White House; he seemed somewhat startled by the holographic GREAT EATS sign that floated above the rose garden. He turned back to the people surrounding him. "I didn't expect such a crowd," he said. "Forgive me for having to ask, but which one of you is the president?"

There was laughter from everyone but the astronauts. Chin prodded Hauptmann in the ribs. "How about that?" Chin said. "He's saying, 'Take me to your leader'!"

"There is no president anymore," said someone near Plato. "No kings, emperors, or prime ministers, either."

Another fellow, who clearly fancied himself a wit, said, "Shakespeare said kill all the lawyers; we didn't do that, but we did get rid of all the politicians . . . and the lawyers followed."

Plato blinked more than the noonday sun demanded. "No government of any kind?"

Nods all around; a chorus of "That's right," too.

"Then—then—what are we supposed to do now?" asked the captain.

Hauptmann decided to speak up. "Why, whatever you wish, of course."

Hauptmann actually got a chance to talk with Captain Plato later in the day. Although some of the spacers did have relatives who were offering them accommodations in their homes, Plato and most of the others had been greeted by no one from their families.

"I'm not sure where to go," Plato said. "I mean, our salaries were supposed to be invested while we were away, but . . ."

Hauptmann nodded. "But the agency that was supposed to do the investing is long since gone, and, besides, government-issued money isn't worth anything anymore; you need corporate points."

Plato shrugged. "And I don't have any of those."

Hauptmann was a bit of a space buff, of course; that's why he'd come into the District to see the landing. To have a chance to talk to the captain in depth would be fabulous. "Would you like to stay with me?" he asked.

Plato looked surprised by the offer, but, well, it was clear that he *did* have to sleep somewhere—unless he planned to return to the orbiting mothership, of course. "Umm, sure," he said, shaking Hauptmann's hand. "Why not?"

Hauptmann's weblink was showing something he'd never seen before: the word "unknown" next to the text, "Trustworthiness rating for Joseph Tyler Plato." But, of course, that was only to be expected.

Chin was clearly jealous that Hauptmann had scored a spacer, and so he made an excuse to come over to Hauptmann's house in Takoma Park early the next morning.

Hauptmann and Chin listened spellbound as Plato regaled them with tales of Franklin's World and its four moons, its salmon-colored orbiting rings, its outcrops of giant crystals towering to the sky, and its neon-bright cascades. No life had been found, which was why, of course, no quarantine was necessary. That lack of native organisms had been a huge disappointment, Plato said; he and his crew were still arguing over what mechanism had caused the oxygen signatures detected in Earth-based spectroscopic scans of Franklin's World, but whatever had made them wasn't biological.

"I really am surprised," said Plato, when they took a break for late-morning coffee. "I expected debriefings and, well, frankly, for the government to have been prepared for our return."

Hauptmann nodded sympathetically. "Sorry about that. There are a lot of good things about getting rid of government, but one of the downsides, I guess, is the loss of all those little gnomes in cubicles who used to keep track of everything."

"We do have a lot of scientific data to share," said Plato.

Chin smiled. "If I were you, I'd hold out for the highest bidder. There's got to be some company somewhere that thinks it can make a profit off of what you've collected."

Plato tipped his head. "Well, until then, I, um, I'm going to need some of those corporate points you were talking about."

Hauptmann and Chin each glanced down at their weblinks; it was habit, really, nothing more, but . . .

But that nasty "unknown" was showing on the displays again, the devices having divined the implied question. Chin looked at Hauptmann. Hauptmann looked at Chin.

"That *is* a problem," Chin said.

❖   ❖   ❖

The first evidence of real trouble was on the noon newscast. Plato watched aghast with Chin and Hauptmann as the story was reported. Leo Johnstone, one of the *Olduvai's* crew, had attempted to rape a woman over by the New Watergate towers. The security firm she subscribed to had responded to her weblink's call for help, and Johnstone had been stopped.

"That idiot," Plato said, shaking his head back and forth, as soon as the report had finished. "That bloody idiot." He looked first at Chin and then at Hauptmann, and spread his arms. "Of course, there was a lot of pairing-off during our mission, but Johnstone had been alone. He kept saying he couldn't wait to get back on terra firma. 'We'll all get heroes' welcomes when we return,' he'd say, 'and I'll have as many women as I want.'"

Hauptmann's eyes went wide. "He really thought that?"

"Oh, yes," said Plato. "'We're astronauts,' he kept saying. 'We've got the Right Stuff.'"

Hauptmann glanced down; his weblink was dutifully displaying an explanation of the arcane reference. "Oh," he said.

Plato lifted his eyebrows. "What's going to happen to Johnstone?"

Chin exhaled noisily. "He's finished," he said softly.

"*What?*" said Plato.

"Finished," agreed Hauptmann. "See, until now he didn't have a trustworthiness rating." Plato's face conveyed his confusion. "Since the day we were born," continued Hauptmann, "other people have been commenting about us on the web. 'Freddie is a bully,' 'Jimmy stole my lunch,' 'Sally cheated on the test.'"

"But surely no one cares about what you did as a child," said Plato.

"It goes on your whole life," said Chin. "People gossip endlessly about other people on the web, and our weblinks"—he held up his right arm so that Plato could see the device—"search and correlate information about anyone we're dealing with or come physically close to. That's why we don't need governments anymore; governments exist to regulate, and, thanks to the trustworthiness ratings, our society is self-regulating."

"It was inevitable," said Hauptmann. "From the day the web was born, from the day the first search engine was created. All we needed was smarter search agents, greater bandwidth, and everyone being online."

"But you spacers," said Chin, "predate that sort of thing. Oh, you had a crude web, but most of those postings were lost thanks to electromagnetic pulses from the Colombian War. You guys are clean slates. It's not that you have *zero* trustworthiness ratings; rather, you've got *no* trustworthiness ratings at all."

"Except for your man Johnstone," said Hauptmann, sadly. "If it was on the news," and he cocked a thumb at the wall monitor, "then it's on the web, and everyone knows about it. A leper would be more welcome than someone with that kind of talk associated with him."

"So what should he do?" asked Plato. "What should all of us from the *Olduvai* do?"

❖　　❖　　❖

There weren't a million people on the Mall this time. There weren't even a hundred thousand. And the mood wasn't jubilant; rather, a melancholy cloud hung over everyone.

But it *was* the best answer. Everyone could see that. The *Olduvai*'s lander had been refurbished, and crews from Earth's orbiting space stations had visited the mothership, upgrading and refurbishing it, as well.

Captain Plato looked despondent; Johnstone and the several others of the twenty-five who had now publicly contravened acceptable standards of behavior looked embarrassed and contrite.

Hauptmann and Chin had no trouble getting to the front of the crowd this time. They already knew what Plato was going to say, having discussed it with him on the way over. And so they watched the faces in the crowd—still a huge number of people, but seeming positively post-apocalyptic in comparison to the throng of a few days before.

"People of the Earth," said Plato, addressing his physical and virtual audiences. "We knew we'd come back to a world much changed, an Earth centuries older than the one we'd left behind. We'd hoped—and those of us who pray had prayed—that it would be a better place. And, in many ways, it clearly is.

"We'll find a new home," Plato continued. "Of that I'm sure. And we'll build a new society—one, we hope, that might be as peaceful and efficient as yours. We— all twenty-five of us—have already agreed on one thing that should get us off on the right foot." He looked at the men and women of his crew, then turned and faced the people of the Free Earth for the last time. "When we find a new world to settle, we won't be planting any flags in its soil."

The Shackles of Freedom

by Mike Resnick and Tobias S. Buckell

I came to New Pennsylvania because I was looking for a world with no government, no laws, nothing to hinder me from doing what I pleased. The colonists here hadn't liked the laws back on Earth, so they set up shop, free of all bureaucracy and all regulations.

What I never bargained for was having to live with the consequences of that freedom.

Mark Suderman was dying on my operating table. His plain blue clothing, stained dark with blood, lay crumpled on the floor. I tried to avoid his brothers' frightened glances. There was nothing more I could tell them, except to pray.

They couldn't know it, but he was a dead man before I ever got a chance to examine him. I simply didn't have the tools to save his life.

I sighed deeply. So much for freedom. This was the twenty-third time I had the freedom to watch a man die that I could have saved.

Hooves clip-clopped in the distance and then echoed their way up the driveway. The rest of the Suderman family had arrived.

"Stay here," I told the brothers, then walked out through the dining room to my porch. A plank squeaked as I stopped next to the swing. Mr. Suderman, his hat in hand, stared straight up at me from the bottom of my tiny set of bleached stairs.

I looked down at him, sighed, and gestured to the door. He climbed the three steps and passed by me, but his rough, callused hand grabbed my shoulder for a brief instant before he went inside. His wife sat stoically in the buggy, her seat rocking on its suspension slightly as she shifted her weight from side to side. The wind tugged at the strings of her bonnet, and the light from our three moons cast shadows across her face.

I had a sudden impulse to walk over to the buggy— but what could I say? That I might have cured him on some world they couldn't even see, let alone pronounce?

I had come here because I knew they needed a doctor. So what if they were Amish? There was no constitution, there were no laws prohibiting me from practicing my trade. There were no restrictions at all.

Except for the Amish themselves.

❖   ❖   ❖

The sun set by the time the elders left with the Sudermans. I began cleaning the table to the flickering light of kerosene lamps. In the brown light it cast, the blood wasn't so noticeable, and not nearly as accusatory.

I could smell manure on the floor, tramped in by Mark's brothers. The men's sweat also filled the room, reminding me how unsterile the area was. Finally I left the house and walked down to the far edge of my small, neglected garden with the mop bucket.

The misshapen weeds seemed to erupt in fierce protest when I emptied the bucket. Tiny weasel-shaped creatures with scaly skin chittered at me and scampered off.

My house lay close inside a cluster of farms and roads. Just beyond them lay an unfamiliar forest full of alien species creeping in and mixing with our own. I knew the weeds in my own garden. But behind the scraggly dandelions and patchy grass, spirals of unearthly flowers moved in and out of the shadows to the rhythm of the wind.

Instead of going back inside, I sat on the porch swing and shivered. The fourth moon—the largest of the quartet—edged over the hills and made silhouettes of the neighbor's barn.

I'd never lost so many lives in such a short time, and I was getting sick of funerals.

It didn't make any sense. I was free to try to convince them to let me save them. They were free to die unnecessarily. And there was no one, no higher authority I could appeal to. Except God.

And unlike me, they talked to Him every day, welcomed Him into their houses and the lives. They *knew* He was on their side.

I sighed and went back into the house.

Mark hadn't died doing anything glamorous like beating back the wild forest of a new planet. He'd been milling grain, and had fallen between the giant wheels. The hardwood cogs chewed him up, spit him out, and left him for me and God—and God washed His hands of the matter.

At the Yoders' I pulled on Zeke's reins. He snorted and plodded to a nonchalant stop just short of the weathered post I usually tied him to. One of the little Yoders, Joshua, walked down to greet me.

"*Guten* morning," he said, mixing his German and English with a smile.

"Good morning, Joshua," I replied. I clambered out of my buggy, then reached back in to retrieve my black bag. Of all my visits, I looked forward to seeing the Yoders the most.

Joshua eyed Zeke with a critical eye.

"Your horse is getting old. How much longer will he be pulling you around? My dad could sell you a good one, with straight legs and a strong back and the look of eagles."

A fast talking six-year-old, this Joshua. Somehow I knew he wouldn't spend the rest of his life on New Pennsylvania.

Unless he contracted a serious disease. Or broke a leg. Or . . .

"No thank you," I said. "I think old Zeke will hold

out just fine for me." In response Zeke broke wind and swished his tail.

Joshua giggled and ran back toward the house, his bare feet kicking up small puffs of dirt.

Joshua's mother came out to the porch. The hem of her black dress scraped the dirty wooden floor planks, and her white blouse had blue stains all over it. Several strands of honey-brown hair had escaped the edges of her bonnet. She brushed at them.

"Dr. Hostetler," she greeted me. "Good morning."

"Good morning, Mrs. Yoder." I walked onto their porch. Several giggling kids ran out the door past me. I looked around, but didn't see Rebecca anywhere.

"I'll tell Ben and Esther you're here," she said. "Please, come in."

I stepped in. The house smelled of food. Fresh-baked bread sat on the counter by the large iron range, and it appeared that Mrs. Yoder was taking advantage of the hot stove to put a cake in as well.

David Yoder, his full beard as dark as the unkempt hair crammed into his straw hat, shook my hand.

"You ministered to Suderman's son," he said. "God bless him, that was a fine boy. A tragedy."

The tragedy was that none of you would let me bring my skills to bear on him.

Mrs. Yoder took a stick and stirred the coal bin under the range. She opened the oven for a quick peek and waved her hand over it. "We'll have to pray for Betty," she said.

That brought back the image of Betty Suderman sitting in her buggy outside my house, waiting for the news of her son's death. I forced it back into my subconcious when I saw Ben and Esther coming down the stairs. Ben's beard had just started growing in, a sign that he was no longer a bachelor. Esther unconsciously held her arms protectively over her stomach.

I shook Ben's hand while Esther smiled nervously at me.

"Let's see what we have here," I said. I undid the clasp on my little black bag and opened it up. The look on Esther's face said that Pandora's box had nothing on my medical bag.

There is nothing so amazing as hearing the heartbeat of a tiny human being inside of its mother's womb. But amazing as the experience was, I had another sobering thought: here was another little person who had better never come down with a disease, or undergo a crippling accident.

I took the stethoscope away from Esther's belly.

"Everything seems okay," I said. I smiled reassuringly. Although, without any scans, I couldn't be absolutely certain. A sonogram to look at the baby would have been nice; DNA tests to make sure to make sure everything was okay after the birth would have been even better. There was no law prohibiting it; just a belief that was a thousand times stronger than any law.

Esther coughed. She stood up with her proud husband, linking her arm through his. They walked back up the creaky steps.

"Asa and I'll be out in the field after lunch," David Yoder said to his son's back.

"I'll be there," replied Ben.

David winked at me. "There'll be a raising happening soon enough for the two of them. Will you join?"

It would be another chance to see Rebecca. I tried to hide my enthusiasm. "We'll see what my schedule is like," I said. "But, yes, I would like to join."

David looked around. "We're almost ready to bring in this year's wheat. Weather's been good. Real good. The strange seasons throw you off a bit, but I think I've got it figured this year. There'll be threshing soon, eh?"

He could have used any of a dozen instruments to predict the weather to a fraction of a degree, the rainfall to a tenth of a centimeter. No law against it. Just a moral repugnance to anything that would make his life easier. We'd argued it many times. I'd never come close to winning.

David kept trying to rope me into coming over to lend an able hand. And in truth I wanted to go. The women would cook blackberry and grape pies. There would be freshly churned butter and baked bread. Washing off a day's worth of hard sweat from forking wheat into the wheels of the thresher, joking with all the other men, eating that special food—it was an appealing picture. It was almost my only pleasure on this world, other than being in Rebecca's company.

Despite my privileged place in the community as a doctor, it was their nature to be wary of me. I had a very advanced education, which didn't sit too well with them, and technology was a very important part of my job (or at least it should have been)—but it was that very technology that was viewed as dangerous to the health of the community. No one ever told me I couldn't use it. I had the freedom to offer it to them; they had the freedom to refuse it. We were both batting a thousand: I always offered, they always refused.

Girls passed by us with white tablecloths, utensils, plates of bread, and half-moon pies. Someone brought out a tureen of bean soup. I pulled my watch out. "Brother Yoder," I said. "I'm falling behind already, I have to go."

David frowned. "You'll miss church tonight?"

"I'm afraid so."

"I don't know if that's good," he said.

"I have to see the Andersons' son and tend to him. They say he's had a cold for a few days, but it could be worse."

"There should always be time for God," David told me.

"A long time ago God spoke to me," I lied, trying to hide my irritation, "and charged me with curing the sick."

To which David could make no argument. He had been chosen by lot to be a preacher. His sermons were well thought out, I was told. I avoided Sundays, and sermons, and all that went with it. I could always easily be elsewhere. David and some of the other Elder preachers sensed that, but again, they usually made an allowance for me.

"I really must go," I said.

"*Ja*, well," David shook my hand and paid my fee. "Make sure you get some bread from my wife before you leave," he said.

"Thank you."

✦   ✦   ✦

When I walked out the door I looked around. Rebecca stood out on the porch, just beside the door. She smoothed down her spotless white apron and smiled.

"Hi," she said.

She had her mother's honey-brown hair and hazel eyes.

I smiled back. "Hello, Rebecca."

"It's good to see you again."

I could see David Yoder looking at me through the window. He was no fool. Someday soon I would have to tell him that I had nothing but honorable intentions toward his daughter. Which was true: marrying Rebecca was about the only thing that would make all the unnecessary dead men and women bearable.

"I heard you say you might make the raising?" said Rebecca.

"Will you be there?"

"Of course," Rebecca said with a shy smile. "I'll be helping *Mutter* with the cooking."

"Then I will do my best."

"I hope you do make it," Rebecca said. "There's singing and dancing afterwards."

Their notion of singing and dancing wasn't about to put the dance halls of Earth and some of the colony worlds out of business, but it was better than nothing. Maybe, just maybe, for a few hours that day, no one would get hurt. No one would come down with a disease that I wasn't permitted to cure. Maybe.

I checked my pocket watch. I would have to push

Zeke faster than his usual meander to make it on time. But it was worth every delayed minute.

"I would really enjoy dancing," I told Rebecca. "I have to leave now. I'm very late."

She took my hand and shook it. Her skin was cool to the touch, and feathery.

"*Gute nacht*, Rebecca," I said.

I drove Zeke at a quick clip through the forest, my mind thinking fuzzy, pleasant things about Rebecca. I didn't hear the distant rumble until Zeke began to perk his ears up.

It began low, but soon became a high pitch as I saw the triangular shape approach. Zeke slowed and side-stepped uneasily.

"Easy," I said.

The sound jumped to earsplitting. The ship buzzed just over the treetops, thundering past on a flyby, the pilot and his companions sightseeing no doubt. I craned my head back and caught just a flash of the number on the side: DY-99. The buggy bounced as Zeke began moving off the road.

"Whoa!" I yelled, pulling on his reins.

Zeke veered back toward the road, then stopped. He whinnied and looked back down at the bushes. A long creeper held his rear left leg. Hundreds of yellow barbs along the vine punctured his stifle, and blood began to trickle down toward his hoof.

I looked down at the gray floorboards of the buggy. The creepers might move up for me. *Calm yourself*, I thought; *nothing is gained by panic*.

"Come on, Zeke," I shouted, snapping the reins.

He strained against the creeper, pulling, his muscles quivering. Then he started kicking and bucking, until I heard a tearing sound, as he finally pulled free. Strips of torn flesh hung from his leg. He moved back away from the creeper, onto the road, but the buggy was still in the bush.

I snapped the reins again, and Zeke pulled at the buggy. We didn't move.

"Whoa."

I took my black bag and jumped out onto the road. Two long vines anchored the rear wheels. Zeke started straining at his harness again.

"Whoa!" It didn't seem to have any effect. Zeke still pulled, staring past me with determination and flared nostrils.

I started taking off his harness. My fingers slipped in under the buckle, and got caught as Zeke let up, then lunged forward again. Creepers began moving up the buggy toward Zeke. I waited for his next pause and lunge, then let go. I landed painfully, hitting my tailbone on a sharp rock.

I pulled a never-used scalpel out of my bag and tried to cut a vine away from Zeke's legs, but it was too small and the vine was too thick, and Zeke wouldn't hold still. He whinnied and kicked, but his efforts were becoming weaker, and finally he just stopped.

The vines wrapped around his legs and began to pull him down the side of the road. He pawed with his front legs at the road, dragging gravel and dirt in with him. Then he gave up with a snort.

The bushes rustled and sighed as they pulled Zeke in, and everything grew quiet.

Shaken, I stood up with my black bag.

The Andersons were a long walk away, but I could make it out of the forest road before dark. As long as I stayed in the middle of the road, I would be okay.

I limped off down the road, wondering what mad whim had made us come to this planet in the first place.

The Andersons were kind enough to give me a lift back to my house, though it meant a long drive. It was dark, and Mr. Anderson kept to the very middle of the road. I looked away as we passed the spot where Zeke had lost his battle for life.

Once I was back in my house I struck matches and held them over my gaslights. They lit the room with a *phoomph!* of pale flickerings. I made dinner: pasta and a red sauce one of the ladies bottled for me, and some stale bread. Tonight would be a good night to just go to bed early, I thought, instead of poring over my library of books, hoping to find old-fashioned ways to mimic modern medicine.

But instead someone thumped at the door.

I opened it to find David Yoder standing on my porch.

"What is it?" I asked. "Is it Esther?" Probably she was going into labor too soon. I turned, thinking about forceps, wondering how I could convince the old man to let me use them in his house.

"No," David said. "It isn't Esther. Rebecca collapsed . . ."

I stood there, dazed, until my mind caught up with

the rest of me. I grabbed my bag in a daze and followed David out to his buggy.

"Creepers," I explained.

David nodded. He'd lost a horse or two to them as well.

Rebecca sat in her bed. Esther stood over her with a sponge. They thought she had a fever of some sort, but Rebecca looked like she had recovered already. She smiled when she saw me and apologized.

"I'm feeling much better now," she said. "I think it has passed."

"Well, let's make sure," I said. "Have you had any other dizzy spells?"

Rebecca chewed her lip.

She had.

"Are there any strange lumps on your body?"

The quizzical look in return sank me. I ran through the questions. And then under the watchful eye of her father I ran my hands over her pale white body, looking for the intrusions. She sucked in her breath slightly when I ran my fingers up the sides of her ribs.

"Your hands are cold," she said.

I didn't look at her face, but continued. It was bittersweet that the first time I touched her body was for medical reasons.

And that I found what I knew I had to find.

My lovely Rebecca had breast cancer. Maybe if she were more aware of her body, she would have been worried sooner. But even then, what could I have done on this world that permitted her the freedom to die in agony? It was advanced, metastasizing no doubt, spreading throughout her entire body.

When I stood up David Yoder caught my eye and nodded me out the door. We walked down through the kitchen to his porch.

"You know what's wrong," he said. It was not a question.

I nodded.

"Well?" he demanded.

"She has cancer."

I sat on the bench, leaned my head against the rough plank wall, and blinked. My eyes were a bit wet.

David didn't say anything after that. He stood near me on the porch for a while, then went into the house. Ben came out.

"Dad says to use one of our horses. I'll take you out to the barn."

I didn't reply. Ben sat next to me and clapped my shoulders.

"It'll be okay," he said. "God will protect her."

I looked the boy straight in the eye. Was he really that naive?

I woke up numb. The alarm clock rang until I slapped the switch down, my motions every bit as mechanical as the clock's.

The bed creaked as I sat on its edge. Two days' worth of half-open books lay all around me, some of them buried in my covers.

Candle wax dripped over the edges of a plate on my bed stand, the translucent stalactites almost reaching to the floor. I picked the nearest book up. The margin had a scribble in it: *DY-99*. Underneath it I had written a single question mark.

"Brother Hostetler?" came the strong shout of David Yoder from my front door. "Are you awake?

"Yes."

I stood up and pulled on my clothes, tying my rope belt off in a quick knot. A faceful of cold water dashed away my morning fuzziness. David's buggy waited outside, the horse looking as impatient as David was to get going.

Raisings were probably the most popular depiction of the culture among outsiders. Maybe it was just that it was a very attractive picture of community, and that was something they had in abundance. Many hands make light work, and there were many hands here at the edge of Yoder's property. Tables held food, lines of breads, preserves, and fruit juices. Soups simmered in iron pots. Women chatted and kids ran around, dodging around legs, tables, chairs, and whatever else served as a convenient obstacle course.

And the men gathered around the foundation of what would become Ben's home. We set to building his house together. It was more than just a community event, but a gift. When we were done Ben would have a home. A beginning.

We toiled together under the sun, hammering joints, then pulling walls up with ropes. Time passed quickly. The frame was up at lunch, and we broke to eat. Then we continued. At some point in mid-evening I stepped back, sweaty and out of breath, and looked up at a complete house.

They could have ordered a pre-fab, of course. It would have gone up faster and lasted longer. No law against it. But . . .

At the meal, when all the men sat in rows at the tables and ate, I walked over to David Yoder's house. Rebecca sat on the back stairs, looking out over the fields at the gathering. She had her skirt tucked neatly under her legs.

I sat next to her. We could just see the picnic tables over the rows of wheat shifting with the changing directions of little wind gusts.

"How are you feeling?" I asked.

"Much better," she said.

"Why aren't you out there, then?"

"Father told me to stay here, and rest myself."

I reached over and held her hand. She looked down at it.

"When you touched me . . ." she began. She caressed my hand. "I liked that." Suddenly she blushed and looked away.

We sat there silently for a long time, watching the stalks of wheat dance, running our fingers each over the other's.

"Are you frightened?" I asked at last.

"I was mad," Rebecca said. "Now I'm scared. I've done everything right. I go to church. I respect my parents. I do my best to be kind to all. Why is God punishing me?" She squeezed my hand, and pulled it to her cheek. "I don't want to die."

DY-99, I thought.

"You don't have to."

Rebecca looked up at me, curious, hope in her eyes. "You know a cure?"

"There are many cures, though I have never been permitted to apply them here," I answered. "If we leave, we can go to the spaceport. You heard the Englishers' ship land. They haven't left yet. They will study the area for a bit, look around to make sure the spaceport is okay, and then leave again. They can take us to a hospital. We can easily cure you there."

Rebecca grabbed my forearm.

"But would they take us up with them?"

"Yes." One of the reasons they kept the spaceport cleared, and a regular schedule, was for reasons like this. A small percentage of the inhabitants changed their mind and took the subtle offer.

Rebecca leaned against me. "My parents will not approve."

"They can't stop you," I said. "This is your life we're talking about." I kissed her hair. It smelled of fresh bread and pumpkin pie. "Come with me."

She stood up, letting go of my hand. "The hospital," she said. "Can they . . . really . . . ?"

"Yes. Don't pack anything," I told her. "Just be ready."

"Tonight?"

I looked back down the road we would have to take to get to DY-99. "Later tonight."

Rebecca walked back into the house. I saw her falter for a second, and she held on to the edge of a table for support. I winced.

✧   ✧   ✧

I approached David. I felt wrong for deceiving him slightly as I asked him about a good deal for one of his horses.

He smiled and stroked his beard.

"We wondered how many more days it would take before you got tired of asking for rides," he said. He named a price and I agreed on the spot. I could have dickered a little, but I wanted to go home as soon as I could.

We walked to the stables, and David led my new horse out. He was a sturdy young fellow. I chose not to pay too much attention, though, as I would be leaving him behind soon enough.

"*Herr* Doctor," David said. "You still feel badly about young Suderman?"

"Yes," I said. "I could have saved him."

"All the good health in the world would be useless with an empty life, or in a community that had rotted away."

"If there is no one alive to appreciate the community," I said, "then it is all pointless."

"You believe this is all pointless, then."

"No." I leaned my head against the horse, smelling its musky sweat. It shifted. "No. But it *is* wasteful." I broke into the words of the Hippocratic oath: "Into whatsoever house I shall enter, it shall be for the good of the sick to the utmost of my power . . . and then to also believe in the community and follow our practices."

"Did you anticipate being torn like this? Before you came to New Pennsylvania?"

"No," I said. "I was wrong. I thought on a world

with total freedom that a doctor would be free to cure the sick."

"But you *do* tend to the sick."

"With methods and cures that haven't changed in five hundred years," I said bitterly. "Out there"—I waved my hand at the stars—"they replace hearts and lungs as easily as you replace a torn shirt. Yet *here* . . ."

"You should have looked deeper into your heart before making the decision to come here."

"Then who would have tried to save Mark Suderman?" I said. "I lose far too many patients, patients I could save anywhere else—but I do save *some*."

"He was saved the day he made the decision to join the church," David Yoder said with a certainty that I wished I possessed. About anything.

"It's getting near dark," I said. "I will be going now."

"*Gute nacht.*"

I pushed the horse to a run after I was out of sight.

I threw two suitcases of clothes together. In my desk I pulled out something I never thought I would need, but had kept anyway. It was a wallet, and inside were plastic cards that on any other world would link me to lines of credit and old friends. I hitched the new horse to my spare buggy and tossed the suitcases in the back.

A horse and buggy turned onto the gravel of my drive. I was sure it was David Yoder, but I was wrong. Two Elders, Zebediah Walshman and his brother, Paul, pulled aside the storm curtains.

"William Hostetler?"

I walked up to the buggy.

"Yes."

"We talked to Brother Yoder. He feels you are going through a crisis," Paul said.

Zebediah looked over at my buggy. "Are you leaving for a while, William?"

"Possibly," I said.

"You are going to the Englanders?"

I didn't reply.

"We can't deny you that choice," Paul said. "But you will not take Rebecca with you."

They turned the buggy back around and rattled off down the road. My heart pounded, my throat dried with nervousness. I walked back to my buggy and kicked at a wheel with my boot. The pain was briefly satisfying.

The air was chilly, and as I turned up the road toward the house I extinguished the buggy's road lamp. I stopped the horse a bit down from the usual post, tying him to a tree. I patted his neck and jumped the ditch onto David Yoder's farm.

It took me a few long minutes in the pitch black to find a ladder. The notion of it—a clandestine meeting with a ladder in the twenty-third century—struck me as ludicrous. But there was nothing ludicrous about the purpose of it. I walked it over to the point under Rebecca's window and leaned the ladder against the side of the house as gently as I could.

She was waiting. She opened the window, bunched up her skirts, and got onto the ladder. It creaked as she came down step by agonizing step.

I led her around the house toward the waiting buggy.

We didn't get far before David Yoder's gentle but firm voice came from the porch.

"Rebecca, come back inside the house," he said.

She froze.

"Come on," I said. "Keep walking. You're free to leave. He can't stop you."

"I can't stop you," David agreed. "But think about what you are leaving. Rebecca, you are already saved, no matter what you do here. But when you leave, you will no longer be able to come back. You will be healthy, but unable to ever see us or speak to us again. Do you think there will be a family out there, with the Englanders, for you? What sort of lives do they lead? Good lives, or will they be confused, and spiritually cluttered, caught up with worldly goods." He paused. "Remember," he concluded, "if you leave, you can never come back. Your children can never come back."

Rebecca's tears trickled down her cheeks and collected along her jaw. "I can't do this!" she told me. "I can't!"

"Then you'll die," I said. "Probably within a couple of months. And in terrible pain that I am not permitted to alleviate on this world." I took off my hat, trying to do something useful with my hands.

"I know," she said. She brushed the side of my face with her hand and kissed me lightly on the lips. "I'm sorry, but I cannot be other than what I am. Better to die as what I am than to live as what I am not."

I watched her go back up into the house.

David and I stood there watching each other.

"She's free to go," I said.

"She was never free to go," said David. "There are

certain laws that are unwritten, and these are the most powerful laws of all."

"You've signed her death warrant," I said bitterly.

"Do you think I *want* her to die?" he demanded, and the light of the four moons reflected off the tears running down his cheeks. "This is God's will, not mine. Never mine!"

And I suddenly realized that he was caught in the same web that had ensnared Rebecca and me. I had thought, just a moment ago, that I hated David Yoder. Now I knew that I could never hate him; I could only pity him, as I pitied us all.

"What will you do now, Dr. Hostetler?" he asked.

"I don't know."

I turned and began walking across his yard.

I rode the horse hard. My hat blew away, and the cold wind played with my hair. The horse started to lather by the time I saw my house, and I slowed us down, struck by remorse. There was no reason to take my anger out on the poor beast.

I hadn't cried in a long time, but I cried that night.

And along with crying, I examined my life and my options. DY-99 was only a few miles away. It would be so easy to get on it, to go out into the galaxy where I could use all my skills.

And if I did, who would take care of Rebecca? Who would deliver Esther's child, and help make sure it grew into a healthy adult? Who would even try to save all the Mark Sudermans after I left?

I turned the buggy around. With a snap of the reins I sent us both trotting back toward the Yoders. In the coming days and weeks I was going to preside at two more miracles, the miracle of death and the miracle of birth. I was going to do it under adverse conditions, like a racehorse carrying extra weight, but Rebecca had not asked to die and Esther's child has not asked to be born, so in a way we were all running handicapped.

In a moment of clarity, I realized that it just meant that we had to try harder. If we were already saved, then it was only right that God wanted a little extra effort in return, whether it was dying with grace or struggling to save people who placed so very many restrictions on their savior.

Somewhere along the drive back, I took the wallet from my pocket and threw it into the dark forest along the road.

A Reception at the Anarchist Embassy

by Brad Linaweaver

"He's the most conservative man you'll ever meet."

The speaker was an attractive woman, although Special Agent Palmer didn't approve of her surgically implanted third eye that regarded him from an otherwise placid brow. He couldn't get used to these modern fashions, preferring instead an old-fashioned girl with a wedding ring in her navel.

Giving one of her breasts a friendly squeeze (and grateful that there were only two of them) he turned his attention to the gentleman in question. The man certainly stood out in the crowd.

"I had a professor like him once," said Palmer. "He

probably thinks the world went to hell in the twenty-third century."

She laughed. "You're almost right but try the twenty-first."

He was surprised. "So tell me, Bretygne, why do I need to converse with this genuine eccentric?"

"Because," she breathed into his ear while returning his friendly squeeze at a lower altitude, "he will provide invaluable assistance when we exchange pleasantries with the ambassador. You see, your crazy Mr. Konski is actually a fan of that old man's books."

In all the miserable time he'd spent on the self-styled anarchist planet Lysander, Palmer had not learned that Konski read any contemporaries. He pulled his forelock, the usual method of expressing thanks to a comrade. The Lady Bretygne Lamarr always did her homework.

"You'll put in a good word for me in your report?" she teased him.

"Why bother? They never read mine but settle for the oral briefing. Now you, my dear, they actually read."

"Flattery has always been your strongest suit." With that, she kicked off on her disc and scooted in the direction of the Amazing Conservative Man.

Palmer wasn't lazy enough to use a disc in low gravity. With a hop and a jump he was right next to her. Admittedly that sort of calisthenics was discouraged but he was good at it and hadn't knocked anyone over yet.

Professor Bernard Astaroth greeted them with a broad smile. "My darling girl," he said to Bretygne, squeezing her other breast (which fine point was noted by Palmer's acute skills at espionage).

"Allow me to introduce Diplomat First Class Palmer, attached to the United States of Earth." She got that out in one breath.

"No first name?" quizzed the professor.

"I'm not partial to them."

Bretygne laughed for him and the professor kept the conversation going with, "I understand that we both enjoy Lady Lamarr's way with words."

"You're too kind," she replied, switching on a phase-three blush in her normally pale cheeks.

"She tells me you're a writer."

"Yes, on aestheto-politics with a heavy emphasis on history."

"Orthodox?" asked Palmer, eyebrows raised.

"Would we be here together tonight if I were?" The professor smiled.

Bretygne thought it politic to change the subject. "Palmer spent a full quarter on Lysander."

"Before or after the insurrection?" asked Astaroth.

Palmer shook his head. "There was no insurrection, no civil war. It was one of their stupid property disputes."

"That evaporated a whole continent?" The professor was incredulous.

"You'd think they would have given up on anarchy after that, but no," said Palmer. "One of the idiots said he had a natural right to protect his property line against intruders. Then he evaporated a six-year-old girl who wandered onto his land. Instead of apologizing and offering restitution, the father amazingly turned the matter over to his defense agency. The other fellow's defense agency didn't agree that their client had over-reacted. Then the God-given natural right everyone has to own plasma bombs came into it and the continent went poof."

"You were planet-side during this?" asked Astaroth.

"Safe behind a force field on the other side of the planet. Admittedly the anarchists over there seemed a little more inclined to take things to arbitration."

"Whew," said the professor. "I did a paper about Lysander, but I'm a few years out of date."

"Palmer is always on top of things," Bretygne grinned, her arm around his waist.

The professor nodded and then did them the favor of lowering his voice. "You're both spies, of course, and lovers as well. There's not much point to the former unless it adds spice to the latter, or do I have it turned around?"

Color drained out of the lady's face, again at the flick of a switch.

Astaroth finally continued: "There's no need to dissemble. Tonight we'll be dealing with an anarchist who has less regard for our rituals than even I! We must be frank."

He gestured to a servo-mech and the machine dutifully floated over. Palmer and Lamarr quickly ordered strong heroin and tonics. The professor settled for a vodka martini.

A few sips of Smirnoff later, he was still causing trouble. "I think we should put up a sign that reads ALL DIPLOMATS ARE SPIES. Or how about this one— MILITARY ATTACHÉS HAVE NO CASE?"

Palmer wasn't amused. "If we're going to be frank, perhaps you'll answer a personal question. Why do you appear in public with those?" He gestured at the older man's wrinkles. He was just as disturbed by Astaroth's white hair.

No one pinches harder than a well-bred lady, but Bretygne was too late to stop her lover's indiscretion. "A fair question. But tell me, both lady and field agent, what you see in this room. Look around!"

They were under the largest dome on the moon in a building that made maximum use of its location. Ambassador Konski had purchased this location with a small amount of the material that suddenly made his world of interest to the United States. He'd been offered prime real estate on Earth but this was as close as he wished to be to the Terran capital—Berlin.

Underneath the giant pressure dome, the Aristarchus embassy stood in solitary splendor. The Grand Ballroom had ceiling strips revealing the stars through a double layer of protective plastiglass. Gigantic chandeliers vied with the stars to hold the eye. But the effect was purely decorative as lighting for the room was a constant emanation from the walls.

Palmer sipped his drink and looked around, taking in the beautiful people. Hairstyles varied wildly. As for bald heads, no two carried the same design. The attire was scanty. Everywhere was an expanse of smooth, healthy skin. Fresh as cream and peaches. No blemishes. No wrinkles. And there was a scent of flowers.

The professor held his old hand in front of Palmer. "You want to know why I choose to have wrinkles and warts?"

Palmer shrugged. "Bretygne said you were a conservative. But to do this strikes me as genuinely reactionary, even perverse. You're still healthy and it's a crime to deactivate the anti-aging elements. You must have had the imperfections added surgically." He gave an involuntary shudder.

The professor smiled over his martini. "May I ask another personal question?"

"What now?" she blurted out.

"How old are the two of you?"

"I'm seventy," said Palmer.

"Forty-six," added Bretygne.

"I see," the old head nodded. "You will both appear youthful and vigorous for at least another two centuries even if we make no further progress in longevity. But we know that medical science marches on, ever relentless, ever vigilant."

Fishing the olive out of the bottom of his glass, the professor held it up to his forehead before popping it into his mouth. Was he making fun of Lamarr's third eye?

"I'm something of a spy myself," he went on. "I know how young Bretygne was when you both became lovers."

This time color flushed her cheeks without any artificial assistance. Palmer grabbed her hand to steady both of them.

Astaroth looked Palmer in the eye and whispered, "I know that she was only thirty when you became lovers on Earth. Good old Earth . . . where the age for consent is thirty-five!"

"Prove it," Palmer challenged through clenched teeth.

The professor shook his head. "I don't want to cause trouble, my fellow spies. I no more approve of the Schlessinger Laws than you do."

In common with most aristocrats, Lady Lamarr had a deeply psychotic side. Her voice was dangerous as she reminded both men of the facts. "There is no statute of limitations for sex with an underager."

As they discussed the volatile issue, the three of them slowly moved to a more private corner of the ballroom. Palmer was relieved to see that Astaroth seemed inclined to keep the conversation private. They wound up standing next to one of the service entrances.

The professor tried manfully to put the genie back into the bottle. "I only bring this up to make a point, my young friends. Here are the two of you sworn to uphold the crazy world state and even you have run afoul of its statistical models and lunatic social engineering."

For some reason Palmer didn't feel like making a joke about this being the right place to discuss lunacy.

Eyes wide, Bretygne asked, "My God, are you with the anarchists?"

"No. I'm the other kind of libertarian, a minarchist who wants a limited state and a genuine Bill of Rights."

"You've got a point there," Palmer agreed. "The Children's Bill of Rights is nothing like the old American one."

"Full marks for knowing some history," said Palmer.

"All libertarianism is illegal," Bretygne stated the obvious, "but I've known you were somewhere on the radical side for a long time. You should be the last person to threaten us!"

"No threat, my dear lady. I've done things just as illegal as the two of you. We can hold each other hostage. How wonderful that we meet through our sordid occupation of providing information to the state!"

They listened to each other's silences. The distant clinking of glasses and low hum of voices seemed comforting somehow. The thick cloud of paranoia began to part as the light of mutual advantage touched their faces.

"Is this a safe place to have our conversation?" asked Bretygne.

"None better," said the professor. "The ambassador has made this a high-tech cocoon of privacy. We need only worry about human ears. Besides, we are higher-ranking spies than anyone sent to keep an eye on us."

"So what do you want?" asked Palmer.

"Profits for all of us, and maybe something even better. What would you say to freedom?"

The ballroom music began, an arrangement of classic rap-Muzak. This conservative choice of music inspired Palmer to better understand the mind behind the wrinkles.

"Bretygne told me that you think the world went to hell back in the twenty-first century. That's long before the current system took over."

"One thing leads to another." Astaroth smiled, glad of an audience. "You seem to know about the North American Bill of Rights. Have you studied the Welfare War that led to the collapse of the American Empire?"

"Only what I was told in school."

"The causes of that war continue to fester even in

the present day. They were the actual reason the world state eventually outlawed both capitalism and socialism. And so we descended to a new rung of hell, the Maternal Ageist Society."

"He's quoting from one of his private books," Bretygne told Palmer, then added proudly: "I read the whole thing!"

Emboldened, Astaroth continued. "Then you remember that capitalism was outlawed as too individualistic and the cause of social atomism. Socialism was forbidden as too egalitarian and unable to punish certain groups at the expense of others, an important matter when the new chrono-charts determined everyone's place in society according to maturity levels. Our duties and obligations and guilts are calibrated before we even pop out of the womb!"

"I forgot the length of your essay" admitted the lady Lamarr.

"I need another drink," said Palmer.

Instead of a servo-mech, a ten-year-old chose that moment to wander over. He had no drinks to offer but provided an excellent prop for the prof.

Placing his hand on the blue sphere surrounding the kid, Astaroth lectured some more: "I curse the day that social scientists and religious leaders were ever allowed to fraternize. That's carrying free speech too far. In an orgy of bipartisanship, they threw out all their good ideas and joined ranks on the bad ones. There was no need to actually burn the old Bill of Rights if it only applied to adults—and the rules for adulthood were constantly changed. Some of us can't vote until we're eighty. Some of us can't marry until we're fifty. The drinking age for everyone is forty. Heaven help those who are finally judged mature at all levels, and so condemned to eternal slavery for an ever-growing population of the immature."

Professor Astaroth finally ran out of steam. They all looked at the smiling face of the ten-year-old boy in his protective bubble. He'd been watching the professor's mouth move. Astaroth did have a most expressive face. Palmer gave the ball a friendly push and sent the kid on his way, back to his parents or state warders. One was as likely as the other.

"Well," said Palmer, "life's an itch. What's anyone to do?"

"Order more drinks," said Astaroth, his most successful speech of the evening. "If I can't have an ideal society, I'll settle for more vodka."

Just then a figure appeared at the service entrance, but it was too tall to be a servo-mech. The figure moved fast. Palmer instinctively reached for a gun that he'd left behind, a condition of attending the embassy ball. But the figure didn't attack. It stopped running and stood next to the threesome, a huge grin on its face—and an even huger cigar sticking at them between very white teeth.

Hardly anyone smoked cigars anymore.

The man wasn't easy to recognize. He was wearing a strange costume with baggy pants. A black mustache was painted on his upper lip. His eyebrows looked as if two Martian caterpillars (genetically bred to enrich the soil) had crawled on his forehead to die.

Palmer recognized the man first. After all, he'd spent time with him. A blessedly short amount of time. This

exasperating excuse for a human being had kept trying to convince Palmer that he was his own identical
twin; and then he'd pretended to be the brother! And
so on. And on.

"Konski." Palmer said it like a curse.

"Professor Astrolobe, you old fraud," said the guest
of honor amiably. "Are you still looking for Freedonia?"

"What are you doing in that costume?" asked
Bretygne who had seen the ambassador on the uniweb
many times. Researching his predilections and outré
writings had hardly prepared her for this.

"Never mind that," said Konski. "Pick a card."

"You don't have any cards," Astaroth observed in a
tired voice.

"It's because of the Nano Collapse. So hard to have
physical stuff any longer."

The lady present was genuinely offended. "You don't
have to use the 'n' word!"

"We must never forget the hard lessons," said
Konski. "I'm sure old Professor Astringent will agree
that there were unexpected benefits to the Nano War.
Or collapse. Or crap-out. Or crash. Or dissolution.
Or . . . I forget the rest. Well, no matter. It was impres-
sive, we'll all agree. Lots more special effects than any
other war. Why, if Earth military forces hadn't used
those molecular decompilers we'd all be so rich now
we wouldn't have anything to do."

He took off his hat—no one else was wearing a
hat—and held it over his heart. "Let's shed a tear for
the end of the nano-trick era. We wanted the treats
instead."

The solemn moment over, he threw the hat over his

head and watched a servo-mech glide out of the service entrance he'd used a moment before. Konski crouched and feigned great excitement as to whether the robot's silver tentacle would snag the ancient headgear before it touched the floor. The robot succeeded and Konski jumped up and down, clapping his hands.

The threesome so diligent in plotting subversion only a short time before now stared at the maniac who was central to their plans. Konski stared back and then noticed his cigar had gone out.

With a flourish, he produced an old-fashioned lighter in the shape of a gun. Once again it was time for the lady present to gasp. (Fainting, feigning shock and blushing with artificial aids were all part of her Feminist Finishing School charms. She only flunked fainting.)

Even possessing the likeness of a gun was forbidden on Earth. Everywhere one could attend Museums of the Gun to learn of the iniquity of firearms.

Bretygne looked at Palmer and noticed his lack of concern. Sometimes she forgot that soldiers and special agents were deprogrammed from the anti-gun conditioning everyone received from birth.

While the drama of the lighter was taking place Astaroth noticed a servo-mech and gestured it over. Everyone must have been standing too close together because just as the ambassador successfully lit his cigar the robot jostled his arm and he dropped the smoldering black rope of tobacco to the antiseptically clean floor.

"Mechanical imbecile!" he shouted. "Lowly metal egg, clean up that mess!"

Suddenly there came the dread cry of "*Laissez faire!*" The terrifying words rose up from the general noise of the crowd. The air was filled with electric tension.

Then the same mysterious voice shouted, "End robot slavery now!"

"Oh, no," muttered Palmer.

"What is it?" asked Bretygne.

"Not what. Who."

Palmer peered into the crowd. The voice cried out again but the words were garbled.

"I can't believe it," said Palmer. "The voice is the same. I always thought Konski was kidding me. The idea seemed too horrible to credit."

The crowd parted. Bretygne grabbed Palmer's arm. Astaroth shook his head and ordered another martini. Approaching them was not merely the twin brother of the ambassador. Worse, the other maniac of the evening was in the same costume presenting a perfect mirror image. He was even smoking another cigar.

The ambassador stood tall, reached into his pocket as if to brandish a weapon and then pulled out another cigar that quickly found its way to his mouth. "Konski, Part Two," thundered the ambassador, "you have no authority here."

"Robots of the world unite!" came an even more thunderous reply. "They have nothing to lose but your chain-smoking!"

"I repeat, you have no standing in this official and officious embassy."

"Oh, for crying out loud," Astaroth exploded, a new drink in his hand. "You're both insane anarchists. How can there even be an anarchist embassy? The whole idea is preposterous."

The two looked at him and sneered.

"You are a minarchist," said the first Konski.

"You are therefore a deviationist," said Part Two.

"Furthermore," continued number one, "Palmer will verify that I am indeed in a position to represent trade deals with Lysander."

"Well, I . . ." began Palmer, but to no avail.

Konski, Part Two, was having none of it. "This slaveholder cannot possibly represent the free and autonomous beings that inhabit the paradise of Kropotkia."

"What the hell is that?" Astaroth wanted to know.

Konski the former was helpful. "Oh, it's just Lysander. My brother refuses to call the planet by its proper name."

"More drinks!" suggested Bretygne. "Make them doubles."

"Triples," amended Palmer.

Ambassador Konski started to touch the servo-mech but it shied away from him. With one last suck of its suction tentacle, it removed the final remains of the fallen cigar and fled. Ashes to ashes, and thence to the garbage recycler.

"It doesn't like you," said Part Two.

Konski shrugged. "Nonsense, a robot can neither like nor dislike anything. Fortunately it has departed before you can violate my private property."

"Ha! You cannot own a self-aware being."

"You can't make a contract with a household appliance."

By this point, the twins were face to face, cigar to cigar. There seemed nothing in heaven or Luna that could stop them.

"Even if they could make contracts," complained Part Two, "such agreements would be null and void, for they cannot sell their primary property which is themselves."

Konski's new cigar quivered with indignation. "Oh, yeah? If you can't sell aspects of your primary property then how can we have the most beloved trade of all true lovers of liberty, namely the fine social work performed by prostitutes throughout the ages?"

"Your area of expertise, eh? Hookers can get away from you but not these poor servo-mechs."

"They don't need liberty any more than your damned cigar needs to escape your incisors!"

"How do you know? Maybe they only lack initiative. I'm fighting for their honor which is more than they ever did."

It went on like that for another five minutes until the Lady Bretygne Lamarr found deep inside her soul the power of two words almost equal to the power of *laissez faire*.

"*Shut up!*" she explained.

She was so loud that her voice was heard throughout the entire ballroom. Dead silence fell over the throng and brought all revelry to a grinding halt. Then someone in the crowd finally realized that underneath the grease paint mustaches and wild hair lurked at least one guest of honor.

The crowd surged forward. A beautiful young girl of twenty-nine was first to speak as children are wont to do. "Rockets away! Seeing two of you is pure lox. May I have dual autographs?"

"Only I am the true ambassador," said Konski.

"But my autograph is more valuable," said Part Two. "It doesn't come free, by the way."

"Mine costs the same!" piped in Konski.

The autographs kept the two of them out of trouble for a while while Palmer, Bretygne and Astaroth discovered a heretofore-unrealized capacity for cocktails. Finally a servo-mech floated above the multitude and announced that dinner was about to be served.

Alas, Part Two heard the announcement. "Will we be violating animal rights tonight?" he wanted to know. "Or perhaps vegetable rights?"

Palmer was starting to feel his fifth drink of the evening. That played no small role in his responding to the terrible twin. "I know for a fact, Mister Brother of the Anarchist Ambassador, that all our food tonight is completely synthetic. The only violation of rights has been on the molecular level."

"Don't ask this one what he thought of the Nano War," pleaded Bretygne in his ear.

"You used the 'n' word," he chided.

Somehow the unwieldy mass of well-dressed and undressed humanity wandered over to the dining area. Part Two went with them. As for Ambassador Konski, he grabbed Lady Lamarr by the arm and announced, "This is our chance. Follow me!"

"Why are you grabbing me by the arm?" asked Bretygne, but not really resisting. "Isn't that a violation of my elbow rights or something?"

"I'll make restitution," he grinned. "Besides, this way I know your boyfriends will follow."

They all went through a service entrance where a space cadet limo was waiting. They piled in and Konski ordered the robot driver to take them out into the lunar night.

Konski's tone of voice lost its strident quality. He sounded like a different person when he said, "Tonight reminded me of an observation by the twenty-first century philosopher Garmon. He said that the truth of all technological societies lies in the manner by which we come to resemble our tools. But I don't want to look like a silver egg with tentacles! I don't want to belong to any labor force that would have me as a member."

Bretygne suddenly felt relaxed for the first time that evening. "You know, Palmer thinks I'm a spoiled brat."

"I've never said that!" he protested.

"But it's true," she said, and not a single man in the limo asked her if she meant it was true that she was spoiled or that it was true that Palmer thought so.

The professor sounded happy, too. "Freedom is learning to balance responsibility along with being spoiled. Both are essential."

Konski nodded. "The human race seems to be on a bell curve. Those who can handle freedom and responsibly are at one end. Those who would be the masters and dictators are on the other end. The vast mass is the bell of the bell curve. They want a little freedom and a little slavery. They play the role of master and slave interchangeably even though they don't want either condition to be permanent."

Palmer couldn't believe what he'd just heard. "That's a surprisingly mature remark to come from a man who just turned in that performance back at the dome."

Konski laughed and started rubbing off his mustache with a bright red handkerchief. "They wanted to see anarchists tonight, didn't they? My brother and I worship a handful of twentieth century movie stars, the ones who had talent. The early, funny ones."

They were sitting in a comfortable semicircle in the back. The guest of honor started acting as if he deserved the title. He patted Palmer on the shoulder. "Enough of the show. Let's get down to brass tacks. Lysander has precious raw materials that are needed to power starships. It would be cheaper to mine them than to produce them artificially. That's also considering the distances involved and the time factors. But we need the United States of Earth to believe that we have a military capacity to defend ourselves."

"You don't!" all three of his critics spoke at once.

"Exactly. But we learned from the loss of a continent that our defense agencies have certain limitations. We know how to live together now, but that doesn't mean we have the organization to withstand an invasion by Earth forces! The bastards on the home world are capable of anything. They think we're all children on Lysander so none of us have rights. We must convince them we are children who can bite!"

The Earth hung above their conversation like a blue and green goblin, threatening the gray expanse of a free Luna. Palmer leaned back in his seat and exhaled slowly. He'd been expecting the moment of decision for some time. Now that it had arrived it was as if a shadow moved across his vision, taking with it all of his worries.

In his whole life, he'd never heard the word freedom used as often as he'd heard it today. The word wouldn't leave him alone. It had gotten inside him. Freedom. Liberty. A light to penetrate his personal darkness.

Looking at Bretygne, he seemed to see her for the first time. He felt something new. He didn't want to have sex with her or to compete with her or to prove anything. He simply felt affection.

Taking her by the hand he smiled. She smiled back. For a brief wonderful moment they were alone in the universe and not even gigantic egos like Konski and Astaroth could intrude.

"I can fix it," said Palmer. "Actually, the three of us can definitely arrange things for you, Mr. Ambassador. But you already know that. We can fool the United States of Earth into believing you have a significant military force. The destruction of the continent on Lysander is proof of your capacity, after all. No one in Berlin would ever believe the real reasons for that disaster."

Konski reached into a compartment and pulled out a small statuette. "This is a replica of the Statue of Liberty."

"Oh, my," said Bretygne. "The one that was destroyed."

"In the Welfare War," Astaroth finished for her.

Konski cradled his trophy. "This is a perfect copy except the inscription on the bottom has been changed. It speaks to what we need now on Lysander. And what we will require as we open new worlds. You three have spent enough time on Earth, don't you think?"

Palmer took the small statue and held it close. He read the inscription out loud:

THIS TIME, JUST SEND US YOUR CHILDREN!

According to Their Need

by Michael A. Stackpole

Father Flynn closed his eyes for a moment and luxuriated in the heat from the reflected sunlight coming up off the lake's silver surface. A gentle breeze provided a hint of a swell to rock the boat, but better was the insistent slap of wavelets against the aluminum hull. While Apogea's orbit around its single sun was a bit too distant to make the world quite warm enough, its largely unspoiled beauty more than compensated for the slight chill.

He opened his blue eyes again and smiled at the woman in the other end of the boat. "I'm thinking, Rina, this is about the closest to Paradise I'll be getting before a discussion with Saint Peter."

The woman laughed lightly and easily, and the youthful tone of her laughter further concealed her age. Flynn knew they were both in their fifties—him solidly, and she just starting—but she hid it well. Still lean, with bright hazel eyes and black hair without a hint of white, she seemed yet as youthful as she had when he first met her on the station. The years had used him a bit harder than they had her, and the resilience that had let her recover from tragedy had been long in evidence throughout his visit.

"Well, Dennis, I hope for your sake that you are incorrect. Apogea *is* very beautiful however." She gave him a very warm smile. "And, despite our lack of luck so far today, it does have the fattest troutganisms I've seen this side of Earth."

"Oh, I believe you, and I'm not in the least disappointed." He winked at her. "After all, it's called fishing, not *catching*, for a reason."

The small lake on which they were drifting lay in a forested hilly basin. The crystal waters were so pure that they just dipped a cup if they were thirsty. Trees resembling pines and maples dotted the hillsides, with Apogea's evolutionary equivalent of cattails lining the shores. Off to the northeast he could see the white crescent of beach they'd set out from, and the cabin hidden a bit farther on, just the edge of the woods.

"It feels as if we're all alone here."

Arina Gadja nodded. "We are. Barring an emergency, accident, seriously poor navigating or someone incredibly rude, we won't see anyone else unless we chose to invite them or accept an invite."

Flynn tapped the chronometer on his left wrist. "But

we're not really alone, are we, since we're being monitored all the time."

"Just for safety's sake. If your heart were to seize up, someone would be along to get you to sick bay."

Flynn shook his head. "You know, I'm still surprised you agreed to come here and live on Apogea. You spent your adult life working security on Qian space stations, enforcing one law over countless individuals who came from a legion of legal traditions. Law and order were so much the fabric of your life, and yet you retire to a world with no government."

Arina started to slowly reel her line in. "Surprised me, too. Given that all that had happened, it seemed like a good choice. Grants to live here are rare, so I could not pass up the chance."

"I know. It's an honor to be given one and I'm thinking I'm grateful you invited me to visit."

"And I'm grateful you came. The only thing Apogea doesn't provide is old friends. Everything else is taken care of, however, and that's how it works. If you think about it, Dennis, governments serve to guarantee security, both in terms of protecting the material we possess, and to see to it that our needs are met."

"Needs save those in the spiritual realm."

She smiled. "True enough, and I know the lack of churches here would be troubling to you, but churches also become a place where power can be concentrated and wielded in favor of one person over another. Here we operate by the golden rule, as overseen by Covenant."

Flynn knew she wasn't using the word Covenant in any religious or legal sense. Covenant was the name given to the vast computer network that administered the world of Apogea. When the creation of the exclusive colony was first proposed, it was agreed that those who wished to live there would put their assets into blind trusts and would come to live on the world forever—barring trips off world necessitated by family emergencies. Their assets and their needs would be taken care of through Covenant, which would monitor wants, whims, and necessitudes, blending desires and providing what people wanted primarily by knowing them as well or better than they knew themselves.

Creating a monastery world with resort trappings for the rich would have been simple, save that hedonistic pursuits precluded complete isolation. Some people bought their way into Apogea. Others, like Arina, earned a grant for service to society—and her grant had been paid for with heroism and blood. Yet others were contract residents. They were heavily screened and brought to Apogea to perform specific services for a year, with contracts renewed if desired. Because needs were met on the world, the generous salaries these people were paid were saved, with hefty performance bonuses being racked up along the way to guarantee good behavior.

On top of that, Covenant practiced random interval reinforcement. The Qian programmers had managed to look at desires and project, into the future, intersection points with external trends. Items and information related to these interests would arrive for the residents at various and unpredictable intervals. It was as if everyone was entered into a lottery on an hourly basis where they might win something they didn't know they wanted, but would please them the moment they got it. These gifts, many quite banal and innocuous, provided excitement and promoted good behavior.

"Oh, Arina, I'm thinking Apogea is quite clever, no doubt about it. When I told Father Ruxton I would be coming to visit, she was rather adamant in warning me about the seductive evil of this place. She said it had been modeled on the trick the Assassins used to play on recruits during the Crusades. They'd drug them and bring them to a magnificent palace where their every need was met. They'd be told they were in Heaven, then after three days, they'd be drugged again and returned to the real world. They'd had their taste of Heaven, so they'd go out and fight against Christendom, knowing the reward they'd have when they were killed."

She nodded and pulled her lure from the water, then set about changing it. "That is the beauty of Apogea, you see. We can exile disruptive influences. For guests and workers, unacceptable behavior is cause for immediate expulsion and forfeiture of bonds and bonuses. For me, being a grant, I'd get pensioned off to some nice resort world. Those who have bought their way in will be returned to the world they once knew, and barred from coming back here ever."

"Oh, the inducements to good behavior are certainly there, but that doesn't guarantee morality, and it doesn't do much for the immortal souls of those living here." Flynn paused as something tugged at the lure unseen in the depths. It wasn't a solid hit, so he continued. "We know, for example, that someone here has the idea that having a harem of sexual partners at his beck and call is a pleasure he wants to enjoy—and we know there are plenty of folks who would see nothing wrong with hiring on for a year here in paradise to deal with that need. And one could even argue that what goes on between consenting adults is fine, barring anyone being injured, but that only refers to physical injuries. The mental and emotional hurts can be considerable. Moreover, the removal from a state of grace is grave, and some might mistake this temporal Heaven for the real thing, playing now and burning later."

"You know I don't disagree with your view concerning morality, and I know you well enough to know that you don't mistake the Church's hierarchy with its spirituality." She tied off a knot, then spread her hands. "I find I can commune with God in this creation as easily as I can in any church."

"And yet," Flynn smiled, "you did have me say Mass and give you the Eucharist when I arrived."

"Religion and spirituality are not forbidden here— nothing is, if it does no harm—just the trappings that would allow it to become harmful."

"If I accept that you are correct, that governments are vital to preserving society through the distribution of wealth, and that meeting all needs obviates the necessity of government, would you concede that Apogea would collapse into anarchy if insecurity or vital shortages were introduced here?"

"At its worst, perhaps, but we also have the advantage of being highly self-sufficient, and a very sparsely populated world. Basic needs could be met easily and while the artificially high standard of living would suffer, the people here would suffer far less than any colony-world population." Arina shrugged. "On a world where, right now, temptation and desire are fulfilled, the necessity to commit crime does not exist."

Flynn nodded. The screening process to come to Apogea, even as a guest, included an examination of records as well as the filling out of numerous forms and polls about tastes and desires. He assumed that for residents of any stripe, the selection process was far more rigorous, and included batteries of psychological screening tests. Residents also had chips implanted in them that served the function of the monitoring device on his wrist. They also recorded physical reactions to stimuli, registering unconscious attractions to asocial behavior, and steps could be taken to curb it or eliminate the person.

Something appeared as a black speck far to the northeast and grew quickly enough. Flynn recognized it as a light Zsytzii transport. It hovered over the cabin for a moment, then came out toward them on the lake. It swooped low, rippling waves in its wake, and hung there, barely a meter off the surface as a side hatch opened. Through the forward windscreens Flynn had already seen one of the long, lean, black-furred Zsytzii Primaries piloting the ship. Another stood at the hatch, and a number of the junior males waited behind him, peering past waist and knees at the two anglers. The Primary wore a minimum of clothing, though the equipment harness did bear rank insignia in the Covenant Safety Service.

Arina gave the Zsytzii a polite nod. "Covenant's peace to you, Captain."

"And to you, Citizen Gadja. It is with regret that Covenant intrudes. We are Captain Lavaryn, and we regret spoiling your time with your friend. Your opinion is sought in a serious matter. Probabilities indicate your guest might be of aid as well."

"What's the problem?"

The Zsytzii smiled quickly, revealing a serrated ribbon of teeth. His juniors followed a second later, dispelling forever their benign appearance. "In the City, someone has died. Natural causes and accident have been statistically excluded, leaving only one alternative."

"Murder?"

The Zsytzii nodded solemnly. "So it is feared. Will you help?"

"I'm not sure what help I could be."

Captain Lavaryn sighed, and his juniors moaned. "Please, citizen, we have no experience in dealing with murder."

Arina glanced at Flynn, and the priest nodded encouragingly at her. The woman smiled slightly, golden sparks flashing from within her hazel eyes. "As you wish, Captain. Let us go."

The City, as it was known, was a fully functioning metropolis. It had been designed down to the square centimeter, for none of it existed fifty years previously when the Apogea project started. The City's development had taken place to reflect the desires, sensibilities, and tastes of the original residents, hence part of it was a disorganized artist section that Flynn had heard described as being "delightfully Bohemian." As nearly as he could tell that indicated that the streets were meant to run haphazardly, and that past every curve was a hidden gallery or cafe or some other little jewel of an establishment containing undiscovered treasures. Other parts of the City had the straight lines of the finest modern developments, and still other suburban communities surrounded the urban center.

The Zsytzii took them directly into the Arts district and set down in a park. The trip from Arina's cabin had taken little more than an hour, as the building had not been located far from the City. She actually had an apartment in one of the modern towers, but spent most of her time out at the lake.

The advantage of Zsytzii transport in service to Covenant was that both Arina and Flynn had suitable clothing provided for them and were able to change en route. Flynn found the shirt, trousers, and jacket, all in black, save for his Roman collar, fit better than the things he normally wore. He was fairly certain that if he made a comment to that effect, suggesting it made him uncomfortable, Covenant would make sure other clothes were more normal fitted.

The uniform Arina had been supplied had been tailored to perfection and shaved five years off her. Dark blue, with red epaulets, cuffs and stripes down the pants, it had enough of a military cut to provide authority. It came complete with a black weapons' harness that had a holster and an Agonizer at her right hip.

Flynn smiled. "Well, Colonel, it's clear Covenant hasn't forgotten why you were given a grant."

"And here I all but had." She nodded, then turned to the Zsytzii officer. "I did retire a colonel in the Qian

Security Service, but it was a pension appointment. I will advise, not take the investigation from you."

The Zsytzii frowned slightly and his juniors groaned. Zsytzii males were born in litters, with the Primary and his juniors having a mild telepathic link which was now often enhanced with cybernetics. The juniors had the intelligence of a six-year-old human—and not a Mozart among them. They functioned well for carrying out simple orders, and during the Zsytzii war had been very effective combatants because of their quickness and small size.

"Colonel Gadja, this is not a concern. We bow to your expertise and hope to learn from you."

"I would be pleased to teach you anything I can." Arina's brows knitted in the concentration Flynn had so often observed. "I will need all the data Covenant can give me on the deceased and his activities, condensed, not raw. Where he has gone, what he likes, known associates, the personality composite Covenant has for him."

Lavaryn nodded. "It shall be done before you will be finished with the crime scene."

Flynn followed Arina from the transport and along the street to a small store of the sort that seemed about as common as fish in the universe. Flynn knew that the presence of water and other evolutionary pressures meant fish were found pretty much everywhere and, similarly, societies seem to produce shops that, to some, sold curiosities, but to others turned trash into treasure. This particular shop had enough dust coating everything that Flynn wondered if it hadn't predated the Apogea project. Exotic knickknacks from hundreds of worlds and thousands of cultures filled every recess of the small shop, save for the narrow aisles meandering between piles. The sales counter had been built into the back wall, cutting off a doorway into the back. The threadbare curtain had been drawn back to show a shabby storage area choked with things on sagging shelves.

The store had clearly been created with an eye toward atmosphere. The floorboards creaked as they walked toward the counter. The air had a dry scent equal parts old leather, old wood and a hint of pungent alien musk. Had Flynn not been very conscious of the fact that he was on Apogea, he could have found himself anywhere in the Qian Commonwealth.

The body lay sprawled on the floor before the counter with a sheet pulled over it. The sheet had tented up toward the chest and when Arina pulled it back, the cause for that was readily apparent. A tusk of some sort had been shoved through the man's chest. Flynn followed the curve of it with his eye and figured it had slid in and up to pierce his heart.

Arina squatted beside the body and turned the dead man's face toward her. "Oh!"

"What is it?"

"I know him."

Flynn came over and stood by the man's feet. "He looks familiar to me, too. Did we see him at the spaceport?"

"No, we know him from Purgatory Station." She smiled slightly. "His name was Flambeau? No, no, it was Fonteneau, that's it, Stephen Fonteneau."

"That was six years ago. He'd come to the station to steal that Golathi princeling's coronet. You and Fith caught him. I remember speaking with him, hearing his Confession." The priest rubbed a hand over his jaw. "I'd not have been thinking I'd see him again, especially after he escaped custody."

"Oh, he was a slippery one. Fith knew that, so we split shifts, never left him alone until he was sent off to stand trial." Arina smiled. "That was the case where Fith and I learned we really complemented each other."

"I seem to recall you were fair inseparable after that." Flynn nodded solemnly. Fith Chykip had been the Qian security director. He and Arina fell hard for each other and, despite Human-Qian pairings being infertile, decided to marry. Flynn had worked hard to get Father Ruxton to sanction the nuptials, and he'd been there to perform the Last Rites for Fith when terrorists widowed Arina.

Captain Lavaryn entered the shop and slipped a datapad from the holster on his equipment harness. "Colonel, the man's name is David Holcomb. He is a contract worker, in month nine. Covenant reports he spends much time in the company of another hire, Deana Thompson, who lives near here. Holcomb was last reported to be in her apartment at midnight. There is no indication why he would be here, nor of his entering this place, nor of his ever having been here before."

Arina blinked. "Covenant's monitoring lost him?"

The Zsytzii nodded. "It happens on occasion when there is interference. Usually it is momentary, sometimes longer."

"That's interesting." She frowned. "Who is assigned to this shop? Where is he?"

"The owner is Regan Park. We have sent a junior to fetch him, and another to bring Deana Thompson to the ship. We know where she is, but he seems to be missing." He canted his head to the side slightly. "She is coming."

"I'll need background data on her." Arina stood. "I will need a complete forensic workup on his body. The medical center should be able to do the work."

Flynn pointed at the thing in the man's chest. "You know what that is, then?"

"Samuel Abrams—he used to run the Novajet Transport Corporation—has a hunting preserve on one of the southern islands. There are some fairly fantastic creatures there. Some are xenobiologicals, some are lab-born monsters—and that's half a mandible set from something he called a 'giant chigger.' They're supposed to be tougher than a Bouganshi to kill. I understand he's got several mandible sets on display both in his home and at the hunting lodge."

"So, they're not the sort of thing that would be found in this shop, are they?"

She shook her head. "I'd say not. Captain, can you pull Covenant's data on chigger pinchers?"

The Zsytzii hesitated as he silently worked his mouth through the pronunciation of "chigger pinchers." "It shall be done, Colonel. Deana Thompson is in the ship now, but she has not been told why she is there."

Flynn held the shop's door open for Arina, then matched her stride back to the ship. "And you'd not be telling Lavaryn who Holcomb really is because . . . ?"

"Not out of any suspicion of him. Seems to me, when he's stressed, he bleeds some thought and emotion into his juniors. Learning Holcomb was a bold thief might shake his confidence, and he might let something slip that a junior would tell Deana Thompson. Keeping the true identity a secret for the moment is best."

"I can see that, yes." He looked at her. "And how are you doing knowing a serpent has crawled into this garden?"

Arina stopped, blinking her eyes with surprise. "You know, I'd just sort of slipped back into the job, and wasn't thinking of the grander implications."

"You'd have gotten there."

"Possible. And it's not just one serpent; it's at least two. Fonteneau shouldn't have been here. Somehow Covenant lost track of him. So we need to know why he was in that shop, why he was here on Apogea, and what he's been doing for the last nine months. It's a legion of snakes."

They returned to the transport and found Deana Thompson sitting all tight and small in the passenger compartment. One of the juniors had fetched her a cup of tea. The petite woman nervously tucked a strand of blond hair behind one ear. She gave them a hopeful smile. "Hi."

Flynn sat beside her on the bench seating, and Arina took up a position opposite her. "I'm Arina Gadja, Colonel Gadja of Safety Services. This is Father Dennis Flynn, a visitor here and a friend of mine. Covenant has requested our aid in resolving a situation involving David Holcomb. You know him?"

"Is he all right?"

Arina's head came up. "What would make you think he might not be?"

Deana hesitated, then looked down into her cup of tea. "Nothing."

Flynn laid a hand on her shoulder and felt her jump. "Listen to me, Miss Thompson, there's going to be nothing worse in all this than your fear."

The edge in Arina's voice contrasted sharply with the quiet softness of his. "Miss Thompson, you must realize how important this is for Covenant to request the help of a citizen. The sooner we get to the bottom of this, the better for all involved."

Deana shook her head. "I told him he shouldn't do it."

"Do what?"

The woman sipped her tea, then held her left hand out, palm forward, showing the hint of a scar where her identification chip had been implanted. "There was one night, David and I were out having a drink, dancing, just having fun. We struck up a conversation with another couple and talked a little about our lives before Apogea. The guy said that the one thing he didn't like about Apogea was that Covenant knew where we were and what we were doing at all times. He said that back in the real world he could go out, get roaring drunk, and wake up not remembering where he was, where he'd been or what he'd done with whom. That not knowing, that was a thrill for him, but here Covenant could tell him everything, taking the mystery out of it."

Flynn shivered, and it wasn't just the man's illusion that what he had done remained unknown. God certainly knew. What chilled Flynn was the man's willful desire to abandon responsibility for his actions, his wanton disavowal of the rules by which society governed itself, and his being thrilled by the not knowing. It was passively nihilistic behavior that could, as the desire for greater thrills built, become actively destructive.

Deana sighed heavily. "We kind of agreed—not that we liked the idea of not knowing, but knowing that Covenant is always watching over you can get to be kinda much. I mean, I know it's not making judgments, just collecting data and changing things to make sure what we want and need is provided. It's benign and positive, but sometimes it feels smothering, you know?"

Arina nodded slowly. "I can see how you could find it so."

Deana stared at her for a second, then broke eye-contact. "So the guy says he's heard of someone who had these blackout chips. You wear it on your wrist, just like he's got, covering your ID chip. The box reads your home location, or a place you're likely to be, and broadcasts to the system that this is where you are. What you do then is, you get these blackout things, then bring party stuff to a place, like a warehouse or the basement of an apartment building, whatever. You get told where when you get the blocker. You have parties and stuff, everybody bringing something. It's cool, and everyone is liking the fact that Covenant thinks we're all home and in bed."

"So there was a party last night?"

Deana nodded. "I went. David was supposed to meet me, but he never made it. I didn't worry since he'd done that before. He'd warned me those times, though."

"Can you tell me when those times were?"

The small woman frowned. "About six weeks, and then three weeks ago."

"You don't think he was seeing someone else?"

Deana's eyes widened. "David? No. We were in love. He was going to be leaving before I was, but we both had signed for good bonus money, so we planned to marry and head back to Mars, or maybe out to one of the Commonwealth worlds to make a life together. Why would you ask that?"

"Routine. Did David know Regan Park?"

"Who?"

"The man who ran the curio shop over here on Aquila Street."

Deana shook her head. "Not that I knew." She turned her left hand back over, then thumbed the ring on her fourth finger. "David may have gotten this there. He gave it to me as a gift. Said Covenant wasn't the only one who could surprise people with nice things."

"A couple more questions, then we will be done. Does the name Stephen Fonteneau mean anything to you?"

"No, not really." Deana grinned a bit. "David had a twin brother named Stephen, so when someone would shout the name, he'd react, all unconsciously. It got to be a joke. There were times when I would leave him messages, asking Stephen to tell David I needed to see him. We made up a twin sister for me, Diana, and he did the same thing."

"Do you know Samuel Abrams? Did David?"

"No, no, not at all. We don't run in those circles. I work with the local theater company, and I know Abrams and his wife had a box. They come and bring friends, but I've never spoken to them. David worked as a sommelier at Cuisine Rigel. He might have met them there, but he used to talk about how servants are always invisible to those people. The only time they took notice of him was when he recommended a new wine, and it would be an import that Covenant had brought in and had earmarked for them anyway. He felt like it was a charade, and occasionally had fun describing how folks who knew nothing praised the wine for things he'd described, not anything in the wine itself."

Arina nodded. "Thank you, Miss Thompson, you have been most helpful."

"Fine, but you've not told me what this is about."

Flynn's friend nodded slowly. "I know, and I couldn't until I had spoken to you. I'm afraid I have some bad news for you. David didn't return last night because he was severely injured. Fatally injured."

"Fatally?" Deana's voice faded to a strangled whisper that caught in her throat. She raised a hand to cover her mouth, while the tea in her cup splashed wildly. Flynn took the cup from her hand, passing it to a junior, then settled an arm around her shoulder. "How?"

Flynn kept his voice low and even. "Hush now, child. He died quickly and in no pain whatsoever. We're thinking he was at the curio shop—likely getting you another gift—and surprised a thief."

"Oh, God!" Deana turned and pressed her face

against Flynn's chest, grabbing a tight handful of his jacket. "He's dead . . . dead. . . ."

A junior arrived leading a tall, heavy-set woman whose face immediately registered alarm as she recognized Deana and heard her sobs. She slid onto the bench on the other side of Deana and stroked her hair. "I'm Maggie Wilson, we work together. I was brought here . . ."

Arina smiled solemnly. "A tragedy. David is dead."

"Oh, Deana." The larger woman gathered Deana into her arms hugging her tightly, and the sobbing woman released Flynn and clung to her friend.

Flynn and Arina left the transport and the two women, meeting Lavaryn at the base of the short landing ramp. "You did well, Captain, bringing the friend here."

"Thank you, Colonel. We have had experience in informing people of accidental deaths, and having friends present seems to help. We regret, however, to have found nothing else of use. The place where Regan Park is supposed to be is vacant. Two ships have left the spaceport in the time since Holcomb's death, at least as calculated by the doctors, and we do not know if he smuggled himself on board. Procedures checking outbound passengers are not as rigorous as they are coming in."

"It will be important for us to find Regan Park, but we don't know if he is a victim who has been taken elsewhere and killed, a murderer or in league with a murderer. We need to discover what has happened. Right now I need Covenant to check and see if Samuel

Abrams or his wife, Veronika, had been to Cuisine Rigel in the last nine months."

The Zsytzii produced his datapad and communicated a request for that data. "A dozen times. Most recently two weeks ago, a week before that, six weeks, two months. The guest list varies from two to twelve, often new arrivals. The Abrams take great delight in sharing a restaurant they consider their 'discovery' with friends."

Lavaryn looked up from the flat-screen device. "Covenant reports they invited you there, but you refused."

Arina shrugged. "I had nothing to wear."

"Rina?" Flynn looked at her incredulously as he tugged on the collar of his coat. "This is Apogea. Covenant provided us these clothes so we'd not be in our fishing gear to make inquiries. You would have been provided whatever you needed."

"I just didn't want to go. Veronika understood." She held up a hand to forestall further discussion. "Lavaryn, we need to canvas the neighborhood. Ask about Regan Park. Ask about the blackout chips. You did get that from the junior listening to the interrogation, yes?"

"We did."

"Good."

"We did not understand the reference to 'Stephen Fonteneau.' Covenant says he is a thief, specializing in jewels and other rare items. What is his connection here? Should we be looking for him, and the other half of that mandible in his possession?"

"Him, no. He was David Holcomb."

The Zsytzii's face screwed down at the brows in a

frown, but came up at the lip in a snarl. "We do not think that is possible. Not to doubt your identification, but that would mean that Covenant was fooled on his identification when he came here."

"I don't like the implications of that idea either, Captain." Arina shook her head. "I need a current location on Samuel and Veronika Abrams."

The Zsytzii's fingers caressed the datapad's input buttons with blurred speed. "He is at his hunting lodge in the islands. She is in the City. Shall we communicate a request for an interview?"

"Please. An hour from now, at her home here."

One of the juniors brought Arina a datapad from the ship. Captain Lavaryn smiled. "We will communicate the address to you, as well as keep you apprised of our investigation."

Arina nodded and slid the data device into the harness's holster. "I know where she lives. It's not far. We'll walk. I get to think while I walk. Let's go, Dennis."

Father Flynn joined her and smiled. "You took to having the weight of that harness on you fast enough, I'm thinking."

She shot him a sidelong glance. "I've been out of it for two years. I'm two years away from what Deana Thompson is going through, which sometimes doesn't seem very far, but other times . . . When I first got here I just wanted to be alone, to mourn, and I know that probably wasn't the best way to deal with Fith's death, but it was the only way I knew to do it."

"The healing process, it's different for everyone. Folks may tend one way or another, wanting to be around folks, wanting to be alone, working, retiring, and any combination of the same." Flynn rested a hand on her shoulder. "You're a vital woman, Arina, resilient. Hunkering down to heal up, that made sense. It was always your way. I was happy indeed to receive your invitation to visit. I took it as a good sign, especially given that I was there when everything happened."

"You helped hold me together, Dennis, and for that I owe you a debt I can't repay."

"Stopping those Spiral Way terrorists put everyone else in a debt they couldn't repay you." Flynn squeezed her shoulder. Spiral Way, being an anarchistic group looking to overthrow the Qian Commonwealth, had tried to enter Commonwealth space at Purgatory Station, figuring that any backwater station such as it would have lax security. Arina and Fith took their jobs seriously, and discovered that the Novajet Transport ship had been hijacked. In it were weapons, including some virals that would have wrought havoc within the Commonwealth. The lightfight that resulted in the transport being secured and the terrorists killed had cost the life of a half-dozen security personnel, Fith being foremost among them.

"So I've been told, many times. I know Samuel Abrams exerted considerable influence to get me a grant to live here. I think he even created and had spread a rumor saying the Spiral Way had specifically targeted Apogea to make me seem even better." She shook her head. "I'm sure some people decided I should come here since they figured my presence would be enough to keep Spiral Way on the other side of the galaxy."

"Do you think Apogea will remain paradise with news of the murder getting out?"

"It will take more than an isolated incident to bring things crashing down." Arina opened her hands as they walked along through the artist's quarter, heading toward the tall towers to the north. "You seem to assume, my friend, that in the absence of a government, the slightest pressure will cause people to revert to animals. Apogea follows a simple model, much akin to that of children playing a pickup game of hockey. They set boundaries, they devise goals, they dispense with some rules and create others to suit their needs, with the will of the group determining what is right and functional. If someone disagrees, they go home."

"The needs of the people here are far more sophisticated than the needs of children playing hockey."

"There is no disputing that. The absence of want doesn't bring with it an absence of stupidity. People get drunk and do stupid things. They get jealous and do stupid things, but those here have been screened to minimize those tendencies, and are monitored to pick up on them and exile them before they become a problem."

Flynn nodded. "And yet, Fonteneau was here. How many more like him are there?"

"No way of knowing. The fact is, of course, that he had to have lied to get here, so his behavior from the first would earn him exile the moment he was caught. But, were he to live here through his contract and function within society, would we have been diminished by his presence? Would we have suffered because of him? You can look at someone like Samuel Abrams, in fact, and note that he has likely done as much harm as good with his businesses, but as long as he fits in with our society here, what he has done off Apogea matters not at all."

"Do you believe that? What if a murderer, some planetary dictator, bought his way into Apogea, would you not find it morally reprehensible that he could be here?"

"His presence? No. Him, certainly; and I'd not associate with him at all. In some ways it could be argued that here, where there is no mechanism for generating power, such a person is rendered harmless. The simple fact of the matter, however, is that because having him here would not rise high in the consciousness of the people in terms of desire, Covenant would not generate an invitation to have him come to Apogea."

Flynn frowned. "I see your point, but I wonder at another one. You seem to argue that an absence of want leads to stability, but does it not also lead to stagnation? What impetus to strive in life?"

"For the contractors, the impetus comes in the nature of the bonuses they get when they leave us." Arina shrugged. "For the others, we are on the other side of striving. We have striven, and we are here, in a sanctuary."

Before Flynn could address that point with another concern, they reached the tower where Veronika Abrams had taken up residence. Covenant checked their identification, opening the building to them, and had a lift in the lobby waiting. It whisked them up to the fifty-first floor, opening into a marble-lined private foyer, across from which a wall of glass gave them a stunning view of the City and the lush, verdant landscape stretching far to the south.

Veronika Abrams greeted them herself. Willowy and graceful, she moved with the ease of a dancer in the flowing blue robe she wore gathered at the waist with a golden rope. Her black hair had been cut short and framed a pixieish face with large dark eyes and full lips. Flynn didn't wonder if she'd had a new face cloned then put in place—doing that was, for women of her class, to be expected and quite unremarkable. Still, the light in her eyes suggested to him that her following class convention came less out of personal vanity, than a sense of fun and delight in seeing her young self in the mirror once more.

The woman advanced, smiling. "Arina Gadja, so good to see you again. A colonel in Covenant's service, well. Unusual for a resident to work, but, I would guess, necessary. And you are Father Flynn?"

"I am."

"Don't be surprised, Father, I am well aware of who comes and goes these days. Mostly coming, a few going, of course. Tracking these things are all that keep me occupied." Veronika linked her arm through Arina's and steered her into the sitting room off to the left side of the foyer. "Now, sit and tell me what is the matter."

Arina joined Veronika on the white fabric couch, while Flynn settled into a matching chair. "Mrs. Abrams, there has been a murder."

The woman started. "A murder? Not Sam . . ."

"No, not your husband, but someone you have met

before. David Holcomb. He was the wine steward at Cuisine Rigel."

Veronika frowned and glanced up toward the ceiling. "Not terribly tall, dark brown hair?"

"That's him."

"I remember him, vaguely." Her eyes sharpened. "What has this to do with me?"

"We have reason to believe he has been here, in this apartment. He has a history of theft, and was found in possession of chigger mandibles. We think he might have taken more, and you are known to have a fine collection of jewelry."

Veronika's hand went to her throat. "Mandibles . . . They're in my husband's study. That's where we have the safe. Come on."

She led them through the suite of rooms and into a room filled with dark wood panels and festooned with the mounted heads of animals slain on a half-dozen worlds. Veronika made immediately for a broad hearth, the corners of which were decorated with chigger mandibles. She counted the four pairs, then pointed to the center of the mantelpiece. "There was another set there, mounted on a stand. It's gone."

She moved to the middle of the hearth and reached up inside, fingering an unseen catch. A panel set with the Novajet logo split apart and opened right in the middle of the mantle. Veronika reached in and withdrew several velvet-covered boxes, then carefully counted them. "One's missing."

Arina took the boxes from her and put them on the massive desk situated in the corner. "Open them, tell me what's gone."

"I don't need to. . . ." Her hand covered her mouth. "It was an emerald *cherengata*, very rare."

Flynn blinked. "You had a *cherengata*?"

"Sam gave it to me as a present when we arrived here on Apogea. I don't know, didn't know, its history; that piece's history. I mean, I know that when the Zsytzii overran the Jirandik worlds, the Jirandi ransomed themselves by giving up these heirlooms. But, you know, not all of them did. Some had been sold before and, many, you know, after the Zsytzii war was settled. Sam said it was one of those, that the provenance was data-perfect on it."

The priest looked over at Arina. "Would Fonteneau steal something to right a wrong?"

She shifted her shoulders uneasily. "For the challenge of saying he had been to Apogea and come away with a prize, certainly. A *cherengata* would still go for a great deal on the open market. It would be just like him to take only that one piece. And the mandibles, just to prove where he'd gotten the *cherengata*."

Veronika hugged her arms around herself. "Will you catch him?"

"The thief? He's dead. His murderer? I don't know." Arina smiled. "I don't think you have anything to worry about, though, Mrs. Abrams. Fonteneau had to work very hard to get here. I doubt there is anyone else who could manage the deception it took, especially as Covenant will modify procedures to prevent a recurrence. We will keep you informed of how the investigation is going. With any luck at all we should be able to return your *cherengata* to you."

"Thank you, Arina." The woman smiled. "I hope I

won't just see you in your official capacity. I have understood your wanting time alone, but there can be too much of that. When we invited you to dinner, we weren't just being polite. On a world where people buy their way into paradise, spending time with who earned it is very dear."

Arina nodded. "I, ah . . . thank you. I'm slowly returning to the world and I appreciate your concern. I wanted to visit. I got as far as your door, but turned away. Your invitation, it was just too soon for me."

"That was understood, Arina, but the invitation is yet open. While you are in the City, we shall get time to visit, your work allowing. And you as well, Father. I was raised Catholic and have lapsed since being here. I'd offer to let you hear my Confession, but the things I have seen would give you a stroke."

"It's not the things you've seen, Mrs. Abrams, but what you've been doing while you've seen them that would be constituting sin." The priest smiled. "If you feel the need, while I am here, I would be pleased to be of service."

"I shall bear that in mind, Father, thank you."

Arina and Father Flynn caught public transport back to her apartment in the City, and Captain Lavaryn soon joined them. The two safety officers synched their datapads and then set about reviewing all they had learned. Both of them characterized it as a great deal, but lamented it still did not tell them terribly much.

David Holcomb was positively identified as Stephen Fonteneau, according to files Covenant pulled in from Commonwealth computers. How he had gotten to

Apogea remained unclear, but a David Holcomb had applied for work and had been accepted, then had died in an accident. Fonteneau had somehow discovered Holcomb's misfortune and had exploited it. Because no one knew how he'd done that, the possibility that others might be present under an assumed identity could not be discounted.

Fishing was soon forgotten as hours became days of sifting evidence, formulating conjectures, finding facts to support or destroy a theory. Witnesses were interviewed again, follow-up questions narrowed the gaps in the known information. The solution to the murder lay tantalizingly close, they could feel it, but proved as elusive as Apogea's trout.

The presence of blackout chips was beyond dispute. Covenant's analysis showed they were not so sophisticated that they couldn't be manufactured right there on Apogea, fabricated from parts taken out of existing machines. Apogea safety services were having no luck tracking the distribution of the things, nor in locating the parties where the hidden met; but they felt confident they'd get a break on that angle soon. As rumors spread of the devices, all manner of folks wandered around, snooping, looking to play detective and beat the safety services at their own game, or to join the rebels who gathered to enjoy themselves.

After a week of sifting through interviews conducted in the neighborhood of Park's curio shop, the mountains of evidence that had been gathered, and applying her knowledge of criminal activity, Arina had come up with a simple theory of the case. Park's shop had not been very popular—virtually no one in the area had been in it or had seen Park. His background indicated he was a small-time merchant and she suspected that, under another name, he'd been a fence. He applied for and got passage to Apogea, either at Fonteneau's request or in seeking to hide from authorities and enemies.

Once on Apogea, he and Fonteneau met each other. Fonteneau had come for the *cherengata*. He arranged with Park to smuggle the loot off the world, since Park had no connection with the Abramses. Once the theft had been discovered, Fonteneau would have known that he'd be questioned, since the only sure way the thief would have known the *cherengata* was in the City would have been if he'd seen it on Veronika.

They pinpointed the robbery as having taken place three weeks before the murder, right after the last visit the Abramses had paid to Cuisine Rigel. Veronika remembered having worn the *cherengata* that night. She also recalled a discussion with their guests about all just going back to the apartment, changing into traveling clothes, and heading down to the hunting lodge. They had talked about not needing to drag anything along, since the lodge was informal and relaxed. Veronika had blushed over the fact that she treated servants as if they were invisible, providing Fonteneau with all the information he needed to accomplish his goal.

Arina assumed that after the theft, Fonteneau had given the *cherengata* to Park, then later changed his mind about having Park smuggle it away. They had a falling out, Park killed Fonteneau, then fled from Apogea. She did allow that it was possible that Park remained on the world, hiding himself with blackout chips, but if that were the case eventually he would be caught.

Deana Thompson's decision to prematurely terminate her contract and leave Apogea caused them to take another look at her. A discreet search of her apartment turned up nothing. She was allowed to leave and the general sentiment about her situation induced Covenant to not only pay her the bonus for which she had contracted, but to increase it.

At the spaceport, Arina and Lavaryn ushered him past immigration control, noting with a laugh that their methods had been singularly unsuccessful in stopping Park. "If you see him, Dennis, please let someone know."

Flynn nodded, standing in that limbo between Immigration and the departure lounge for the shuttle up to the orbital station. "Just as well he got away in one minor sense. Without a government, you'd be having a hard time trying him for murder. You'd exile him, which seems little punishment for his crime."

"God exiled Adam and Eve from Eden to punish them."

"But they weren't murderers."

"Cain was, and God made him wander the Earth forever." Arina smiled. "And Cain was the father of us all."

"True enough. That seed of evil might be in all of us, but perhaps your situation here doesn't nurture it. The lack of want might not be the lack of temptation, but it does seem to do away with much of it." Flynn drew Arina into a hug. "God be with you, my dear. Don't be working too hard."

Arina pulled back and smiled. "Thank you, Dennis. I am tired, but I needed this. I'll be more than ready to hang up the harness when this business is done, but for the moment it's good to remember who I was before . . ."

"I know, Rina. It's good to have you back." He shook hands with the Zsytzii. "Now, Captain Lavaryn, I expect you to be taking good care of her."

"We treasure our mentor." The Zsytzii smiled as two of his juniors hugged Arina's legs. "We have learned much, and will learn more, much more."

"Very good, the both of you. All luck and peace." Flynn plucked a small bag from one of the juniors. "Now, the lot of you, get back to work. I'll expect to hear how it turned out."

"You will, Dennis, you will." Arina waved to him, then retreated with the Zsytzii brood out of the building.

Father Flynn shouldered his bag and entered the departure lounge. He set his bag down on a bench, sparing only a brief nod in the direction of an amorous couple over in the corner. Before he could seat himself, however, a woman approached him, slowly drawing down the hood of her cloak.

Flynn let the surprise fully register on his face. "You ought not to be here, Mrs. Abrams."

She raised her wrist and tapped the blackout device. "As far as Covenant knows, I'm not." She withdrew a small velvet-covered box from within her cloak and pressed it into his hands. "You will see to it that this gets back to its rightful owners."

"Of course."

"Thank you. I couldn't bear to keep the *cherengata* when I knew how it had been stolen." Veronika shook her head. "I would have sent it back directly, but Sam, he's so funny about that sort of thing. He thrills in shaving deals on the dark side of things, taking risks like that. To give this back would suggest he was wrong in having bought it in the first place. He didn't mind it being stolen back away from him. He greatly enjoyed the daring nature of the theft, and that the thief had done the impossible just to take something from *him*. It meant he was still important. He pretty much chortled about the theft, and has been alive planning how to secure things in the future."

Flynn nodded. "And since Covenant knows you don't want stolen pieces as gifts, your husband will not have the opportunity to buy same from now on."

"Right."

"It will be my pleasure to get this back to the Jirandi *cheren* to whom it belonged." He gave her a smile. "Thank you for setting this all in motion. Arina needed this. After her husband's death, she wondered if she had somehow lost her edge, and that's why he died. She needed time to mourn, and then she needed to be reminded that she is good, she's strong, she's smart. Working on this whole theft and murder might have exhausted her physically, but she's so alive mentally, well, it's good to see. Wonderful."

"I agree, Father."

"Excuse me, Father, would you want some help with your bag? We'll be boarding, soon."

The priest turned and smiled at the man from the

corner. "Despite your looking a fair sight more alive than when last I saw you, Mr. Fonteneau, I'm thinking Miss Thompson there will be more appreciative of your help than I will."

"Father, that was just a brain-dead clone they made to kill, not me."

"I know, Stephen, I know." The priest shivered. "That was the nastiest bit of this deception, cloning you to kill. Now, your Miss Thompson, she's forgiven you the dying?"

"Nothing to forgive, Father. I knew he wasn't dead all along." Deana slipped her arm through Fonteneau's. "When Covenant weighed the two problems of Mrs. Abrams needing to get rid of the *cherengata* without incurring her husband's wrath, and Arina Gadja's need for redemption of her self-esteem, it came up with this plan, built out of pieces of Arina's past. It hired me, an actress, to play the part of Stephen's lover. That we actually fell for each other made things that much more convincing. Covenant saw having an innocent led to believe her lover had died as being harmful, hence I was brought in to act the part."

Fonteneau raised an eyebrow. "Of course, she knew she was looking for me before I knew of her, but it worked. I'm glad I came because when Covenant located me, I'd been hidden away good. I'd gone straight you know, Father, after escaping. Here I got the chance to use my skills for good, got a new identity and records expunged in the real world, and love to boot."

Veronika smiled. "And Regan Park never existed, so the hunt for him can continue, as will the searches for the sources of the blackout chips. A little rebellion is good for people, gives them things to think about, talk about, and keeps the world alive for people who thrive on intrigues. The hint of danger is all we need."

The priest's eyes narrowed. In many ways, it seemed, Arina's game analogy had not been far off. The will of the people determined the direction in which Covenant would allow things to flow. The computer did not govern or control, but encouraged and facilitated harmony with the will of Apogea's people. Despite the complexity of society's needs, the balance was maintained and the world's community flourished.

"Anything beyond a hint of danger is probably more than folks here desire, and with good reason." Flynn smiled, then leaned in and kissed Veronika on the cheek. "Fortunately, the serpents in this garden all seem benign. Enjoy the peace that brings you, and know how lucky you are.

Pakeha

by Jane Lindskold

Ambrose Kidd, an old Kiwi sailor who remembered those days, was the first to tell Faelin about Aotearoa, yarning over a tankard of winter ale in a San Francisco pub. This was back when Faelin—an orphan of twelve—was still lying about his age to get a job clearing tables and such in a bar.

"Maybe if we hadn't been so spoiled then," the old salt would always begin, "we could've kept things the way they were, but we were spoiled—telephone, the Internet, cruise ships, jet airplanes—New Zealand weren't just a bunch of volcanic islands off the hither side of Australia; we were part of the first world. It might make you laugh, but tourism was a major part of our economy. Anybody with enough money could reach New Zealand in less than a day.

"Most folks skipped out when they saw what the petroleum virus was doing. You born-since can't imagine what that virus meant. Seems like just about everything then had petroleum by-products in it. Not just the obvious stuff like fuel and plastics, but clothing, medicines, even food was full of the stuff. Hell, I ain't telling anything you haven't heard before, son."

He wasn't, either. Faelin had heard stories like this a million times before. What fascinated him was where the story went from here. The New Zealanders had taken a novel approach to the crisis. While most nations strove to keep things as much the same as possible—laying new, untainted cables for telegraph and telephone for example—New Zealand's remaining population resolved to make a radical change.

"I remember my folks talking about it," Kidd went on. "Lady name of Christine Pesh had the idea, as I recall. Bright lady, fancied for prime minister if the oil bugs hadn't got loose. In a way, that makes it odd she should come up with such a plan, but then again, as they tell it, she'd always been one of those who contrary to reason—given they make their money outta government—think that a government that governs least governs best."

Faelin laughed and scooped up the old man's tankard, replacing it with another, filled while the boss's back was turned.

"Sounds to me," he commented, swiping circles on the tables with a dirty rag, "like this Christine Pesh was just lazy."

Ambrose Kidd snorted. "Not at all. It's harder work
to make folk think for themselves than to think for 'em.
Anyhow, Christine Pesh proposed—and got her proposal out while the communication system was still
working pretty well—that government be phased out.
She argued that those Kiwis who remained would have
enough to do keeping mutton and fish on the table
without supporting deadbeat politicians. I don't know
how she managed it—remember, son, I was younger
than you are now when this happened—but she got
her measure passed."

Faelin was California born and bred. He'd heard of
wilder schemes, but he knew how governments worked.

"Seems like someone would have appealed," he said.

"There were those who tried," Kidd agreed, "but
Pesh and her cronies told 'em there was no government anymore to listen to their appeal. Meantime,
while these pro-government factions blustered and
debated—'cause they couldn't even agree among themselves which way things *should* be run, if they got
government started again—the petroleum virus kept
chewing away at stuff. Telephone failed. Computers
flashed nonsense and died—lord how I cried when I
couldn't get my games to run! Cars and trucks—all of
which needed petroleum to go and even if they hadn't
were so full of plastic parts that they crumpled up . . ."

"Just like here," Faelin interrupted, knowing he was
being rude, but eager to hear the real story.

"That's right," Kidd said, thin lips shaping the half
smile of an old man who realizes that the great events
of his life are dull fodder to the eager young. "And
so Pesh got her way. There were some riots, but most

of those who disagreed simply got on ships and left.
Most, I hear, got only as far as Australia, where they
found more government than anyone could want—but
that's another tale.

"You're wanting to hear about New Zealand, or
Aotearoa as they renamed it, saying that since the
nation was certainly new but had nothing to do with
Zeeland—some Dutch place, I recall—they might as
well go back to the old Maori name for the land.
Prettier, too, means something like Land of the Long
White Cloud."

Faelin nodded encouragingly. The boss didn't care
if he chatted up the customers during these slow hours,
not so long as he worked while he did so and the
customers kept drinking.

"There were a couple of townships," Kidd went on,
"Christ Church was one, I recall, that experimented
with government. Problem was, it's hard to run a
government when nobody except you is playing by the
rules, sorta like playing soccer when three-quarters of
the players insist on picking the ball up with their
hands. None of those enclaves lasted more than about
twenty years.

"My folks had decided to stay on in Aotearoa. They
ran an inn out at Thames, augmenting their business
with salvage—lots of folk worked salvage in those days.
An uncle offered to take me on his ship as cabin boy—
an island cruise, then—it'd be a while before anyone
tried to go much farther than Australia. No reason or
so it seemed to us."

Kidd paused, visibly swallowing down tales that
covered some sixty years at sea. Faelin felt a tinge of

curiosity about them, but not enough to keep him from prompting:

"And the rest of the Kiwis? How did things go for them?"

"They were pretty damn hot on their new idea, called Aotearoa the new frontier, compared it to the American West, like we used to see in the movies. Movies were . . ."

"I know, I know," Faelin said impatiently. "I *am* Californian! So everyone wore guns and rode horses?"

"Well," Kidd laughed, "many did, but that wasn't why folks made the comparison—at least not the only reason. More reason was because there was no law but what folks carried in their hearts. That's still how it is today—or at least how it was when I left Aotearoa a couple years back, and I don't see why it should have changed. No law books or lawyers, no presidents or monarchs, no rules and regulations, just common sense, hard work, and prosperity for those who earn it."

Faelin never forgot Ambrose Kidd's stories. Indeed, he became the old sailor's constant companion—for it soon became clear that Kidd was never sailing home again. The boy's eager attention was meat and drink to Kidd, just as his stories were to the orphan boy. After the sailor died, Faelin found that he was starving for more.

He took jobs around the ports and soon learned to spot a Kiwi sailor by a certain proud lift to his head. An offer of a drink usually got the boy more stories. Work as a dockhand evolved into work aboard ships— first in port, then at sea.

Chafing under California's numerous regulations, all of which seemed to exist—as far as Faelin could tell—to keep the strong and able from profiting while buoying up the weak and unfit, Faelin happily took a berth on the *Speculation*.

Speculation was an ocean-going free-trader, a sailing vessel modeled off the old China clipper—a ship type that, ironically, had met its demise due to the evolution of the coal-dependent steamers soon after it had reached near perfection of design. Now, with petroleum products useless, the clipper ship had been resurrected.

Current technology had taken a while to recover to the point that a clipper ship could be built—there were so many old skills to be relearned, so many shops to be retooled—but now that point had been reached and Faelin's childhood had been marked by the sight of these great white seabirds, first in ones and twos, later in great flocks.

The *Speculation*'s captain, a sour old cove named Burke, was among those who were taking advantage of the relative availability of clipper ships. Burke's vessel was not among the newest, but Burke was owner-aboard, a thing that would have been nearly unheard of twenty years before when it took a corporation to fund the building of the vessels.

Faelin admired Captain Burke as the perfect type of the self-made man. The *Speculation* was a tight ship, but her regulations made sense. After all, you couldn't have someone lolling below decks in a storm when all hands were needed on deck or deciding to steer without the least knowledge of navigation, could you?

For five years, Faelin served on the *Speculation* and during that time he grew into a big man, broad-shouldered, topping most around him by a head or more. His rough, calloused hands were equally swift with a pistol, gun, or a line. He even picked up a few lubber skills—some carpentry, iron working, and sewing. He became known as a good man to have at your side in a brawl, had many followers but never close friends.

Over those five years, however, Faelin's opinion of Captain Burke and his capacity as a commander underwent a change. Faelin couldn't help but notice that as officers retired or went on to other vessels, he himself was never promoted to fill their posts. He received pay raises readily enough, and high bonuses when a cargo sold well. Still, this wasn't stripes on his sleeve and his mates calling him "sir."

Had the *Speculation* been a military vessel, Faelin might have excused the oversight, but on a free-trader nothing but ability was required for promotion. Therefore, he started brooding over the slight.

He might not make a good quartermaster—Faelin was the first to admit that bookkeeping was far from his favorite sport—but he navigated well enough, had taken his time at the wheel. He might be young yet to serve as first officer, but he'd make a good second. Eventually, he grew sullen, deciding he was being slighted.

"I tell you," he said one afternoon to Simon Alcott, his closest crony, as they sat up in the riggings mending trousers. "Captain Burke doesn't like me because he sees I'm a threat to him and that wimp son of his,

Irving. He don't dare promote me, even to second, lest the crew start wondering why Irving's first mate and I'm second. Far better to have old Waldemar in that post, him with his stammer and two missing fingers."

Simon Alcott listened and nodded. Ever since Faelin had come to his rescue one night in a Singapore alley, Simon had been his absolutely loyal toady, reveling in his protector's strength. In his simple loyalty, contradicting anything Faelin said or thought never would have occurred to Simon. Indeed, he thought Faelin was right.

"Heck, Faelin," Simon said, "you'd make a better captain than the old man. Let him keep the books and work out the trades. You could run this ship tighter than a kernel fits in a nutshell."

For weeks Faelin groused on, Simon providing an unquestioning chorus to his complaints, until Faelin's vague grudges became as real to him as if Captain Burke actually told him that he was unpromotable.

As his discontent grew, Faelin considered his options. He could jump ship and get hired by another vessel, maybe by one of the big lines. They'd recognize his skills quick enough. For days he reveled in the image of himself in the neatly tailored dark blue coat and trousers of one of the better known shipping lines. There'd be gold piping on his sleeve and men jumping to anticipate his every word.

This fantasy soured, though, when Faelin considered the host of rules and regulations that even the officers were governed by on the lines. There were taverns and brothels they couldn't enter lest they sully the image of their employer. They had to accept transfers without protest, had to keep those uniforms perfect and those brass buttons shining. Sure they had lackeys to do the real work, but Faelin couldn't help but feel he'd be sealing himself into a tighter box than he was in already.

When Captain Burke announced that their next long haul was to be a winter—summer as it would be in the southern hemisphere—voyage to Australia, followed by a stop in Auckland, Aotearoa, Faelin realized what he should do.

Weren't rules—laws, regulations, favoritism—all that was holding him back? Hadn't old Ambrose Kidd told him that Aotearoa had no government and so was free from all that nonsense? Well, then, Faelin would jump ship in Auckland, that's what he'd do! Hadn't he been drawn there all his life? Hadn't old Kidd's stories been what had taken him to sea in the first place?

Faelin grinned like a fool, swallowing the expression when he saw Alcott staring at him curiously. They were weeks out yet, plenty of time for him to lay his plans.

He started by making himself up a couple of crates filled with trade goods purchased in various ports. He made them smallish ones, easy enough to carry for one man, especially if that man was a sailor used to loading and unloading, hauling lines and anchor, and all the rest.

From Kidd's tales Faelin knew that, other than gold, Aotearoa was metal poor. Nearly all they had came from salvage and trade. In every port of call he bought nails and wire, hinges and bolts, fish-hooks. He ended up taking Simon Alcott into his confidence for his follower started wondering at Faelin's sudden, unusual interest in trade. When Alcott begged permission to jump ship with him, Faelin graciously granted it. After all, two men could carry more than one and he knew that Simon would never rat on him.

In addition to trade goods, Faelin bought small items that would make their transition easier: extra knives, whetstones, coils of tightly spun rope, axe and hammer heads, needles and thread. In a pinch these could go on the block, too, but he didn't want to spend their capital on commonsense necessities.

Faelin spent both of their earnings lavishly, chatted up Kiwi sailors in every port, but kept care that no one other than Simon should notice his new interest. At last, after months at sea that for the first time in years seemed long, the *Speculation* sailed into Auckland's harbor and Faelin saw the promised land before him.

November was summer here and the hills were green. Off in the distance a white plume of smoke marked one of the many volcanoes that had shaped these islands, dormant now but for that almost fluffy plume. Drinking in those lush hills, the neat houses, the confident bustle of the citizens, Faelin thought Aotearoa the most beautiful place he'd ever seen.

Its difference from other nations was perceptible from the moment he strode down the gangplank in Auckland. By now Faelin had visited hundreds of ports through both Americas, Europe, the British Isles, even in Japan. Never before—not even in those nations erupted into despotic chaos—had there not been a governmental presence somewhere near the docks.

In Auckland's port there was plenty of activity, but

not a glimpse of anyone with that stiff, attentive posture that said "official." There was no one sporting a clipboard, name-tag, or uniform. Merchants hurried to dicker for cargos, but no one rushed to collect tariffs. Able bodies offered themselves for a variety of jobs, from porter and dock hand to guide and companion, but there were no police, no soldiers, no . . .

Momentarily Faelin felt a little lost. Then he rallied. His plans called for him and Simon to work just like usual, right until Burke announced that they were to set sail. Then he and Simon—who would have already inconspicuously unloaded their trade goods—would go ashore for one more roister. All they'd need to do then was lie low until the *Speculation* sailed on the tide.

He knew Captain Burke of old. Once the old man had even stranded his son, Irving, leaving the chastened young man to catch up to them at their next port. Burke wouldn't wait for two sailors, able as they might be.

Everything went according to plan. From a room in a port-side inn, Faelin watched the *Speculation* spread her wings and course out to sea. He felt a momentary twinge—after all, the ship had been his home for over five years—but this was washed away in a flood of excitement. Next time he encountered Captain Burke or any of his mates from the *Speculation* Faelin planned to be a big man—a ship owner maybe, a land owner, a trader.

Smiling, Faelin sauntered downstairs, Simon at his heels, to settle their bill. By reflex, he pulled out a handful of coins left over from his last pay. (At first he'd regretted that he'd not be getting his share of the Aotearoa bonus, but then he'd had the brilliant idea to make it up out of Burke's stores.)

The innkeeper, a prim-looking old woman, pulled out a scale and started weighing the coins, checking values against a handwritten chart.

"Copper'll bring less than iron," she said. "Iron less than steel. These..." she sniffed at some nickel-blend tokens, "aren't worth much but as sinkers on a line."

"They're money, lady," Simon Alcott blustered in reflection of his hero's momentary embarrassment, "not ore."

The old woman cocked an elegant white eyebrow at him.

"Not in Aotearoa, bro," she said. "Money's only worth what a backing government says it is. We're purely a barter economy here. You might get better prices from a currency speculator. To me this is just a few ounces of metal—and not pure metal either. Values are down a bit, too, what with the *Speculation* dumping quite a bit of metal goods on the market."

Faelin stepped in.

"How about worked metal, ma'am?" he said, doing his best to exude manly politeness to cover his gaff.

"That'd be better," the innkeeper admitted.

Eventually, they settled the bill with a handful of iron nails, a deal that brought them a map of the area, the innkeeper's recommendation of a boarding house run by her sister, information as to where they could get current values, and the old lady's sour smile.

"Welcome to Aotearoa," she said in parting. "You

look tough enough and used to hard work, maybe you'll make pakeha yet."

Pakeha, they were to learn later, was local slang for a resident. Before the petroleum virus, it had meant anyone of European ancestry, but now it was reserved for those—no matter where their parents had been born—who made the grade in the new nation.

After Simon and Faelin had left the inn and were consulting the map, meaning to head first for the boarding house, a bedraggled figure clad in dirty rags sidled over to them.

"Spare a bit for a shave and a shower?" the man whined. "I gotta try and get passage off this madhouse island, and no one'll look at me twice the mess I am."

Faelin sneered at this wreck of a human being— clearly one of those who would never be pakeha, though he certainly looked to have the raw makings. There were broad shoulders under that ragged shirt and height despite the man's cringing crouch.

Faelin started to tell the bum to haul his worthless ass off to the social center, remembered in time that there wouldn't be one here, and in his momentary confusion dug a handful of nickel coins from the pocket of his trousers.

"See what you can get with these," he said, tossing them into the man's cupped hands.

The bum caught most of them, scrabbling on the patched concrete of the dock front for those he dropped, then scurried off. Simon shivered as he watched him go.

"Felt like someone stepped on my grave, just then," he said.

Faelin snorted, balanced his crate of trade goods on one shoulder and tucked his duffle under his arm, then led the way into the city.

A sign greeted them as they left the harbor:

**Welcome to Aotearoa.
Mind your goods and your manners.
No one will mind them for you.**

Faelin was heartened by the words. This was promising—a warning to the weak, a message to the strong.

At the boarding house, a handful of iron nails bought them a room and two meals a day for a couple of weeks if they agreed to do their own housekeeping—a thing that was second nature to a sailor in any case. The owner of the boarding house, Mrs. Philbert, tossed in the use of her son as a guide to sweeten the deal.

Mrs. Philbert was a shrewd-faced woman, less elegant and quite a bit younger than her sister, but she liked sailors. She told them her husband sailed on an island trader that ran a regular route between the North and South Islands.

As Faelin looked around the comfortable room to which they'd been shown and contemplated the wealth of manufactured goods stored in their two crates, he felt pleased with himself. Leaving Simon to stow their gear and make the room comfortable, he set out with the innkeeper's Bobby to get a feel for Aotearoa.

The next few weeks were a flurry of new impressions. Faelin had waited until his arrival to select just where he wanted to settle. He had a good idea of his needs.

He wanted open water near so he and Simon could fall back on sailing when needed. He wanted a fairly rural area. Auckland, while small by the standards of some urban areas, was still too big. The best pickings had been taken long ago and Faelin hadn't come here to be somebody else's serf.

He also needed to trade for horses and pack mules to carry their gear. The livestock he planned to ranch— his dreams still colored by old Kidd's comparison of Aotearoa to the American frontier—could wait until he'd staked his claim.

Eventually, Faelin selected a settlement near what had once been called New Plymouth. When the oil bugs had set to work New Plymouth had been abandoned by all but a few hardy souls. This new settlement, called Richmont, had started up about three years before and the town was actively recruiting settlers. They advertised a trading post, two inns, several boarding houses, a school, and a budding road system.

Richmont fit Faelin's requirements to perfection and, best of all, a wagon train funded in part by the town's founders was heading out within the week. The wagon train's organizer was more than willing to hire both Faelin and Simon as guards in return for grub and promise of their pick of a couple good cattle at the trail's end.

Waving good-bye to Mrs. Philbert and little Bobby, Faelin swung into the saddle of his buckskin riding horse and never looked back.

Richmont proved to be almost everything for which Faelin had hoped. The original city of New Plymouth was gone, burned to the ground in the riots that had followed the advent of the petroleum virus, riots inspired by panic related to the petrochemical plants that had once functioned in the area. The new settlement was built slightly west along the coast from the original city.

Although New Plymouth had been destroyed, its concrete, brick, and stone remained as a source of building materials for the new settlement. Instead of the log cabins and clapboard houses that had lined the streets of Richmont in Faelin's imagination, there were solid square-built houses, rarely more than three stories high, laboriously cemented together.

The greatest bane of Faelin's existence, Chapin Toms, lived in the most imposing of the three-story buildings. Chapin—he was one of those people who insisted everyone call him by his first name—was the unofficial mayor of Richmont. A tiny, wiry man in his mid-sixties, Chapin looked so frail that Faelin suspected he could break Chapin in two without breaking a sweat. He had the impulse to do so within a week of his arrival in Richmont.

Chapin ran the Richmont trading post and, as such, pretty much dictated the prices for anything other than a meal, drink, or livestock—and indirectly affected the prices for those as well. What drove Faelin crazy was how everyone rhapsodized about how fair Chapin was when to Faelin it was apparent that Chapin set his prices by how much a person could do for him— Chapin—personally. As a newcomer, Faelin felt he was being shafted.

He and Simon had staked their claim on a nice

chunk of waterfront land west of Richmont, near to where—so the settlement agent told them—the small town of Oakura had been. Their land had beach front, good acreage inland for grazing, and nearby scavenging for building materials. The weather was pleasant this time of year—enough so that two sailors didn't think twice about bunking in a tent, but Faelin wanted at least the beginnings of a house built by winter.

Leaving Simon behind to mind the cattle and sheep—their duties as guards on the trip out had netted them a cow, a couple of nice heifers, and about a dozen sheep—Faelin rode into town. He took with him a pack mule, a small selection of worked metal trade goods, and empty saddlebags to carry back his loot.

Faelin strode into Chapin's trading post—the Dairy as the locals called it for some reason Faelin couldn't fathom, given that there wasn't a cow in sight—nodding greetings to a few folks he knew from the journey out. While waiting his turn he wandered around, checking the stock against his list. He was pleased to see that just about everything he needed was on the shelves. There were luxury goods, too: bolts of fabric, bottled liquor, shiny trinkets, salvaged antiquities.

When his turn came, Faelin nodded greeting and began: "I'd like a couple of shovels, two buckets, five pounds of flour, four hens and a rooster, and one of those things you use for making butter."

"A churn," Chapin said. He had a face like an amiable walnut and the lines in it shaped a smile around the words.

Faelin nodded. "That's right. A couple of glass or

crockery jars would be good, too. Never knew one cow could give so much milk."

Chapin smiled again.

"Your bro picked a good beast, there. He has an eye for cattle."

"That's right. Grew up on a farm in Oregon," Faelin replied. "Handy with cattle and sheep."

"You're a sailor, I recall." Chapin thrust a hand across the counter. "We haven't been formally introduced. I'm Chapin Toms."

"Faelin," Faelin replied.

His surname had been that of the Domain of California orphanage which had reared him, and he'd dropped it as soon as he went to sea. Faelin had no idea where his given name came from, but suspected that it had been some administrator's fancy. Still, for years it had been all he owned and he'd grown fond of it.

"Faelin," Chapin said, pausing as if he expected more. "Right. Well, let's go through that list of yours. Shovel. Wood or metal blade?"

Faelin had no doubts on this. He'd known these would be his most expensive purchase.

"Metal."

"New or used?"

"Used, if the condition's good."

"Buckets. Wood or leather or tin?"

"Leather's fine."

"Have a sack for your flour?"

"Uh, no."

"I'll have to charge for that, then, but you'll find it'll reuse. All I have are ten-pound sacks right now. Hope that'll do."

Faelin nodded stiffly, certain he was being had and reluctant to turn from the counter lest he see a knowing grin on a pakeha face.

"Hens and rooster. Particular breed?"

Faelin couldn't recall the name of the big white birds the *Speculation*'s cook had preferred and was embarrassed to say.

"Any kind as long as they lay biggish eggs."

"Well, the rooster'll take care of making sure there're eggs," Chapin said, a roguish twinkle in his eye.

Faelin wanted to punch the little man. At least he'd known enough to ask for a rooster.

"And a butter churn," Chapin concluded. "Small one should do for you two. Of course, you could save yourself the labor and trade with a neighbor. Debra and Fleming Dutchman have a two year-old claim not far from you and Debbie makes fine butter."

Faelin nodded. "We've spoken."

Chapin paused as if waiting to see if the request for the churn would be withdrawn, then he went on.

"Jars. I can do you a couple of good two-gallon crockery ones."

Faelin nodded, accepting the two bluish stoneware pieces set up on the counter for his inspection.

"Anything else?" Chapin asked. "Wax? We sell that in pound bricks. Axe handles? Honey? Liquor? Lanterns?"

Faelin considered. Wax would be useful for waterproofing as well as for making candles. Axe handles they could make. Both he and Simon were whittlers from way back. Sweets and liquor, though, those were luxuries that he and Simon had resolved to do without.

They had a cake of sugar swiped from *Speculation*'s stores and would make that last.

"Two pounds of wax," he replied. "I'll think on the rest."

Chapin nodded and started arraying the goods on the counter. A small group of idlers watched with interest, making Faelin feel acutely self-conscious. He wasn't used to shopping except for minor luxuries—shipboard life took care of the basics. Barter wasn't unfamiliar, not with all the ports he'd been to, but he didn't like the vague feeling that he was about to be taken.

When Chapin finished setting everything out, he asked Faelin to inspect the goods for flaws.

" 'Cause it's yours once it goes into your saddle-bags.' "

Then he hopped up on a tall three-legged stool, bent his hands back to crack his knuckles, and said:

"So what do you have to trade, Faelin?"

Faelin pulled out some nails.

"Nails are good," Chapin said, hopping down from his stool, agile as a monkey to check their heft and quality. "These are good nails. They'll cover the poultry, flour and sack, wax, and, because I'm in a good mood and leather buckets aren't moving since we got a cooper in town, the buckets. What you got to cover the shovels?"

Faelin glowered at Chapin. There had been a few chuckles about the buckets, chuckles that made him feel uncomfortably like an outsider.

"Leather buckets are good," he growled. "And my mate and I can mend them ourselves."

Chapin waved a hand airily. "Don't be such a hard

case, Faelin. Can't you see I'm having a joke at my own expense? I over-bought last winter and all the pakeha know it."

Rather than being soothed, Faelin felt even more out of place at this reminder that he was a newcomer.

"What do you want for the shovels?" he asked stiffly.

"You brought a nice mule in with you," Chapin said. "How about him?"

"You must be joking!" Faelin replied.

"Well, I can't see what else you've got if you don't put it on the table," Chapin said amiably. "What's weighing down your goody bag there? It's more than a few nails or I'm a one-legged weta."

Faelin had the vague idea that the weta was some local critter—a bug, he thought.

"And how do I know you'll play fair with me if I put my cards on the table?" he retorted.

"You are a hard case, aren't you?" Chapin said. "Look, Faelin. We're all neighbors. We live together, work together. How far would I go if I stole from my neighbors? Why they'd just trade with each other and leave me out of the mix. I only manage to make my living because people trust me to be fair and to provide them with a savings of time."

He leaned forward on his stool, his ugly walnut face earnest. "These aren't the petroleum days, Faelin. You could make most of what you're buying from me or hunt it out yourself. I'm just saving you time. If you don't want to trade for the churn and the shovels, ride on over to the cooper. He'll make you a churn—it might take a couple of weeks if he doesn't have one in stock, but he can make you one. Old Mrs. Velma has a couple of rusty old shovels. I bet you could rent them from her in return for splitting a couple cords of wood and returning the shovels all bright and sharp.

"Now, walk or pour out your trade goods. I have customers waiting. They may be enjoying the show—'specially since it's giving them a good idea of market value for a few things, but I don't have time to waste."

Faelin flushed and nearly walked, but he had a long trip back to the claim and didn't want to explain to Simon why he came back empty-handed. He spilled out the contents of his sack: more nails, a couple of feet of wire, and, selected almost at random, a pulley.

Chapin inspected the goods, then he looked around the store as if assessing his audience.

"A lesson for you, Faelin. The nails and wire, those are really good. Most of the nails we have here are wrought iron or salvage. These you've brought are better than local made. The wire's more of the same. Hell, most of us make do with twine. The pulley, that's a matter of need. With the new settlers come in—yourself among them—there's going to be a lot of house raising."

Faelin nodded. Rather than being grateful for the lesson, he was feeling embarrassed. He suspected now that both Mrs. Philbert and her sister back in Auckland had ripped him off. He wondered about the livestock dealers from whom he'd bought the horses and mules. At least Simon had gotten them good stock, but he'd bet his left foot they'd overpaid.

He felt color rising along his neck and fought down a desire to storm out the door.

"I'd keep that pulley if I were you," Chapin went on, "and hire yourself and Simon out to help raise a couple houses. Then when you're done, you'll have help and more to build your own place."

Chapin nodded happily, pleased by his own sermon.

Faelin swallowed hard. He wasn't going to accept this walnut-faced little monkey pushing him around. There wasn't a government here to make him build other people's houses. He'd just learned his nails made him pretty rich by local standards. He'd buy labor when he needed it and damn Chapin for trying to turn him into a toady.

"How much for the churn and the shovels?" he repeated.

"Nails for the shovels," Chapin replied, his friendly manner suddenly take it or leave it, "and the wire for the churn. Keep the pulley and I'll put you down for house building."

Faelin started to say, "Don't bother," then swallowed the words. He could always refuse when asked. He settled his bill and got out of there as fast as possible, then he fumed the entire way back to the claim. The chatter of the indignant chickens didn't help his mood.

As the weeks and months passed, Faelin's opinion of Chapin didn't change.

"He's made himself king in a land where there's supposed to be no government," he growled to Simon after another frustrating shopping trip. "Did you know that since we decided not to go to the Dutchmans' barn raising, Chapin refused to sell me anything? Said he didn't feel like trading with a man who couldn't be bothered to help a close neighbor. Those Dutchmans are just rolling in cream and butter! They could pay for my time!"

It hadn't helped Faelin's feelings about Chapin's know-it-all attitude that after a month or so of trying to make their own butter, Simon had timidly suggested that they trade the churn to Debra and Fleming in return for a few months' supply of butter and cheese. Faelin had been forced to agree. After a day of dealing with livestock and working on the house, neither man had the energy to churn.

He ignored the fact that he, not Chapin, had been at fault in the matter of the churn and continued his list of grievances.

"I had to go to the miller direct and she gouged me, charged everything that Chapin would have and made me pull nails from old lumber while I waited!"

Simon said nothing. Though Simon would never complain to Faelin, Faelin had seen the other man's distress when they didn't go to the barn raising. Simon liked the Dutchmans—a handsome, mostly Chinese couple despite their names—and the two men's isolation on the claim after crowded quarters on the *Speculation* had proven almost more than Simon could bear.

Faelin, not normally a sympathetic man, took pity on Simon, letting him make some of the supply runs into town and not even protesting when Simon came back with a fat black and brown sheepdog puppy of the type locally known as a huntaway. He tried not to recall that this new arrangement also saved him further confrontations with his self-appointed rival.

But Faelin continued to feel the pressure of Chapin's influence. When he got into a fistfight with the cooper over a horse race, Chapin just turned away and sighed, but the next time Faelin came into the Dairy, Chapin refused to serve him until Faelin promised to donate something to the cooper's support while he recovered from the hand Faelin had broken.

When Faelin tried to recruit some labor for raising the walls on the new house—he and Simon had built a solid foundation, but couldn't hope to finish stone walls by winter—mysteriously no one was available, not even when Faelin advertised handsome pay in metal goods. Not until he and Simon took a turn in a few building parties did help materialize, and then for free.

The laborers even brought treats—sweets and veggies and summer ale—to augment the fish-fry Simon and Faelin had supplied, and that evening their quiet claim echoed with laughter and the skirling notes of Erland Totaranui's fiddle.

Faelin hated it, hated the pressure of obligation which seemed far more binding than any law—after all, laws could be circumvented, reinterpreted, or simply ignored. He hated it even more when he saw how Simon was being seduced from him.

When they had arrived in Aotearoa, Simon had been completely ruled by Faelin. He let Faelin dictate practically everything he did, and was never happier than when dogging Faelin's heels. By July, the heart of the local winter, Simon was making excuses to do things on his own. He'd made friends with not only the Dutchmans and other pakeha neighbors, but also with members of a local Maori clan to the east who were associated with, but not precisely part of, the Richmont settlement.

Many a wet afternoon when Faelin thought they should be mending nets or carding wool or any of a thousand other jobs, Simon would make an excuse to go riding off to visit a neighbor. Roto the puppy—named after the Maori word for lake, since he'd been so hard to house train—would happily trot after Simon.

Nor could Faelin really complain that Simon was shirking. He always brought something back with him as payment for his day's labors elsewhere—honey and wax from a neighbor's hives, salt, tanned hides, rope. Once, incredibly, he'd even secured them the long-term loan of a Maori waka, or canoe, in return for giving sailing lessons to the local clan.

Faelin's dislike of Chapin and his influence came to a head that spring at the sheep shearing. Like so many things Faelin thought should be handled by trade and barter—or by a bit of strong-arm persuasion—the shearing was a community event, as much an excuse for a party as a means of getting work done.

With a calm persuasiveness Faelin wouldn't have suspected the other man of being capable of a year before, Simon had explained how much less labor it would involve for them to drive their small flock—now thirty strong with trade and lambings—over to town.

After pointing out that they didn't have shears, that they didn't really know what they were doing, and that they might as well see if they could trade a lamb or two for a piglet, Simon had clinched the matter by saying, "And if you're not going, well, then I am any-how. There's to be dancing when the work is done and a cook-off and a horse race. Farmer Lamont is donating a pig in honor of his first grandchild's birthday and it's to be pit barbecued."

"I never said I wasn't going," Faelin snarled, though in fact he'd been planning on staying home. This spring he was hoping to put in a small kitchen garden, despite the fact that he'd never grown as much as an onion in all his life. He'd thought to start turning what looked to him like a promising bit of land.

Faelin trailed the flock into town in a sour mood, watching Roto drive the sheep along with effortless ease. He wished he could figure out why his own course was never so easy. He'd expected that in a land without government and binding regulations he'd prosper.

He wasn't lazy, nor was he intimidated by bad weather. He was strong and before had always met those who—like Simon—would cling to him because of that strength. To top it off, he had skills most of the others never dreamed of. He'd been shocked to learn that Farmer Lamont had been a lawyer in far-away New York before chucking it all and coming to homestead in Aotearoa over twenty years before.

Now Lamont was a pakeha of the pakeha. In fact, the Richmont settlement was Lamont's second claim. He'd sold his first at what everyone knew was a tremendous profit because Auckland was getting too built up for him. Lamont said he wanted his sons and daughters to be able to raise their families in less developed land, just as he had them.

Such thoughts put a sour taste in Faelin's mouth, but that sour turned to honey at his first sight of Jocelyn.

Tall and arrow-straight with golden-brown skin and shining black hair, she glided through the Richmont town square like a princess. Clearly, her parentage was mixed—there was Polynesian in her and Chinese, but the lapis lazuli of her laughing eyes spoke of some European heritage as well.

When Faelin first saw her, Jocelyn was holding a toddler by the hand and his spirits plummeted. Then the little one tore his hand free and calling out, "Mama! Mama!" went waddling across to a woman Faelin vaguely recognized as one of the Lamont girls.

This then must be the much celebrated Lamont grandchild. At that moment, Faelin would have added every sheep in his flock to the barbecue in his joy at realizing this goddess was not the baby's mother.

He nudged his buckskin alongside Simon's bay.

"Who is *that*?" he asked, indicating the girl with a tilt of his head.

Simon looked and smiled. When he replied his voice was warm with affection.

"That's Jocelyn Lee. She's a cousin of the Dutchmans, came up from Auckland over the winter. She's been staying with them since August. I'm surprised you haven't met her."

Simon clipped the end off that last sentence, suddenly uncomfortable. The fact was, Faelin had become more and more a hermit over that winter. Simon did almost all their trading, even picking up the butter and cheese from the Dutchmans. Faelin had done the fishing, building, even the sewing—anything that gave him an excuse to let Simon be the one to go out.

Faelin felt a faint regret for lost opportunities. Then

suddenly he didn't care. Jocelyn Lee was here. So was he. There was to be dancing that evening. He would dance with her. He would woo her. He would win her.

Faelin worked that day with a constant awareness of Jocelyn's graceful presence. When the day warmed, he stripped off his shirt, knowing his muscles would show to advantage. He did every job with a smile on his lips, knowing he'd shine better in her eyes. He even avoided the horse race—though he longed to try his buckskin against the cooper's black—lest the old tale of their scrap go round and cheapen him in her eyes.

All that day he listened as the flirting note of her laughter, sweeter than any music, carried across the bleating of indignant sheep. When Jocelyn carried around cold water for the shearers' refreshment, Faelin introduced himself, then found himself too fumble-tongued to carry on.

When the shearing was done, Faelin retired to the room he and Simon had taken for the night and scrubbed down with care. He dressed in his best clothes, glad now that Simon had insisted they pack them along.

Like most sailors, Faelin had learned to tailor and embroider. The bleached cotton shirt he wore fit to perfection and was graced with tiny blue stars. After tying his freshly washed hair back in a sailor's queue and donning newly polished boots, Faelin inspected himself in the mirror and was pleased with the sight.

Faelin's grooming had taken so long that Simon had left without him. When he entered the torch-lit circle where three-quarters of the area's population had gathered, Faelin felt strangely shy, aware that he was still a stranger in a group of friends.

To cover his discomfort, he put a sailor's swagger into his walk and joined Simon by the buffet. The food was free—donated by all the participants and transformed into a feast by those who hadn't actually been working with the sheep. The centerpiece might have been Farmer Lamont's barbecued pig, but there was such a variety of food spread around it that even its vast bulk was dwarfed.

Faelin ate lightly, waiting impatiently for Jocelyn to arrive. Even after the dancing had started, she didn't come. Gruffly, Faelin refused an invitation from saucy Debbie Dutchman, waiting like an eagle for Jocelyn lest he not be free to dive upon her when she arrived.

When Jocelyn did come in, the dancing was in full swing. Even so it seemed to Faelin that Jocelyn brought her own music with her. In workday trousers and shirt, she'd been eye-catching. Now, dressed for a party, she was everything he had dreamed—lovely as springtime itself in a floor-length frock of deep red silk embellished with scattered golden flowers.

That silk gown should have been a warning to Faelin, but he was too besotted to think. Jocelyn stood poised near the edge of the circle of light and the swirl of dancing. Contrary to Faelin's expectation that she would be pounced on as soon as she arrived, she remained alone, though by far the finest woman in the place.

Why it's just like with me, Faelin thought. *No one will have anything to do with her because she's so far above the rest. They want to lower her to their level—*

*to transform that lovely princess into a wallflower as
they've tried to make me every man's lackey.*

Faelin strode over to her, the beating of his heart in
his ears louder than the combined fiddles and guitars,
so that he felt strangely disconnected from everything
around him. He made Jocelyn a sweeping bow, aware
that he cut a dashing figure, and held out his hand.

"May I have this dance, sweet lady?"

In his imagination—fevered all that day so he hardly
remembered the sheep, the mud, the faces of those
he'd worked beside—Jocelyn had blushed prettily and
put her hand in his. Then he'd swept her off into the
middle of the dancing, the two of them becoming the
shining heart of the action, paired stars that transformed all the rest into extras.

But in reality, Jocelyn returned his bow with a pretty
curtsy and smiled.

"Thank you, sir, but I'm waiting for my fiancé."

"Your what! Who . . ."

Faelin heard himself bellow so loudly that the danc-
ers nearest turned to stare and the musicians faltered
for a moment in their playing.

"My fiancé," Jocelyn replied. "He had a bit of business to conclude."

"Then he's lost his chance," Faelin said, struggling
for gallantry. "Let me convince you . . ."

A new voice cut in from slightly behind him.

"Convince her of what, Faelin?"

Faelin knew that voice, light and a touch impish,
mocking him yet again.

"Chapin!"

He wheeled and found the little monkey man

looking up at him, head tilted in inquiry, a smile on his lips.

"I see you've met my betrothed," Chapin said. "Jocelyn Lee, meet Faelin the Sailor, late of the *Speculation* and of California, now settler—neighbor to your cousins the Dutchmans."

Faelin saw red. He didn't know what made him more furious—that this little man should have somehow bought Jocelyn Lee or that in his mocking way he should make his introduction a reminder that Faelin was just a settler, not pakeha, not now, and—if Chapin had his damnable way not ever—not unless Faelin became Chapin's lackey, building other folks' houses, shearing their sheep, taking their insults . . .

Jocelyn had slid her slender hand into Chapin's skinny paw and was smiling up at Faelin.

"Pleased to meet you, Faelin. I know your partner, of course. Sweet Simon we call him, always such a help. Such a hand with the cattle."

Faelin began to tremble with fury. So Simon had turned against him. Jocelyn might name him Faelin's partner, but clearly he'd become a toady to these enemies . . .

He gnashed his teeth. He hadn't known anyone ever really did that, but in the madness that was overtaking him, he gnashed them, feeling them grind like rocks in his mouth.

"You!" he bellowed, a rough growl that echoed through the suddenly quiet throng. He hardly noticed that the dancing had stopped, only that his words carried farther. "You, Chapin! What did you pay for her?"

"Pay?" Chapin looked astonished.

Jocelyn, still clinging to his hand, colored, her golden skin flushing crimson.

"Pay? Chapin repeated.

"Aye, pay," Faelin growled. "You make everyone trade with you, monkey man. I won't believe that such a beauty would agree to wed a skinny old monkey like you if you didn't offer a good trade. Did you give her cousins more cattle for their farm? Or did you buy her with pretty things and the promise of a three-story stone house?"

The significance of the silk dress came to him. Vaguely Faelin recalled having seen a bolt of that fabric on his first visit to the store.

"Aye," he continued, tapping Jocelyn's sleeve. "I see she's wearing part of your trade. Well then, I've a trade for you. I'll trade you your life for the girl. Otherwise, I'm going to rip your head off those scrawny shoulders and take her home with me. What do you say to that offer?"

Chapin shook his head gently, almost sadly, then said:

"I have a counter offer for you, Faelin. Look around."

And Faelin did. Behind him the assembled pakeha had drawn into a semicircle. No one carried weapons, but fists were clenched and faces were stern.

From in the midst of that crowd of disapproval, old Farmer Lamont shook his gray head.

"We don't do things that way, Faelin. Jocelyn has the right to make up her mind who she wants to marry. If she wants to marry Chapin—for whatever reason—we support her, especially since Chapin wants to marry her, too, and no other woman has a claim on him."

There was a murmur of uneasy male laughter as if to say "What man in his right mind *wouldn't* want to marry Jocelyn?"

Faelin spat. "You talk of claims, of rights, Lamont. I thought Aotearoa had no laws."

"No government," Lamont said with a slight stress on the second word. "Law is not the same as government. Law is the rules by which a society decides to live. What we support here is the right of every human to decide his or her own life, free of some governing body asserting its rights over theirs."

"And my rights?" Faelin countered. "Seems like since I've come here, everyone has been steering me to do things their way. I can't get a bag of flour or a pig or a few days' work on my land without trotting about doing everyone else's bidding."

"Your rights are yours," Lamont expounded, shades of the lawyer he had once been in his intonation. "You can make your own flour or raise your own pigs or work your own land, but if you want to make someone else do something, then you'd better have the means to enforce your will. Seems to me that when you're accusing us of making you do our bidding, what you're really complaining about is that you can't make us do your bidding."

"There's no law against my way," Faelin sneered.

"No law," Lamont agreed, "but we don't like your manners much."

Faelin swung on his heel to look at Jocelyn. She was holding on to Chapin's arm, her posture protective.

Whatever Chapin had paid for her, he'd bought her well and good.

"Damn you all," he said to no one in particular.

He spotted Simon on the edge of the crowd, Roto sitting on his feet.

"C'mon, Simon. We're cutting out of here."

Simon shook his head.

"Not me. I've got dancing to do."

Faelin stared at him, then he stormed out past the circle of torchlight and into the darkness beyond. The buckskin was at least tied up and waiting. Tacking it up, he swung into the saddle.

As he rode off, he heard a wave of laughter and the music starting up again. Angrily, he turned the horse's head not west toward the claim, but north to Auckland.

Bandits stole the buckskin two days later, taking also Faelin's boots, his leather belt with its brass buckle, and the trade trinkets from his pockets. Almost as an afterthought, one ugly fellow made him strip out of his party clothes, tossing him a ragged shirt in trade.

Faelin made the rest of the way to Auckland half-naked and on bare feet. He hobbled into town and discovered that there was no police or soldiery interested in his sorrows. A group of bounty hunters paid him in secondhand shoes and trousers for information on the bandits. They weren't interested in his joining them, though.

"Get a horse," one said, "maybe then."

Faelin turned to robbery. After one nasty beating when he underestimated the strength of the man he planned to assault, he humbled himself to laborer's work. He stayed away from the docks, though, lest someone who'd known him in better days recognize him.

Summer wasn't too bad, nor was autumn, but winter came in wet and chill. After nearly dying of hypothermia one night, Faelin traded some of his earnings to bunk in a barracks. He was robbed there, set back to almost the same naked condition in which he'd arrived in Auckland six months before.

He began to dream of Richmont as one might a fairyland. No one had robbed him there—not even though he and Simon were two men alone and known to be rich. Folk had even been kind, after a fashion. Oddly enough it was little Debra Dutchman's laughing attempt to get him to dance with her that haunted Faelin most. What had he done to earn that kindness?

Winter turned to spring. With the better weather, clipper ships came into dock. Faelin was drawn to them, haunted by his past. At first he watched from a distance, admiring the white spread of the sails. He began to think that if only he could get off this damned island, maybe he could earn enough to make his way. He'd lost weight and muscle, but the skills were there.

Soon, whenever he wasn't working—earning just enough to keep him in poor food and worse clothing— Faelin took to lurking about the docks, the pride that had kept him away faded to a shadow. In a way he was still afraid to be seen by anyone who might know him, yet he longed for the contact that might get him a berth.

Late one afternoon in September, almost a year after he had fled Richmont, a voice spoke his name.

"Faelin?"

He looked up, trying to place the voice, realizing with shock that the man who was speaking to him was Simon. Superficially, Simon looked the same, but there was something to his bearing—a straightness, a way of meeting your eye when talking to you—that transformed him into another man. Faelin, who had been much beaten and kicked this past year, had to fight an automatic urge to cringe.

"Faelin!" Simon repeated, dropping to his knees next to him. "Man, you're alive! I'd given you up for dead. I've been looking . . ."

He stopped, shocked as he assessed his former partner's condition. Then he went on in a deliberately steady voice:

"I've been looking since last year. Someone said they saw your buckskin for sale in a shady market at the edge of Auckland. I went there, but no luck, though I did find someone who remembered a man wearing what had to be your shirt. It wasn't you though—for one thing he was older, for another fair as a whale's belly. I kept checking for you though, came on all the supply runs to Auckland, but never got a whiff of you.

"When the clippers were due, though, I thought I'd check again. Seemed you might have gotten a berth, if by luck you'd gotten here alive. God's own, man, but what happened to you?"

Faelin told him, first crouched there on the street, later, when Simon recovered himself, in a tavern where they drank good ale and Faelin had his fill of chowder and bread.

"And so here I am," Faelin concluded. Simon's

honest joy at finding him alive had robbed him of any defensiveness. He'd told the entire thing straight, even including the embarrassing parts.

"And what do you want next?" Simon asked. "If you want a berth, I'll buy you out of your share of the claim, if . . ."

"You'll buy me out?" Faelin interrupted, astonished. Surely he'd abandoned any right to the claim a year since.

Simon misunderstood him, though.

"I've managed to hold it. Made a deal with the Dutchmans. I work their place in return for keeping our livestock with theirs. Got another dog and that helps with the sheep. Named it Repo. That's Maori for 'swamp,'" he added inconsequentially. "Was just as hard to house train as Roto."

"But you say I still have a share?" Faelin asked. "After I walked out on you?"

"Sure. You started the whole thing, Faelin. I'd never have had the courage to jump ship and find my way to Richmont without you. I owe you my life and my . . . well . . . prosperity. In a way, I owe you my happiness, too."

Simon blushed.

"I got married this winter to Lamont's younger daughter, Idelia. She's not a looker like Jocelyn, but she's a sweetheart."

"And you'd still give me a share?" Faelin asked again.

"That's right," Simon said. He looked Faelin squarely in the eye. "I'll sell enough to make up your half of the sheep and cattle—based on what we had when you left. Same for the dog and the riding stock, less that buckskin. There's something I'd rather do though . . ."

"What?"

"Convince you to come back, Faelin. You've the makings of pakeha, if you'd just get rid of the idea that something can be had for nothing but your wanting it. Idelia knows how I feel and though she's a bit nervous—you scared everybody white when you went at old Chapin—she says she trusts my judgment."

Faelin considered. Impossibly, he had a second chance and he thought he understood a whole lot better what he was being offered.

He thrust out his hand.

"It's a deal, partner."

This time, he knew he'd make his word good.

Devil's Star

by Jack Williamson

My mother had chronic bad luck, and a secret shield against it. On no evidence at all, she clung to a stubborn belief that she was the great-grandniece of an illegitimate son of President Cleon Starhawke I, who had won fame for the interstellar conquests that added half a thousand planets to the Terran Republic, and notoriety for the beauty and fertility of his numerous mistresses.

"Never forget that we have presidential blood," she used to urge me. "Live up to it, Kiff, and it will make you great."

With no proof of the myth, I grew up proud of my Starhawke blood, loyal to the Republic and dreaming of a chance for some signal service to the President. My father abandoned us before I was five, migrating to a newly opened planet with a younger woman. My mother spent the next few years working as a domestic servant before she found another husband and skipped out with him, leaving me alone on Earth.

My own luck ran better. Both husbands left funds toward my education. She enrolled me in the Starhawke Space Academy. I came of age and earned my commission there, swearing eternal allegiance to the Terran Republic and Cleon III.

Graduating as a military historian, I begged for the chance to make my name with some active force out on the Rim frontier. Instead, I found myself still stuck on Earth, the freshman member of a little research team in the library at the Presidential War College near New Denver. Our project was to produce an updated history of Devil's Star. On my first day there, a discontented senior officer tried to shatter my illusions.

"You'll find no career here." He looked around and dropped his voice. "The library was founded to glorify the Starhawkes, but they won no wars on Devil's Star. The planet may justify the name, but it has no history."

I asked for facts about it

"None worth knowing." He shrugged. "Sea level air pressure nearly twice Terra's. Surface mostly too hot and too hostile to be terraformed. No resources worth attention. The explorers had labeled it Lucifer and passed it by."

"Wasn't it once a penal colony?"

"A death pit." He shrugged again. "Called the Black

Hole. Infested with hostile life and strange disease. Prisoners sometimes sent down in old landing craft, with no fuel to take off again. Public outrage stopped that when the truth got out. No landings since." He made a bitter face. "We're in the same fix here, condemned to our own hopeless hole."

"The convicts did survive?"

"A disappointment to the executioners." He grinned. "A hardy few climbed out of the heat, to a high mountain ridge that runs down the middle of the main continent. A cooler corner of hell. Some are likely still alive."

Trapped there, with nothing to do and no future in sight, I was feeling as hopeless as another maroon until the day an officer in the uniform of the Presidential Guard caught me in my little cubicle with the news that Space Admiral Gilliyar wanted to see me at once. Astonished and a little alarmed, I asked why.

"He'll tell you why."

A luxury aircar carried us across the base to the Space Command Tower. We found the admiral in a huge corner office that looked across a great field of silver-bright skip-ships. A big man with a bulldog chin, his bright red hair cut short, he was in shirt sleeves, his uniform jacket flung over the back of a chair behind a huge bare desk.

He stood up when the orderly brought me in. My heart thumping, I saluted.

"So you are Starman Kiff McCall?" He returned the salute, studied me with keen gray eyes, nodded abruptly. "You look fit for the job. Let's sit."

Breathing a little easier, but anxious to know what job, I followed him to chairs at a wide window that looked out west across the starport to snowcapped mountain summits.

"Have you done duty off the Earth?"

"No sir."

I waited, sweating.

"No matter." He shrugged again. "What do you know about Devil's Star?"

"Very little, sir. I doubt that much is known by anybody. All contact was outlawed two centuries ago."

"You'll soon know more." My mouth must have gaped; he laughed at me. "If you're ready to go there?"

"I—" I had to catch my breath. "I'm ready."

"Think before you jump." He bent toward me, hard eyes narrowed to study me again. "This will be a highly confidential mission, with no official support or public reward. Your career and even your life may be in danger."

"I've sworn an oath." Feeling like a schoolboy, I put my hand on my heart. "My life is pledged to the Republic and the President."

He smiled at the quiver in my voice.

"I trust you." He spoke very gravely. "What I say is for your ears only. Here is the situation. The sanctions against contact with the planet Lucifer have been broken. As you may know, enemies of the Republic were once exiled there. Their descendants appear to have created an outlaw society. The mere rumor of a free society is a hazard to the state. The President has ordered the planet reclaimed as Terran territory. He is sending me there as the first governor."

Muscles tightened in his jaw.

"It's been a black hole. The convict transports didn't all return. We never knew why, but those who got back called it hell. Before any landing is attempted, we're sending an undercover agent to look the situation over and report what resistance we should expect. That's your errand."

I never returned to my library cubicle. Instead I spent a few hectic months in a class for interstellar intelligence officers, a disappointment to me. I'd hoped for training to face the hazards of the star frontiers, but Cleon I had annihilated the alien foes he found there. These future agents were destined for duty here closer to home.

"Worlds gone soft!" a black-mustached instructor shouted at us. "Rotten to the heart! Maybe loyal Terrans once, but turncoats now, corrupted by all that damned Free Space gibble-gabble. Your future duty is to hunt such traitors down and stop their venomous slander against the Starhawke Presidents."

Admiral Gilliyar's mission had not been revealed, yet my part in it gave me a thrill of secret pride. His staff invented a cover story for me. Based on my mother's claims to presidential kinship, it named me the leader of an exposed Free Space plot to overthrow the President. In flight to escape arrest, I was to become a hunted fugitive, my whereabouts unknown.

On my last day at school, I was hustled out of class and escorted to an empty hangar at the skyport. There, equipped with an oxygen mask and a radio, I was nailed into a rough wooden box stenciled ELECTRONIC SUNDRIES.

The radio kept me informed while it was tilted, jarred and jolted, finally loaded into the cargo hold of the *Star of Avalon*.

That was the ship of a suspected smuggler that had been captured, but released with a warning when the captain paid his excise taxes. And no doubt a bribe; I had learned that even the great Terran Republic is not without corruption.

Our first skip was a stomach-churning lurch. The radio went silent. Elated to be off the Earth and on my way, I got out of the box and hammered on a bulkhead. A startled spacehand let me out of the hold and took me to Bart Greenlaw, master and owner of the ship. A fit youthful man in a bright yellow skip suit, he interrupted my cover story.

"So you are Kiff McCall?" His keen eyes scanned me. "I trade with Free Spacers. The price on your head has them wondering about you and your conspiracy. They'd never heard of you."

"We try to keep our secrets," I told him. "I left friends behind, friends I can't betray."

"I understand." He studied me again, and finally smiled as if he believed me. "I know how my own Free Spacer friends feel about the Republic. Or the Terran Empire, they call it. Power corrupts, they say, until it finally rots itself. The Starhawkes hold too much power. They've held it too long."

His gaze sharpened to study my reaction.

"They say Cleon III is sitting on a bomb, armed and ready to blow."

I nodded, trying not to show too much emotion. Any connection between the Free Space activists and Devil's

Star was something I must report, but my own mission could have ended then and there if he had guessed the truth.

"One question, if I may ask." His eyes narrowed. "If you're an actual freedom fighter, why are you heading for a prison you'll never escape?"

"We lost a battle." I groped for anything he might accept. "I had to run while I could, but the war isn't over. I want the whole picture. I'm fascinated with the little I know about Devil's Star. I want to do a history of it. Smuggled out to civilization, it might make a difference."

"Civilization?" His face set hard for an instant, but then he gave me a quizzical smile. "You ought to find us interesting."

Seeming satisfied, he found a berth for me, and treated me like another member of his little crew. They all were busy, calculating skip congruencies and maneuvering for relaunch positions and relative velocities, but he let me sit with them at meals, where I could listen for anything Admiral Gilliyar might want to know.

In my berth that night, I dreamed the admiral had won his little war. I was with him on his triumphant return to Earth. A military band was blaring when we came off his flagship, and a goose-stepping squad from the Presidential Guard escorted us to the White Palace. Cleon III received us in the Diamond Room to praise the admiral for his heroic victory and make him the sole proprietor of the conquered planet.

As the dream went on, the beaming admiral presented me to Cleon III. Without my daring undercover work, he said, his expedition would have ended in disaster. The President thanked me for my heroic service to the Republic, and pinned a glittering Starhawke Medal of Honor on my chest.

I felt let down when I woke to find that moment of glory gone, yet my elation lingered. After all, I was safely on my way to Lucifer. Greenlaw seemed to trust me. Something like the dream might still come true.

Our flight took a week. The skips themselves are instant; outside our space-time bubble there is no space to cross or time to pass, but any long voyage requires a series of jumps from one point of congruence to another. On the major space lanes these are marked and charted, but contact points are hard to find and markers can drift. Some points are periodic. Some can vanish altogether. Skip navigation takes high skills and a rare grasp of the total cosmos.

I came to admire Greenlaw for his easy-seeming expertise as an extraspatial pilot, and to enjoy his company. A native of Devil's Star, he loved his planet and liked to talk about its history and geography.

"There's one big continent," he said. "Split in half by a high ridge that runs north and south down the middle of it. That's where we live, between two harsh frontiers, east and west of us. Monsoon rains keep the east half buried under jungle and forest. Dry downslope winds keep the west half hotter than any place on Earth. Both halves are deadly in a dozen ways, yet rich with resources we've learned to use."

I asked about the government.

"We have none." He grinned at my astonishment. "No laws. No money. No taxes. No cops or prisons. We never forgot the merciless government that dumped us here." He paused to smooth his bitter voice. "We were political convicts, condemned for wanting freedom. The Terran government dumped us into the desert or that deadly jungle, with freedom to die."

He glared as if I had challenged him.

"A few of us didn't. We made it up to the highlands, where survival was barely possible—after we learned to care for one another. That's our secret. All for each and each for all." He intoned the words like a mantra. "If you can understand?"

Not sure I did, I shook my head.

"It's your culture." He frowned and shook his head. "I saw it when I was a student there. A culture of selfish aggression. You need your laws and cops and prisons to protect yourselves from one another. We don't, if you get the difference."

"No money?" I asked. "How do you manage without it?"

"Well enough." He shrugged. "You would call it a barter economy. We have exchange centers. Through your working life, you make contributions when you can. In return you draw what you need, a loaf of bread, a farm tool, the service of a surgeon. You continue to serve and be served as long as you live. We have no idle millionaires, no homeless beggars."

"No public services?" I asked. "Don't you need roads, schools, fire departments, hospitals?"

"Of course we do."

"With no money and no taxes, who pays for them?"

"Why pay?" His tone was almost scolding. "We build them. Where you have laws, and lockups for those who break them, we have customs. Our own folkways. A culture of altruism. Every young person spends a year in some service of his or her own choice—and one of our years is nearly two of Earth's. I spent mine sweating down in the desert, at work on date farms and a new angel wood plantation.

"The rest of our lives, we serve one day a week. Teaching, nursing, farming, building roads or bridges, doing what we can for others, trusting them to do for us. When I'm unable to care for myself, others will care for me. Not for money, but because that's our way of life."

"Don't people shirk?"

"Not many. Not often. Not long." He laughed. "A few have tried to live alone. They find how much we need each other."

"With no government at all?"

"You will see." He paused and spoke again, more reflectively. "As a student on Earth, I saw enough of the rotten Terran government you say is hunting you now. I learned to cope with cops and laws and rules and regulations and stupid bureaucrats. Give me freedom!"

Listening, I felt uncomfortable. I had begun to like him. My mission meant trouble for him, trouble for the world he loved. I had to remind myself that I was a Terran soldier, bound to a path of duty I must follow, whatever the cost to me.

Our final skip brought us into planetary orbit. The first hemisphere we saw was all blue ocean. The single huge continent slid into view, the east half-hidden under white monsoon clouds, the western desert a naked waste of dull reds and bright yellows, wrinkled with bare brown hills.

"My home!" Smiling like a happy child, Greenlaw pointed to the highlands, a thin green slash between desert and cloud. "The Vale of Avalon."

The next skip took us lower. I made it out, a high valley between two mountain ridges. A little river ran north between green slopes from a white-capped volcanic cone to a long narrow lake.

"The Avalon River." He pointed. "Most of our settlements are scattered along it, some grown into towns."

He landed at Benspost, a cluster of red tile roofs at a bend in the river. His father, Ben Greenlaw, owned the trading post, a sprawling building with low walls of roughly shaped stone. A little crowd had gathered to welcome him home, calling eager greetings as we came down the ramp.

Men in fringed brown buckskin, women in brighter cottons, wide-eyed children, all anxious to see the wonders he had brought back from the stars. He waved to a smiling, dark-haired woman in slacks and a neat leather jacket.

"Laurel," he said. "My kid sister. She's just back from her service year, down in the jungles. You'll meet our father. He's crippled from hell fever he caught there when he was young. I hope she came back better."

She ran to hug him when we stepped off the ramp.

"All okay." Smiling into his face, she looked fit enough and trimly attractive. "It was a great adventure,

really. We were cutting a road across the flood plain
to the Styx."

That was the great river than drained half the rainy
lowlands.

"Kiff McCall." He introduced me. "A runaway rebel,
in flight from the wrath of Cleon III."

"From old Earth?" She appraised me with clear
green eyes, smiled, and gave me a strong handshake.
"I want to hear all about it."

"I want to hear about the jungle."

"They call it hell, but I had a great year there!"
Flushed with the excitement of the moment, she was
beautiful. "We got all the way to the river. Set up a
sawmill. Cut lumber to build a little boat with a sawmill engine. The first steamer on the Styx."

I stood stupidly silent, longing for her to like me
and thinking how she would hate me when she learned
what I was.

"Kiff will be our guest," Bart told her. "If you can
find him a room.

"I certainly can."

She wanted to carry my bag. It held things I didn't
want to show, a gun, my long-range radio, electronic
gear to record and encode my reports to the admiral.
I clung to it, and followed her through the store.
Flushed with pride in Bart and his daring voyages, she
showed me tables stacked with goods he had brought
in: books and holo sets, watches, radios, computers.

"Things we don't make yet," she said. "But we're
learning fast."

Uneasy with her, thinking of the painful lessons the
admiral would soon be teaching, I followed her through

the tables loaded with local goods. Shoes and clothing, hardware, flour, dried meats, native fruits and nuts with names strange to me.

A clerk was filling an order, punching prices into a barter card. As eager as a child with a birthday, she showed me a hunting rifle she wanted to buy with her savings from the service year. It was the work of a native craftsman, beautifully finished, the stock inlaid with silver, but useless to stop the admiral's battlecraft.

The family lived at the back of the single-story building. We left my bag in a clean little room with white-plastered walls and a comfortable bed, and she took me to meet her father. We found him at a desk facing a big window that looked out across the wide green valley to that old volcano in the south.

A heavy man with a withered leg, he gripped the edges of the desk to haul himself upright and shake my hand. I saw patches of dead-white scar tissue on his face and hands, saw his grimace of pain. Yet his grasp was strong. He smiled warmly at me and then at Laurel, when she came to put her arm around him.

"Relics of the hell country." He raised his hands to show the scars. "I spent my service year there, back before we discovered angel wood. Laurel was luckier."

"Kiff's a freedom fighter," she told him. "In flight from Cleon III"

"Welcome, sir!" He shook my hand again. "They'll never touch you here."

Sitting again, he listened to my cover story with a shrewd intentness that left me afraid he might see through the lies.

"We'll keep you safe." Laurel's eyes were shining. "You'll like it here."

She took me out see the town, a cluster of low stone buildings along a single cobblestone street. There were no motor vehicles, but I saw people on huge ungainly native creatures she called camels, larger than the Terran sort and able to carry half a ton of weight.

"I rode them down into the rain country," she told me. "They have evil tempers, but they're addicted to the silvernuts that grow there. When one gets unruly, a handful of nuts will make him kneel and beg."

She pointed to wires strung from poles along the street.

"Something my grandfather brought us. He found a junkyard of wrecked landing craft down in the desert where they used to unload the convicts, and salvaged parts to rebuild one that got him off the planet. He got aboard an old prison transport that had been lost in orbit when mutineers killed the officers.

"He taught himself skip navigation from the texts and tools he found aboard. The first skip took him nowhere, but a few more got him out to the home planet of our ancestors. He found kinsmen, made Free Space friends—and spent a dozen years on Earth learning everything he could. He'd abandoned the old transport, but he finally got home in a modern ship, with a cargo that changed life here."

I hated to think how Gilliyar would change it again.

"Electricity!" Her voice had risen. "Lights. Telephones. Radio. We've found no oil or coal to burn for power, but now we have windmill generators up in mountain gaps where the trade winds are steady. I wish we could get nuclear power."

I thought of the fusion engines on the admiral's battlecraft.

That uneasy awareness of my mission kept me troubled and silent that evening at dinner. Laurel's mother, Martha, had grown most of the food in her own kitchen garden. A genial, generous woman, she kept piling my plate with servings too large and seemed troubled that I had no better appetite.

In spite of such a welcome, the passing days left me no happier. I was there for months, waiting for Gilliyar's armada to arrive in orbit and preparing to tell him that the outlaws had no defenses worth concern. Laurel arranged a barter card for me. In return, I agreed to teach classes or tutor students in what they wanted to know about the outside worlds.

She became my first student. My cover story made me a romantic figure in her mind, the lone survivor of a heroic rebellion crushed by ruthless Terran power. Her face used to light when she saw me, in a way that wrenched my heart. I knew the truth would come out, knew it would destroy me.

I longed to reveal myself and beg for her forgiveness. Yet I was still a Terran soldier, bound by my oath of allegiance and a lifetime of loyal emotion, hopelessly trapped by all the lies I had told. Keeping silent because I had to, I let her enjoy the days that brought a tortured joy to me. She became an eager guide to her world: the lofty ridge that sliced like a blade between the jungle and the desert. She had seen

enough of the jungle, but she took me on a camel down
a winding mountain trail to an oasis on the high desert.
A long day of clinging to a clumsy wooden seat on the
back of the lurching beast left me sun-blistered and
aching.

The torrid sun was low before we could dismount
at the edge of a tiny lake at the end of a dry stream
that ran down from the highlands in the monsoon
season. It was on a stony plateau, the low desert and
the vast salt marshes on the coast still a full mile farther
down, but even after sunset the heat was stifling. Laurel
used her barter card to pay for our rooms and meals
at a lodge where her brother had worked through his
social service year.

She gave me a little handful of bright green beans.
"The seed of the angel tree," she said. "A shrub from
down along the coast. It's a natural drug for hell fever.
We're trying to grow it here.

I chewed one of the seeds. Its sharp astringency
burned my mouth, bitter as my own predicament.

"It's better than it tastes." She laughed at the face
I made. "It saved my father's life."

Radiant at breakfast next morning, she wanted to
show me the rows of young angel trees her brother
had planted, and took me through a little museum that
held the relics of a tragic chapter in the planet's history. A shipload of Free Space convicts had been left
at the oasis with no supplies. Nearly half of them died.
Gunter Greenlaw led the team that opened the road
and got the survivors to the Vale.

"We earned our liberty," she told me.

✧   ✧   ✧

Later, we rode south to ski on the slopes of that dead volcano. The road ran beside the Avalon through gardens, fruit orchards, grain fields, green meadows where spotted cattle grazed the slopes above us. Laurel spoke proudly of the pioneers who had tamed a hostile wilderness, dammed mountain streams for water, cleared land for crops and cattle, built their new society.

The beast's lurching gait kept bumping us together on the high wooden seat. Tormented by her body warmth, breathing her haunting scent, listening to her easy laugh, I tried to contain tides of wild desire and bitter despair.

At the lodge I offered my card and asked for two rooms.

"One will do," she told the clerk, and turned to grin at me. "I love you, Kiff. You do like me, don't you?"

Trapped in a tangle of emotions, I stammered that I did.

"Do you think we must be married?" The clerk stared, and she laughed at me. "You've talked about your government and how it limits all you do. We have more freedom here."

The clerk punched my card for just one room, but I needed time to sort my tangled feelings out. I said I felt hungry. We had dinner and a bottle of wine, out on a terrace below the snows. She admired the view and asked if we had snow sports on Earth. I found little to say.

"Kiff, you are hard to understand." She pushed her glass aside and leaned to stare into my face. "Even when I know how different your old world was. Are you unhappy here? Is there someone you love back outside?"

Honestly, I told her there was no one. Still I couldn't tell her what I felt, but the wine had begun to dull my reservations. When it was gone, we went to bed together. She was passionate. I half forgot my mission. Honestly, I told her I loved her, but all I couldn't say choked me with bitter shame.

We spent three days there. There were no lifts, but a big windmill drove an endless cable that pulled us to the top. The sun was bright, the slope great fun. Laurel was more intoxicating than the wine. She seemed radiant, imagining our future together.

"My brother has Free Space friends," she told me. "They say the star worlds have to change. He hopes we can make some kind of peaceful contact with them. Do you think a time will come when I can go with you back to the stars?"

"That would be wonderful," I told her. "If it could happen."

I knew it was impossible.

My radio stayed dead until the night when I found a green light flashing. Admiral Gilliyar was overhead, on a geosynchronous orbit that kept his armada over the highland ridge. I spent the rest of the night transmitting my recorded notes and pictures.

The sonic boom of an emerging skip craft pealed out of the sky while we were at breakfast a few mornings later. Jets roared overhead. A clerk rushed in, shouting that a Terran lander was down on the pad. A sleek little craft, it carried the Terran flag painted on its armored flank. Black-muzzled guns jutted out of the top turret.

Nobody got off. It sat there nearly an hour, while uneasy citizens gathered around it. A door dropped at last to make a ramp. I heard a roll of martial music. A flagman led a squad of riflemen down the ramp. A cameraman followed, set up a tripod, and shot Admiral Gilliyar marching out of the air lock in dress blue and gold, medals flashing on his breast.

Moving with the music, he took the flag and stabbed the sharpened staff into the ground. He turned, found me standing with my hosts in the watching crowd, and called my name. I stood there a moment, caught in confusion and bleak regret, before I stumbled toward him. Laurel ran to overtake me and threw her arms around me.

"Kiff!" she whispered. "I've always been afraid they'd come after you. Can't we help?"

I stood there an endless time trembling in her arms, too sick to speak. Breathing at last, I muttered that I was sorry, terribly sorry. I kissed her. Sobbing, she clung to me.

"I never meant—never meant to hurt you." The words stuck in my throat. "But I'm a spy. In the service of Cleon III and the Terran Republic."

She gripped my arms and stared at me, her wide eyes strange with shock. Blind with my own sudden tears I pulled out of her grasp, blundered on toward the admiral, and stopped to give him a stiff salute. Smiling, he returned the salute and came on to shake my hand. The little crowd had fallen silent, waiting till he turned and spoke.

"I am Terran Space Admiral Acton Gilliyar."

He paused for a moment before he went on, his mellow eloquence echoing off the long stone wall. He came in peace, to bring President Cleon Stawhawke's most cordial greetings and a heartfelt welcome into the Republic. I hardly heard the booming words. I was watching Laurel.

Her face white and stiff at first, she flushed pink. Her small fists clenched. Glaring at me with a look that changed from shock to scornful contempt, she spat on the ground.

"The President regrets your long neglect," his polished voice rolled on. "I understand that you are trying to survive here in a stare of lawless anarchy. I have come to bring you the law and order of Terran civilization. President Starhawke has appointed me the first governor of the planet Lucifer."

Muttering, people stared at one another and back at him.

"Sir!" Laurel's voice rang loud, heated perhaps by her anger at me. "We want none of your Republic." She looked around at those beside her, saw them nodding with agreement. "We need none of you!"

"Madam." He raised his voice, his tone grown harder. "With all due respect, I must inform you that your planet has belonged to the Terran Republic since the discoverers landed here and raised our flag."

"Non—nonsense, sir!" She caught her breath and lifted her quivering voice. "You threw us out of your wicked empire, and left us here to die. We've earned our freedom and we'll die to keep it."

"You may die. You'll never keep it."

"We'll never give it up."

"I must warn you, madam, that your words are a reckless incitement to treason." His voice slow and grimly solemn, he looked around at the little crowd and fixed his eyes on her. "If you want to die, the choice is yours. In modern times, suspected traitors are no longer merely exiled. The penalty now is death."

I heard a stifled outcry from her mother, a furious oath from her father. Friends gathered around them in a muttering group. The admiral turned to lift his hand at nose of the lander. The martial music rose again. He ordered his rifle squad back to the ramp. Laurel darted past them to the flag, pulled the staff out of the ground, and hurled it against the side of the lander. She stood staring at him and then at me, breathing hard.

"We witnessed that outrageous act of open treason!" he shouted at her. "What is your name?"

"Laurel Greenlaw." She tossed her head. "What is yours?"

"Acton Gilliyar." He grinned at her bleakly. "We'll be meeting again."

He beckoned to me. I followed him and the riflemen aboard. A warning siren screeched. Looking down from the control turret, I saw people scattering. Laurel stood closer, shaking here fist, dwindling to a defiant doll as we lifted.

❖   ❖   ❖

The admiral landed us at half a dozen towns up and down the Avalon, at the ski lodge below the volcano, the oasis down on the desert, at a lumber camp on the headwaters of the Styx. At each stop he went off with his rifle squad to read his proclamations. A few people hooted. Nobody cheered.

We climbed back to the geosynchronous point. He broadcast an ultimatum demanding unconditional submission. The colonists must accept the rule of the democratic Terran Republic, swear allegiance to President Cleon III, welcome Terran landing forces, pay Terran taxes, obey orders from him as their newly appointed governor. Unless he received a signal of surrender within three days, he would be forced, however unwillingly, to take whatever measures the situation might require.

"There will be no signal," I warned him. "There is no government, nobody with authority to surrender."

"I expected opposition from the like of that Greenlaw woman." He shook his head, his jaw set hard. "These people were condemned and sent here as outlaw enemies of the state. They are enemies and outlaws still. If they want a lesson in Terran power, I'll give them a lesson."

Waiting three days in orbit, he received no signal of surrender. His lesson was a volley of guided missiles.

"I'm remaining on the flagship," he told me. "It will be my official residence. Captain Crendock is going down as my executive secretary with orders to secure the planet and establish administrative control."

He was startled when I wanted to go back to Benspost.

"Why?" He gave me a hard look. "You won't find friends there."

Uncomfortably, I tried to explain my own torn feelings.

"I'm still loyal," I told him, "bound by my duty to the Republic. But I did make friends there. People were generous to me. I was fascinated with their history. I want to write it for the whole Republic."

"Forget your pet traitors," he advised me. "That Greenlaw woman is no friend now."

"Yet she is making history. History worth recording."

"Better get back to Terra while you can." He gave me a stiff half-smile. "You were warned to expect no public recognition, but we will surely find something for you."

He called me a fool when I shook my head.

I had to go back to find Laurel, to try to explain what I had done, to beg her to understand. I didn't tell him that, but in the end, he replaced my lost radio and holo camera and let me go back down to Benspost with Crendock. A missile had struck there, and little remained of old Ben Greenlaw's trading post.

Yet life went on. I saw camels loaded with lumber and tile to repair shattered buildings. Bart was back again from some Terran planet with another illicit cargo. We found his skipcraft undamaged, standing on the pad near the ashes and fallen walls.

"Leave him alone," Gilliyar had ordered. "I hope to legalize the trade and impose excise taxes.

Camels were tethered around his ship, the drivers loading them with goods he had brought. His crew was loading it again with exports: nuts and dried fruit from the desert lowlands, rare hardwoods and balls of raw rubber from the rain forest.

His parents had set up a new barter center in a tent on a vacant lot. His mother burst into tears when she saw me, and ran back into the tent. His father sat in his wheelchair behind a rough table, surrounded with whatever his clerks had been able to salvage. I thought he seemed sick, the splotches of his old jungle fever infection livid and swollen.

He looked up at me with an enigmatic expression.

"Well, sir?" He shook his head. "I never expected to see you again."

"I'm a historian," I said. "I came back to write the history of the colony. And I want to see your daughter."

"You've turned our history to tragedy." He spoke with a harsh finality. "You'll never see Laurel."

He turned to deal with a farmer who had come with a basket of eggs to trade. I saw Bart himself, stooping in the ashes of the store, filling a bag with scraps of fused and blackened metal. He met me with a quizzical grin and handed me what was left of my gun, the magazine shattered when the ammunition exploded.

"I think this was yours."

I asked about Laurel.

"Gone." The grin vanished. "I don't know where." His gaze grew sharper. "If your Terran friends are looking for her . . ."

He shrugged and stooped again into the ashes.

A few days later he came up to me while I was out with the camera to shoot a group of workers with spades and wheelbarrows, refilling a crater that one of Gilliyar's missiles had left in the road.

"Let's talk." He offered his hand. "I've heard about your history. I want our Terran friends to know our story. Will you let me take you back to tell it?"

I thanked him.

"But the history isn't finished. And I want to stay till I can see your sister."

His face grew bleak. "You'll be here forever."

Before he took off, I gave him a draft of my unfinished narrative, copies of my holos of the ruins, and a shot of Crendock strutting off a lander to repeat Gilliyar's ultimatum. I kept digging into the records I could find, asking people for their recollections, shooting the damage from the bombardment and the efforts at reconstruction.

And longing all the time for a glimpse of Laurel.

Crendock set up his headquarters on a hilltop above the ruins. His landers were busy for a time, bringing down temporary buildings and equipment. He tried to employ civilian labor, but nobody wanted his money or wanted him there. The few people left in the town were clearing the streets, rebuilding their homes, replanting gardens. Some of them let me join the labor teams, gave me food and shelter in return. I asked and asked again for news of Laurel, receiving blank or hostile stares.

Crendock's officers were just as determined to find her, but no more successful.

"It's frustrating," he told me one night when he had asked me to his quarters for a Terran dinner. "There's nobody with authority, no way to get control. Gilliyar says this Laurel Greenlaw has to be our first target. She openly defied him. He wants her caught and tried for treason."

He asked for anything I knew. That was nothing at all.

"My investigators have been looking everywhere. Broiling themselves down in the desert. Freezing on the slopes of that volcano. Not a clue. I hear that she was once employed down in the jungle. She may have returned. Nowhere we can follow, but we're posting a price on her head."

With no better lead, I found Marco Finn, the top driver of a camel train returning to the lumber mills, and begged him for a ride down to the jungle.

"Don't go." He turned to spit green fluid from the angel cud that bulged his bearded cheek. "You ain't fit for it."

He was a raw-boned, short-spoken man, scarred from hell fever, his wild beard stained bright green from the angel wood bark he chewed. He frowned and squinted at me. I tried to explain that I wanted to see the jungle, get the history of the lumbermen, the silvernut and rubber plantations, the barges on the Styx.

"Who will give a damn?" He shrugged and spat again. "Nothing but poison vines and devil bugs and rain that never stops. We call it hell country. No place for a Terran."

"But you're going back."

"We hell rats ain't quite human." He gave me a ferocious scowl. "We toughen up and take it like it is.

Sometimes it kills us, but people need the timber and the rubber and the silvernuts. And we get double barter points. If I'm alive ten years from now I can use my last timber load to build a cabin up in sky country. Grow a garden. Keep chickens and a cow. What you ought to do."

Yet he let me climb to the hard seat beside him.

The east rim of the upland is higher and steeper than the west. None of the convicts dropped into the jungle ever reached the highlands until rescue teams from the top found and cleared the trail. The ride down took us three long days.

Finn and I sat together every day on the pitching seat. We shared meals when we squatted around the cook fires, shared space in his little tent when we camped. He knew who I was. He must have wondered about Terra and my life there, wondered how I became a spy, but he never inquired.

Listening for Laurel's name, I never spoke of her.

The first day we wound through sunless gorges that old glaciers had cut, and came out into blinding sun on ledges so narrow I hardly dared look down at the endless ocean of glaring monsoon clouds, a mile and more beneath us. The second day we were still in them, in a fog so dense I could hardly see the beast ahead. The third day we came out of the clouds, down into ceaseless rain and suffocating heat. Still far below, the jungle was a featureless dark-green sea. The fourth day we were in its dismal twilight, breathing the reeks of wet decay and the rank musks of strange life.

Still the road ran on. Sometimes it was made of logs,

laid side by side. Sometimes it was flat rocks, laid to crown a thin clay dike. More often it was only a ditch of thick red mud, splashed and churned by the camel's wide-splayed feet. Undergrowth walled it and arched overhead, most of it a tangle of thick-leafed fungoid stuff the driver had no name for when I asked. The rain never stopped.

The days were endless nightmares. Stinging insects hummed around us. My face and arms itched and burned. My bones ached. My appetite was gone. My strength drained away till I had to tie myself into the bucking seat. I tried to chew the angel bark Finn shared when he saw I had the fever, but the bitter stuff burned my mouth and knotted my stomach and seemed to do no good.

Sweating and gasping for breath though the endless nights, I dreamed and dreamed again that I had found Laurel. Sometimes we had been swimming together in that little lake at the desert oasis, sometimes we were skiing on the old volcano, sometimes we had been back in bed together. She was always beautiful. Longing for her to love me, I tried to tell her how sorry I was. The words always stuck in my burning throat and she coldly turned away.

I lost the count of days. I don't know when we reached the lumber mills or how I got to Hell. That was the name of a settlement on the swampy shore of the Styx. Dimly, I remember the patter of the endless rain on the tent, the coughs and stinks of the men on the cots around me, the days when all I wanted was death. I remember dreams of Laurel, bathing my body in angel seed tea when my swollen throat wouldn't swallow.

✧   ✧   ✧

A morning came when my head seemed clear. The tent was silent, except for the murmur of the rain. The other cots were empty. The epidemic was over. Feeling well again, I lay waiting until Laurel came in. She was real, alive and smiling, lovely in a white uniform somehow spotless in spite of the mud. She helped me sit up and gave me a mug of the angel seed tea. Magically, its burning bitterness was gone. It had almost the taste of a good dry wine.

She laughed when I tried to say how sorry I was.

"You've already told me, at least a thousand times." She asked if I felt hungry and brought a tray of food. Suddenly ravenous, I gorged on river fish and hellcakes and roasted silvernuts and camel cheese. I was able to limp with her out into the clearing. Huge crimson blooms blazed from the vines that twined the trees around it. The air was sweet with their scent, and the jungle's dark power seemed almost kind. We went down to the dock to watch the little steamer come in with a load of cured rubber from a plantation down the river. The name painted on the bow was *Laurel*.

Next day she was even happier.

"Bart was on the radio," she told me. "He's back from Terra with great good news. Your stories about Gilliyar's bombardment set off new Free Space riots on a hundred planets. Revolution came so close that Cleon III had to abdicate. His son is promising to negotiate the independence of a new Free Space Federation.

"The new government has recognized our own freedom and ordered Gilliyar's forces out. They wanted to rename the planet Avalon. Bart told them no. He says Lucifer fits us better. They wanted him to stay as our ambassador. He said no to that. Ambassadors are government.

"But he did get them to guarantee free trade and free travel. They want angel wood and silvernut for medical research. We're free to visit Terra if we like." Soberly, she shook her head and caught my hand. "Not soon, I think. Our lives are here."

She found a place for us on a camel train when I felt strong enough. We rode together back up the hell road, back out of the rain and the bugs and the stink of the swamps, back through the fog into bright sunlight, back through narrow passes into the Vale of Avalon. I was still half-drunk on the angel tea and my dreams of our future together. She was more realistic.

"Freedom won't come free," she told me. "It never does."

Renegade

by Mark Tier

On the giant screen in Union Square a marine running full tilt toward the camera suddenly spurted blood where his head had been. I was glad there was no sound—I felt sick enough already.

Before I could wonder what had happened to the cameraman the screen blanked for a fraction of a second, and the scene shifted to a bird's-eye view of the jungle battle. And then cut to an ad.

On the old-fashioned ticker underneath—a copy of the relic in Times Square—the headline MARINES RETREAT appeared, one letter at a time.

A screech of brakes and the sound of scrunching steel jerked my attention back to the street. Most everyone on the sidewalk had come to a dead halt. Including me—and I hadn't even noticed. I suddenly became aware of the unnatural silence: after all, it's not every day you see someone's head blown off live on a five-hundred-foot three-dimensional screen. Drivers were mesmerized too. One of them must have hit the brakes and taken his car out of automatic. The roadnet braked the cars behind, but not fast enough to prevent a spectacular pile-up.

A lady nearby was throwing up in the gutter. My stomach started to churn so I took a few steps back. I felt a bit sick too, but I couldn't feel sorry for the guy. He'd volunteered knowing full well what the risks were. And was—had been—highly paid to take them. After all, every man and woman in both the Eighth Army and the Marines get a share of the holo and web rights. With the ratings on this mêlée his family, if he had one, will be well taken care of.

How much time had passed? More than I thought. Now I had to hurry to be at the hearing on time. As I and hundreds of others started moving again the normal Union Square bustle returned. Though it would be a while before the traffic followed suit.

8TH ARMY ODDS ON; MARINES 27–1 was now scrolling across the ticker. I'm not a gambling man but I can't resist an all-but-sure-thing. 27 to 1! That was like taking candy from the mouths of babes.

A few taps on my phone and I learned that the US Marines were retreating all across the front. But the retreat was slow and it didn't seem like they were about to fold. Sure wouldn't do their marketing image any good if they gave up so easily. *We Never Quit* was their motto.

If they only held out for just a few days I'd clean up. A good friend of mine, an executive of the Eighth Army Inc. had told me that their client—don't ask me whether it was the government of Colombia or the government of Venezuela; I haven't really been following this fracas too closely—had run out of money. That's real money I mean: they had plenty of that stuff they printed down there, whatever they called it, and a wheelbarrow full of it and a silver dime might get you a cup of coffee in San Francisco if the vendor was short of toilet paper.

Whichever gang of thugs it was, if they didn't pay up by Monday the Eighth Army Inc. was flying straight back home. Today was Friday. Planes and choppers were on standby over in Florida to pull them out at a moment's notice. Then all that would stand between the US Marines and the thugs running Venezuela (or Colombia) was the ragtag gaggle of bandits they called their army.

Those marines would walk it in the rest of the way. And the bookies would have to pay up.

A few more taps and I placed two hundred ounces (gold, not silver) on the Marines to win. If the Eighth Army pulled a rabbit out of the hat over the weekend, losing that gold would hurt, but it wouldn't kill me. Like I told you, I'm not a gambling man. You always gotta calculate the odds. If you work with an insurance company for as long as I have without learning that you're still pushing paper.

The phone beeped to tell me I had a couple of

minutes to be on time. Then it rang and Joe's ugly face (he's my partner) appeared on the screen. "Where the hell are you?" he growled.

I looked to find out. "Just walking into the lobby of the building," I told him. I turned the phone so he could see for himself.

He harrumphed, and his face disappeared from the screen. Joe was like that: didn't waste any time on pleasantries. Wasn't much good with small talk either.

I took my seat just before the judge walked in, followed by his staff. Adjudicator-in-Chief was his official title, but everybody called them judges.

When he was young, my granddad became a cop just before the tax revolt brought down the government and cops disappeared altogether. Here, anyway. I guess there are still cops in Colombia (or Venezuela) and other places which still have governments. What he told me about judges in his time bears no relation to adjudicators today. For a start, adjudicators are unbribable. Well, Chief Adjudicators. Offer one of *them* a bribe and he resigns your case. Then you're in deep doodoo. Boycotted. You'll never get another reputable adjudication outfit to take you on.

In a way, I guess I'm following in my grandfather's footsteps. Joe and I run San Francisco Investigations, one of the biggest agencies in the city. Occasionally we do some of the things cops used to do. Like today's case: murder.

Judge Wainwright was pushing eighty, though you'd never have guessed it. He strode into the room with the walk and energy of a much younger man. That, and his full head of hair—even if it was gray—meant he could pass for fifty-something. I resolved once again to spend more time at the gym—his youthful look made me jealous. Hell, he looks younger than I am!

Wainwright commanded the highest fees in the business, such was his experience and reputation for impartiality. Any of the freshmen advocates from his firm could have easily handled today's case. I'd expected one of them to be mediating. So why does All-Risk Insurance—they're our biggest client—want to spend so much money when any junior could have taken his place for peanuts? It didn't figure.

Wainwright sat down at the head of the table in the center of the room. Adjudicators' hearing rooms are often highly personalized. This design was one of the more interesting.

The only way to know this table's "head" is by where the judge sits. It's almost, but not quite, circular. Look a second time and it seems triangular. It's both.

Wainwright's staff arranged themselves on one side of the circular triangle. The All-Risk team sat at another.

To any casual watcher on the web it should have been immediately clear why a junior adjudicator could have handled this hearing: the third side was empty. The defendant, Gerald Murdock—the murderer—wasn't represented. And he hadn't shown up. Not that anyone expected him to: he'd disappeared straight after the murder and no one knew—or was willing to tell—where he'd gone.

That's why Joe and I were both here. Our firm had handled the case; we carried out the investigation, took the depositions, and so on. The moment the adjudicator ruled we were going to have to find the guy and get him to cough up what the judge was about to decide he owed.

Anyone who knew nothing about the killing of Randolph Ackerman had to be blind, deaf *and* dumb. With group sex, drugs, wife- and secretary-swapping, questionable business deals, not to mention nude bodies (one of them dead) and a murderer who'd done a disappearing act with bundles of money, the tabloids had a field day.

Last Saturday evening Gerald Murdock joined Randolph Ackerman for dinner and a group sex party at Ackerman's penthouse on Nob Hill. Murdock's secretary, Annabelle Pearson, Ackerman's wife, Sophia, and her sister, Jude, were also there to join in the fun and games.

The two men had a few business interests together and over the last couple of years there'd been lots of friction and disagreement between them. Apparently, both of them felt their partner was getting more than his fair share of the profits. They'd come to a peace agreement, and the purpose of the dinner was to celebrate and cement it. Bury the hatchet, if you will.

After dinner, after several bottles of wine, tabs of cocaine and God knows what other cocktails, and lots of group groping, Ackerman and Murdock got into an argument over one of the women. The argument quickly degenerated into a vicious rehash of every accusation they'd ever made against each other.

Seemingly livid with rage, Murdock grabbed a gun from his jacket and shot Ackerman between the eyes.

Waving the gun at the women he quickly dressed, ran out of the apartment, down the stairs and into a passing cab.

The women were so stunned—not to mention drunk and/or drugged—that they were slow to act. They first called an ambulance, which arrived just minutes after Murdock had left the building. Not that an ambulance was any help to Ackerman by then. Only after that did they call security. The place was crawling with armed guards (ours) just moments after the ambulance arrived. Just moments too late.

Both witnesses—Annabelle Pearson played mute—agreed with each other down to most of the fine details. And since they were both interviewed while the body was being taken away, still semi-naked, wrapped in sheets or towels, they didn't have time to concoct any fairytales.

Ackerman's hobby, however, made it an open and shut case. Seems he liked to record his sex parties with multiple holographic cameras and then edit them into home porn shows. He had hundreds of them. Someone bootlegged the files. The murder—along with Ackerman's entire porn library—is readily available all over cyberspace. It's the worst thing to hit Hollywood and the holo nets in years.

We tracked down the cab Murdock had picked up on Nob Hill. He'd gotten out at Union Square, and then his trail disappeared. We couldn't find any trace of him. We figured he had a car parked there and a second identity already fixed up, probably with one of the sleazier insurance outfits.

By Monday it was obvious that Murdock hadn't fired

that shot in a moment of angry passion. Over the previous months he'd quietly sold all his business interests and closed his stock and bank accounts. He'd turned the last of his real estate into cash just the week before. All but one of his bank accounts were cleaned out. He'd even managed to skim some of the cash from his joint ventures with Ackerman just minutes before the banks closed on Saturday. Ackerman hadn't suspected a thing.

One of his companies remained. The reason emerged when we asked the Insurance Association data bank for information on Gerald Murdock: he had no insurance cover whatsoever in his own name. One reason he wasn't represented before the adjudicator.

His sole remaining company, GMR Holdings, *was* insured. With the Mafia Corporation of Washington, DC. They weren't too cooperative. Never were: just the minimum level to ensure that other insurance agencies cooperated with them when they needed it. It was part of their heritage. At least according to their marketing, they were proud of their history as a private protection agency back when the government kept trying to put *any* competitor out of business.

As Mafia insured the *company*, not Murdock, they were under no obligation to give us the time of day. When we called they were as mute as mollusks.

And on Monday Annabelle Pearson paid every remaining bill and proceeded to shut that company down too.

All the money was gone. Thousands of gold ounces.

Gerald Murdock's legal identity had been tied to his company. His credit cards, bank accounts, agreements and everything else. Very clever. He could deal normally in our society and any trace would lead back to his company, not him.

It also meant there were no records of Murdock: no voiceprints, fingerprints or retina scans on file that we could access to help track him down.

We made a voiceprint from Ackerman's holo of the party. We found fingerprints that were probably Murdock's. We ran them through the data bank and—as I'd expected—drew a blank.

It was as if Gerald Murdock didn't exist. No doubt exactly what he had in mind.

"Good morning, gentlemen," said Wainwright. "We're here today to adjudicate the accusation that Gerald Murdock murdered Randolph Ackerman. Is Mr. Murdock present?"

When there was no answer, Wainwright asked, "Since Mr. Murdock does not appear to be here, who stands to speak for him?"

Again, no answer.

Wainwright was a stickler for procedures. He already knew that Murdock wasn't represented. But any missing step could give grounds for a rehearing or appeal. If Murdock ever surfaced to make a challenge.

"Who speaks for the estate of Randolph Ackerman?"

"I do, sir."

Joe and I looked at each other and I could see he felt as startled as me. Martin Li, the attorney who'd answered, billed more per hour than Wainwright. As usual, I was surprised I hadn't noticed him before. Strangely for a lawyer, he seemed to disappear in a crowd. Yet he was an extraordinarily handsome man. Eurasian most likely. But you just didn't see him until he began to use his deep, penetrating voice. From that moment on, I always had difficulty pulling my eyes away from him.

So why did All-Risks want two of the highest-powered guys in the business on *this* case? No reason popped into my head, but I had the uncomfortable feeling that it would somehow involve us.

This case had moved at lightning speed. Murder Saturday; evidence all assembled by Thursday morning; hearing today. No defendant to argue with helped. Still, fast in our business was normally two to three weeks between crime and hearing for an open and shut case. Ever since Sunday night, our office had looked more like a student dorm without maid service than a place of business. I don't think any of us had had a good night's sleep all week.

"Be it noted that Gerald Murdock has failed to appear to contest the charges against him," Wainwright said. Turning to Li he asked, "Do you contend that this hearing has jurisdiction over the case?"

"Indeed it does, sir. Mind if I walk around? I think better."

Wainwright waved his hand in a gesture of assent.

"It is conceivable that by his absence," said Li as he paced slowly from one side of the room to the other, "from the fact that he is not represented here today the defendant, Gerald Murdock, could argue that this hearing does not have jurisdiction.

"If he did, he would be wrong.

"Randolph Ackerman was a client of All-Risk

Insurance. His person and his property, including his apartment, were insured by All-Risk under a general all-risk policy. That policy included legal representation and mediation with other members of the Insurance Association and their clients. That policy was registered with the Association.

"When Gerald Murdock entered Ackerman's apartment on Saturday night, he implicitly agreed to place himself under the rules of Ackerman's policy with All-Risk."

"Was there a notice to this effect?" asked Wainwright.

"Yes, sir," answered Li. "On all entrances to Ackerman's apartment."

These signs are so common the only time I become aware of them is when they aren't there. They usually read:

WARNING

This property is insured by XYZ Insurance Co.
By entering this property you agree to be bound
by the rules of the policy and the
American Insurance Association.

"Has this been attested?" asked Wainwright.

"Yes, sir." One of Li's assistants passed a file to Wainwright, who quickly skimmed through it. Though I'd bet he'd read it all before.

"As Gerald Murdock is neither represented here today, nor has he any known contract with any member of the American Insurance Association, or any of the other insurance associations in North America, he is uninsured. And was uninsured at the time Randolph Ackerman died." Li's assistant passed another folder to Wainwright. "In that file," Li continued, "are the results of our search for any insurance cover of Gerald Murdock.

"Being uninsured, any of his actions while upon the property of Randolph Ackerman are to be adjudicated by the rules of Ackerman's policy with All-Risk Insurance. He implicitly agreed to that upon entry."

Two more files were pushed across the table to Wainwright. They'd be copies of Ackerman's policy and All-Risk's rules.

"In that case," said Wainwright, "I hereby rule that this hearing has the legal jurisdiction to adjudicate the accusation that Gerald Murdock murdered Randolph Ackerman."

Every adjudication session began with these formalities. Now they were over, Wainwright turned with obvious relief to Li and asked, "Is there anything you'd like to add to your brief?"

Knowing Wainwright, he'd already mastered every nuance of the evidence the All-Risk team had prepared—including any errors or omissions. Today's hearing was, other than the decision itself, the final part of the adjudication process.

"No sir," answered Li.

"Then, please proceed with your summary."

"The facts are clear," said Li. "At 11:07 last Saturday evening, Gerald Murdock shot Randolph Ackerman. The time was established from Ackerman's holo. He died instantly, according to the doctor who examined the body. Murdock left the apartment, hailed a cab, got off at Union Square, and hasn't been seen since.

"These facts were established from interviews with two of the three witnesses, Sophia Ackerman, the victim's wife, and Jude Schwarz, her sister, and from the holo. A secure copy of the holo was made immediately. It was discovered by bonded detectives from San Francisco Investigations.

"The third witness, Annabelle Pearson, Murdock's secretary, refused to answer any questions."

My attention was again riveted to Martin Li. I was vaguely aware that Wainwright sat stock still, like a gray stone god, only his eyes moving as Li walked.

"Both witnesses agreed that no one had been near the computer recording the holo, a fact borne out by the holo itself. Between the murder and the time the detectives entered the apartment twelve minutes later, none of the three women or the medics went anywhere near the computer. There was no one else in the apartment at the time: the maid and the butler who served dinner had already gone home."

Wainwright made a cryptic note with his pencil, the first time he'd moved since Li began to speak.

"Bonded computer experts testified that the only access to the holo files was through the terminal in the living room, and the terminal in Ackerman's study which could only be entered from the living room.

"Since there can be no question of the veracity of the holographic file of the murder that we have presented in evidence, it is clear that Gerald Murdock is guilty of the murder of Randolph Ackerman beyond a shadow of doubt."

Li stopped pacing for a moment and let silence hang over the room.

"We have prepared significant excerpts from the holos and depositions that show these facts. Would you care to review them, sir?"

"No need," said Wainwright. "However, please show me evidence that supports your contention that no one went near the computer terminals."

"Certainly sir." Turning to one of his assistants, he continued, "Blair, can you bring up the holo at the time of the murder."

"Alleged murder please, Mr. Li. Murder—or otherwise—has yet to be determined."

"Of course, sir."

The holo shimmered and then solidified on top of the table. Murdock was frozen with his hand reaching into his jacket. Ackerman stood naked in the center of the room, his face bright red, his mouth open in the middle of a scream. The three women lay on the sofa or the floor in different states of undress.

Li walked around the table to stand behind his assistant. He spoke softly and the scene revolved. After a moment, a door and a terminal were highlighted.

"This is the computer terminal in the living room," he said, and leaned over the table putting his hand inside the holo to point at the keyboard. "And this—" he pointed at the highlighted door "—is the only entrance into the study, with the only other terminal that could access these files."

At a gesture from Li, another of his assistants passed two files to Wainwright. "These files show the layout of the computers, and which terminal could access which file type, kind and level of security," said Li, "and the layout of Ackerman's penthouse apartment."

"Thank you," said Wainwright, making another note. "Continue," he said, looking at Li.

Li said a few more quiet words to his assistant, and stepped back.

"We'll hold the holo on the door and the keyboard and fast forward it to the moment the secure copy was made." As he spoke Murdock sprang to life and for the second time today I saw a man die. This one didn't affect me nearly as much. I'd seen it before, and knew it was coming.

I felt like laughing at the way Murdock dressed and disappeared in a flurry of clothing and as the three almost-naked women seemed to run every which way across the room. A team of medics appeared and suddenly the room seemed to overflow with armed men. As one of them looked into the study the picture slowed back to normal speed.

"As you can see, this is the first time anyone has been near the keyboard or the door," Li said.

Sam Renkin, one of our investigators, sat down at the keyboard. A moment later he said, "Hey, this thing is recording something."

Li signaled his assistant and the holo stopped. "From this moment on," he said, "this man, Sam Renkin, a bonded detective from San Francisco Investigations never left the keyboard until a secure copy of the files on the computer was made.

"One other point. These files could be accessed by voice, but only by Ackerman's voice. The computer would respond to Mrs. Ackerman's voice for other commands. Otherwise, only with a password that Mrs. Ackerman said she did not know. Indeed, when Mr. Renkin asked her if she'd known that the computer was recording everything, she went into shock and had to be treated by the medics."

Turning to Wainwright he asked, "Do you have any other questions, sir?"

With a slight shake of his head, Wainwright indicated that Li should continue. As the holo shimmered and disappeared Wainwright ceased being a faint shadow behind Sam Renkin's face.

"In our brief, we outlined the substantial circumstantial evidence that strongly suggests Murdock had murder in mind when he arrived for dinner.

"But the facts are clear. At 11:07 last Saturday evening, Gerald Murdock shot and killed Randolph Ackerman. There can be no doubt that Murdock is guilty of murder. For that reason, whether he killed Murdock in a fit of anger or, as we submit, as part of a long-standing plan makes absolutely no difference to the penalty we seek.

"Gerald Murdock is guilty."

Li took a sheet of paper from his place at the table and passed it to Wainwright.

"Murdock is guilty of murder beyond a shadow of doubt. The high probability that the murder was premeditated merely adds weight to our claim that Murdock pay the highest penalty the law allows.

"And it's to that penalty I'd now like to turn."

"We submit that Murdock be required to pay to All-Risk Insurance the sum of 125,115 gold ounces, plus all costs, with interest."

The amount Li asked for drew a low whistle of astonishment from several spectators, including me. People started whispering to each other until Wainwright's sharp "Quiet, please," brought silence back to the room.

"Continue."

"Certainly, sir," said Li. "If he fails to pay the penalty, ownership of all property identified as belonging to him be transferred to All-Risk Insurance in full or partial settlement of the penalty. And as he has disappeared entirely and has no known legal identity, we ask that Gerald Murdock be declared a renegade and outlaw until such time as the penalty is paid in full."

Now I understood why they'd rushed to have this case adjudicated. They'd be able to take ownership of Murdock's companies. GMR Holdings was the only one left, but if they could grab it before Annabelle Pearson closed it down completely they'd have a chance of being able to trace the money and, with it, Murdock.

Correction: *We'd* have a chance. Joe and I were going to be the ones who had to find him.

"As we all know, and as Murdock must also know, the penalty for murder is restitution to the heirs of the victim for the value of the life taken, and restitution of any other damages directly attributable to the death.

"Ackerman's life was insured by All-Risk for the sum of fifteen thousand gold ounces. We seek reimbursement of that amount.

"In addition, Ackerman's policy with All-Risk includes coverage of violent death, such as murder.

"Because of this provision, All-Risk had complete access to Ackerman's financial records and routinely updated this risk. The calculation of the value of Ackerman's life, based on the present value of his estimated future earning power, totals 110,115 gold ounces. This amount is exhaustively documented in the brief, using standard Insurance Association scales."

That was a big number, even for someone as wealthy as Ackerman. It's a number you could easily lowball. That was one of the things I liked about All-Risk: they never stiffed their customers.

And how do you figure someone's *future* earning potential? You make lots of assumptions. Assumptions that would have been challenged—if there'd been a Murdock representative to challenge them.

"The penalty we seek includes reimbursement of the fifteen thousand gold ounces in life insurance cover that All-Risk has already paid to Ackerman's widow, Sophia Ackerman, and the sum of 110,115 gold ounces that would become immediately due and payable by All-Risk Insurance.

"We also submit that the penalty include all the costs of the investigation and these proceedings to date, plus the costs yet to be disbursed in finding the defendant and recovering the penalty.

"Finally, that the penalty include interest on the outstanding amount from the moment the decision of these proceedings is finalized to the time the penalty has been recovered in full."

Wainwright was looking at the papers Li had given him. When Li stopped talking, he looked up.

"Subject to any questions, the plaintiff rests."

"No questions," said Wainwright. In a louder voice,

looking around the room, "Is there anyone here to speak for Gerald Murdock?"

Once more he was greeted with silence.

"In that case, this hearing is adjourned until two o'clock." As Wainwright stood up his assistants followed suit. A hubbub of conversation quickly filled the silence as they left the room.

I grabbed Joe by the arm. "Let's go and talk to Li before everybody else does."

A loose knot of people had gathered around him. I squeezed through and offered him my hand. "Nicely put, counselor."

"Hi Ray." He smiled at me. "Joe."

"We were surprised to see both you *and* Wainwright here today."

"I think the idea is they don't want the faintest question as to the probity of the verdict."

Up close, I noticed that his eyes looked tired. "Looks like you haven't had much sleep recently. Either."

He laughed. "We're hoping to give you a warm trail to follow. If there's any trail at all."

"There's always something—"

"Ah, there you are." A voice came from behind me. "Joe. Ray. We need to talk right away." I turned as somebody's hand grabbed my arm and started tugging it gently.

"Hi, Fritz. Anyone here had any sleep this week?" Fritz Gandhi—he had an Indian father and a German mother—was chief of All-Risk's San Francisco bureau.

"Plenty of time for that next week. Or next month," he said.

"Looks like I have to go," I said to Martin. "See you at two."

"I wouldn't count on it," said Fritz. "You'll be too busy."

Joe and I followed Fritz into a nearby room along with a number of people I recognized from his office. A woman I did not know, who was stunningly attractive despite her full head of gray hair, was already sitting at the table.

"Ray, Joe, I'd like you to meet Noni Brooks. Noni, this is Ray Black and Joe Herrera. They head San Francisco Investigations."

"Good," she said. I presumed our reputation had preceded us. "I'm pleased to meet you."

"Noni's from Berkshire Re," Fritz explained. "They have—potentially—a large interest in this case."

"The violent death cover?" Joe asked. Noni and Fritz both nodded.

Noni Brooks certainly didn't waste any time. "The question is: can you find Gerald Murdock?" But her look seemed to say, If *you* can't, we'll get someone who can.

Berkshire Re is the biggest—and smartest—insurance outfit in the world. They obviously wanted Murdock and his money found. And they don't take "impossible" as an answer.

"What's the budget?" asked Joe.

"Five hundred ounces," said Noni.

"To start with," added Fritz.

"You're assuming Wainwright will find him guilty," I said.

"No," said Noni, "we're not *assuming* that. Though we expect he will." She looked at her watch. "Judge Wainwright will give his decision three and a half hours from now. If we just sit around and wait till then and the verdict *is* guilty, that's three and a half hours we've lost.

"Do I need to point out the obvious? It's Friday already, and this man is going to be very hard to find. His trail's getting colder by the minute. One extra hour could be the difference between success and failure."

What about the five days we've already lost? I thought to myself. But I said, "If anyone can find him, we can." Joe nodded his agreement.

"As far as you're concerned," said Fritz, "Wainwright has already pronounced him guilty. We'll call you when he announces his decision but we want you to be ready to move the moment he does."

"GMR Holdings," said Joe.

"That's right," said Fritz. "Follow the money. We've got all the papers ready: five minutes after Wainwright rules we'll be in possession of the company. Then we have to get Murdock's secretary out of the office and see what she's left for us to find."

"I want to see the bank records," I said. "Murdock disappeared at Union Square Saturday night. Like the Invisible Man. Feels like we've been hitting our heads against a brick wall ever since."

"That's exactly the point," said Fritz. "Somewhere in the company's records should be a warm trail to follow. At least a lead, a hint of some kind."

"Looks like our only bet," said Joe.

Noni Brooks shook her head. "There'll be a reward.

One thousand ounces for information that leads us to Murdock."

"Who'll screen the replies?" asked Joe.

"We want you to do that. You're the experts," said Fritz.

"That'll cost extra," said Joe. "Murdock will be 'seen' all over the world."

"We only need one."

"Yeah. But figuring which is the right one will cost a fortune."

Fritz turned to Noni, who nodded her head.

"Okay," he said. "We're also going after the money Murdock skimmed from the joint venture companies. We're claiming Murdock broke the partnership agreements which would make it theft."

"But I thought he had the right to withdraw that money," I said.

"He had the right to spend the money on joint venture business. Not to pay himself without Ackerman's agreement. Anyway, we'll have a judgment in a day or three. If the judge rules against Murdock, he'll be guilty of theft as well as murder."

"Good," said Joe.

Everybody turned to look at him. "Why?" someone asked.

"Never mind now," said Fritz. "It's time we got moving."

"Who's handing things on your end?" Joe asked.

"Tony Ramirez. He's expecting your call."

"What I want to know," said Joe, to no one in particular, "is why did he do it? What's his *motive*?"

✧   ✧   ✧

"Greed or lust," said Joe as we walked out onto Geary.

"What about revenge?"

Joe shook his head. "Doesn't figure."

"Hang on a minute," said Joe. He stepped into the tobacco store we'd just passed.

"Heavens above," he said, jogging up to where I'd stopped. He stared at his phone in one hand and a packet of Maui Wowie Lights in the other. "They've gone down in price again!"

I jangled the coins in my pocket. Joe never carried any, always paying by phone. Call me weird if you like, but I enjoy the feel, the *weight* of gold and silver.

"So what's new?" I asked.

"They dropped last month, and they're down again already."

Thinking of our payroll I said, "Wish salaries went down like everything else."

"Yeah," he grunted.

"So what do you want with them?" I asked him.

"Added inspiration."

"I'm inspired enough already."

"I said *added* inspiration, you dummy. I want to watch the holo. There's bound to be something, something somebody said or did, that will give us a clue."

The rest of the morning disappeared in a blaze of activity. But at two o'clock we were ready. At 2:05 Wainwright announced his decision: Guilty. At 2:10 one team from All-Risk, along with some of our operatives, moved into Murdock's office. A second team went to the Bank of San Francisco. At 2:15 they zapped us the account records of GMR Holdings.

"What's the time in Switzerland?" asked Joe as the records scrolled across the screen.

I thought for a minute. "Bedtime, I'd say."

"Damn. Bet Swiss banks aren't open Saturdays, either." Joe pointed at the screen. "I don't like the look of that." His fingers danced over the keyboard and the screen split into half a dozen different displays.

"See," he said. "All the money was sent to Swiss banks. All these transfers—" all but one of the displays lit up "—went to three different Swiss banks. Union Bank, Credit Suisse, Bank Leu. All big names."

"We should get some cooperation out of them. What's the problem?"

Joe punched a button on the keyboard and the display that hadn't been highlighted filled the screen.

"Right there. That wire went Saturday. Anstalt Bank. Where the hell is Vaduz, anyway?" He highlighted the bank's name and an information screen appeared. "Vaduz, Liechtenstein. Oh hell."

"Liechtenstein," I murmured. "So how do we stand with them?"

"Those guys in Liechtenstein don't say 'boo' to their own mothers. Let's see. Court order required," he read from a new display. "Hmmm. To get that, the whole case has to be retried in Vaduz. Witnesses. Everything. God knows how long that would take—years possibly. They don't recognize our adjudication process."

"Anyway," I said, "what's the bet all the money is some other place."

"Ha. Want me to take the wrong side of a sure thing?

The phone rang and a message blinked on the screen that Tony Ramirez was calling. "Good," said Joe as he pushed the Accept button. Tony's face appeared on the screen.

"Seen the bank records?" he asked.

"Yeah," said Joe. "Liechtenstein."

"And Switzerland, which is a bit more cooperative. Monday, we'll be filing cases in both places."

"So what are the chances of getting any information?" I asked.

"Not good," said Ramirez. "Better, though, when we get a ruling that Murdock stole the money from the joint ventures. That case should be finished this afternoon.

"You got anything?"

"Lots of questions," said Joe. "You got any answers?"

"Lots," Ramirez laughed. "See what you guys can dig up in Switzerland."

"Sure. We'll be on the next ship out. Let us know if they find Murdock guilty of theft."

"Will do."

After Tony had signed off Joe asked me, "Who *is* our guy in Switzerland?"

"Günter Lattman. Remember?"

"Let's call him." Günter's number appeared on the screen.

"Wait! How cooperative do you think he'll be if you wake him up in the middle of the night."

"You're right," Joe said, grudgingly.

"Send him a message, ask him to call *us* as soon

as he can. Let him wake *us* up in the middle of the night."

Joe nodded as the phone rang again. It was Andy, one of our investigators who'd gone with the All-Risk team to Murdock's office.

"What did you find?" I asked.

"She didn't leave much for us *to* find. Most of the computers have been wiped clean. We'll see what we can recover, but I wouldn't hold your breath. She's had a whole week."

"Anything at all?"

"Well . . . I don't know. We haven't moved anything yet. I'd like you to come down and have a look. Joe, I mean. My gut feeling is he might smell something."

I didn't take offense. Joe's "nose" had taken on a mystical quality in our company.

"We're on our way."

What had clearly been Murdock's office had a wonderful, close-up view of the building next door. We entered through a general office/reception area with three desks. One other door led into a smaller office which had been Annabelle Pearson's.

Joe stood in the center of Murdock's office, deep in thought. We all knew better than to interrupt him when he was in this state.

This office, like the others, had been all but stripped clean. Other than a few papers in the trash cans, a few files lying around, some old newspapers and magazines, all that was left was two bookshelves full of books. Mostly travel guides.

After a while Joe said, "It's too obvious." One of the

All-Risk guys started to ask him, "What—and was silenced. "Wait," somebody whispered to him.

Joe walked to one of the shelves and scanned the titles. They were mostly tourist guides to countries in Africa and South America. On one of the tightly packed shelves there was a hole where a book had been removed. The missing book was one of the travel guides.

"It's like Murdock left instructions. 'Ms. Pearson,'" he recited, "'please destroy everything but don't remove or touch anything on the bookshelves.'

"It's like Murdock's trying to tell us, 'Please waste your time looking for me here.'"

"Somewhere in Africa," I said. "Starting with 'N.'"

"Nigeria," someone said.

"Niger."

"Nairobi."

"Nepal."

"Nepal's in Asia, muscle head."

"Never mind." Turning to Andy, Joe said, "What I'd like you to do is set up these books and shelves in my office, *exactly* as they are now. Make a list of all the countries; see what's missing. And what the missing book probably is. See what you find out about trips Murdock took. Was he a traveler or a stay-at-home? Where did he go on vacations? What were his hobbies? Things like that. We need a better feel for this man."

"Right," said Andy.

"Wherever he is, I'll bet he's not where that bookshelf is pointing us to."

"Perhaps he's sitting there laughing at us while we're

looking everywhere else," said one of the people from All-Risk. "Wheels within wheels."

"That really helps narrow down the search," I said.

"Or maybe Annabelle Pearson took it," said Andy. "Maybe *she* wants to go there."

Talking to himself again, Joe murmured, "I'll bet she does."

"Want me to order you guys pizza or something before I head for home?"

Molly's voice pulled me away from the screen. I rubbed my eyes, bleary from hours poring over files and documents. By contrast Molly (our receptionist) was bright and chirpy: she was about the only member of our staff who hadn't been putting in twenty-six-hour days.

Joe seemed to be asleep, his feet up on the desk and his chair laying all the way back. With Joe, appearances are always deceptive. "Good idea," he mumbled without opening his eyes.

"Want the usual?" she asked.

"Sure, pepperoni," I said.

"Yeah," said Joe, "with just a sprinkle of hash."

"You too?" said Molly, looking at me.

"Not for me. I want to keep my head clear so I'll stick to beer. If you could order a six-pack—make sure they're ice-cold."

"What's the time?" asked Joe.

"Six." Molly said. "Oh . . . and everybody else is wondering if you want them to stay another night, or can they all go home?"

I looked at Joe. "Tell 'em to go home, sleep—and

keep their phones on in case we need 'em at three o'clock in the morning."

"Thanks, Molly," I said.

As she closed the door Joe stirred himself, stretched and sat up. He reached for the still-unopened packet of Maui Wowie Lights lying on his desk and pulled out a joint. "Time to look at that holo," he said.

Joe and I shared a large office. Our desks half-faced each other so we could work privately or talk when we wanted to. A couple of very comfortable sofas lined the opposite wall—they'd proved their worth this week. The books and bookshelves from Murdock's office had been set up against the wall to Joe's left.

"Any inspirations?" I asked, waving at the books.

"Needle in a haystack. I think that's a red herring. My gut has been bugging me about that holo; maybe, *that's* where we'll find our lead. Not in those books. . . . Heard from Andy?"

I shook my head. "Let's give him a call and see what he's got."

"No need—he'll call in when he's ready."

Joe punched a button on his keyboard and the holo shimmered in the center of the room for a moment before stabilizing.

"This is hardly what I'd have chosen for a Friday night movie."

Joe grinned. "Me neither. I'd rather watch the football. So let's run it—maybe we can catch the end of the game."

Fat chance. Having seen it before, I had trouble keeping awake. Joe on the other hand looked like he was going to fall asleep at any moment, only moving to munch on pizza. But he was actually in a highly alert, trancelike state. Which deepened as the smoke in the room thickened. Just when he looked like he'd finally dozed off he'd wind the holo back saying, "Look at this."

Dinner was over, but the five of them were still at the dining table. Murdock and Ackerman were toasting each other. "To our partnership," said Ackerman. "May it prosper," said Murdock. "He doesn't mean it," said Joe.

Joe wound the holo back and locked it onto Murdock's face and zoomed in. When Murdock said, "May it prosper," he looped it, so Murdock said the same words over and over again.

"Look at his face," Joe said. "It's wooden. That smile is forced. He's lying through his teeth."

We know that, I thought. Just that morning he'd stripped the money out of the partnerships. He's ready to run. I also knew better than to interrupt Joe when he was following his nose. I knew what he was trying to do: get inside their minds.

Joe then ran through the same scene again, with the perspective locked onto Ackerman. "He doesn't notice."

"What?" I asked.

"He can't see it. He's enthusiastic. Maybe he was one of those people who can't read faces; insensitive."

"Maybe he's too drunk or stoned."

"Maybe," said Joe. But he didn't believe it.

I only perked up when the women stripped off. No—I don't "get off" from watching other people have sex. These three women, though, were something to look at. Like watching a beauty contest. And Ackerman's wife, Sophia, was the clear winner.

"There it is. That's why my nose has been twitching. It's not Murdock at all."

I couldn't figure out what Joe was talking about.

"Look at this." Joe locked the holo on Sophia Ackerman's face. Even I could see it now: she and Murdock weren't screwing: they were making love. Or she was: it was written all over her face.

Then Joe flicked to Annabelle Pearson. For just a moment there was a look of pure hatred on her face. Joe froze the picture, zoomed out, and it was clear that Annabelle Pearson was looking at Sophia and Murdock making love.

One more flick and we were looking at Sophia Ackerman. Just for a second, a look of disgust crossed her face: at that moment she was looking at her husband.

"That's it," said Joe. "The eternal triangle. Or quadrangle, in this case. If we can't follow the money, we can follow the sex."

He punched his phone. "Andy. I want a twenty-four-hour tail on Mrs. Murdock and Annabelle Pearson . . . Yes, starting right now. . . . Call anyone you need: this has got to be tight. You've all got to be ready to follow them wherever they go. . . . Sure, hire all the extra help you need. . . . Yeah, right, tell everyone to have their bags packed. And make sure your cards are loaded with cash: one of those women is going to lead us to Murdock as sure as my name is Joe Herrera, and you've got to be ready to go wherever in the world they go."

For a while Joe listened, muttering, "Yeah," "Okay," "Good," and so on. Finally, "Okay, I'm on my way," and put the phone down.

"Where?" I asked.

"Murdock's apartment. I'm meeting Andy there."

"My god, it's getting on for midnight!"

"Well, I'm in the mood right now."

"What's Andy found out?"

"Oh, this and that. Sort of mood stuff. I'll fill you in tomorrow."

"Is that it?" I asked, motioning to the holo.

"Oh yeah, we're finished with that. My nose has stopped itching." With relief, I switched the holo off and the room was clear at last.

Joe grabbed his coat and waved "goodbye" as he ran out the door. I've no idea where his energy came from; it just made me feel even more tired.

And then the phone rang. Who could be calling at this time of night? Maybe it was Sophia Ackerman looking for a date. I must have been dreaming.

"Hullo. Is this San Francisco Investigations?" said a voice I didn't recognize. It was English English, but with a faint trace of a foreign accent I couldn't place. No face appeared on the screen to help me out.

"Yes," I replied.

"Oh, good morning, Ray."

"Yes. Who is this?"

"Oh, sorry. It's too early in the morning to show my face. Günter Lattman here."

"Günter! You got my message? What time is it in Zurich?"

"About eight-thirty. What are you doing in the office so late?"

"Working, more's the pity."

"I went quickly through the Murdock stuff you sent me. There's no way I can get information out of a Swiss bank without a Swiss court order. And Swiss courts don't recognize your murder penalties. If we found Murdock here we could lock him up for you—but that wouldn't get you any money out of him."

"All-Risks is going to file in a Zurich court bright and early Monday morning."

"That'll take weeks if you're lucky. Months more likely. And even then, the Swiss court isn't going to give you— or me—access to Swiss bank records. Not for murder."

"Yeah, that's what I thought."

"All they could do is arrest him if he was found here."

"There's another case against Murdock in court right now. For theft."

"That's different," said Günter, enthusiasm showing in his voice at last. "If you can show there's stolen money in a Swiss bank, well . . ."

"Murdock's flown the coop. He didn't show up in court today, and he won't show up next week. So it should be open and shut."

"Okay. You've still got to get a Swiss court order. But that's a lot easier for theft. Do you want me help you get that done?"

"I'm pretty sure All-Risks will take care of that. I'll check and let you know. Main thing is we want to see those records as soon as possible after we get the order. Can you set that up?"

"That I can do."

"Great. I have to hit the sack. I'll talk to All-Risks and get back to you next week."

"Fine. Good night."

After I'd closed up the office—kind of Joe to leave that to me—I slumped into my car, ordered it to take me "Home, Jeeves," reclined the seat and dozed while the roadnet took me there. When the car pulled into the garage I was sound asleep: it had to wake me up.

On Monday the Eighth Army called for a truce and pulled out. My bank account was flusher by 5,400 gold ounces. The rest of the week was downhill from there.

Tuesday Murdock was found guilty of theft; Thursday a Swiss court gave us access to Murdock's bank records (which impressed Günter no end. "All-Risks must have pulled a lot of strings to get the hearing done so fast," he told us); and Friday we had copies.

All the money had flown. To places like Nauru, the Cook Islands, Pitcairn and other sandbars that made Mafia, Inc. look like first-prize winners in a gabfest.

The money trail was a dead end.

Meanwhile our phones were ringing off the hook with more red herrings, thanks to Berkshire's reward. . . .

WANTED

for Murder and Theft:

1,000*au* REWARD

Gerald Murdock has been declared an outlaw and a renegade under the rules of the

American Insurance Association.
A reward of 1,000 gold ounces
will be paid to the person who
provides information leading to
his arrest.

Outlaw means that no client
of any AIA member is insured
for any dealing with Gerald
Murdock other than self-defence.

Renegade means that any
member of the public who
apprehends, arrests, or detains
Gerald Murdock or assists in
doing so will be considered a
bonded representative of the AIA
under its rules.

People were told to contact us—and they did. Within
two days, Murdock had been sighted in fifty-five countries, every major city in North America and half the
small towns.

Luckily for us, Berkshire paid for all the extra staff,
phone lines and follow-up on all the leads, just as Noni
had promised.

Noni—and Fritz—weren't quite so understanding on
everything else.

Eventually, after several meetings, some of them
heated, they had to agree that with the money trail
dead and none of the leads leading us anywhere Joe's
instinct to "follow the sex" was all that was left.

"And if he dumps *both* women?" Noni asked.

Joe and I could only shrug.

✧   ✧   ✧

Some three months later I'd just gotten to sleep when a phone call from Andy woke me.

"I'm on a rocket to Tokyo. Just took off."

"So? What? Why?"

"I nearly lost her on the way to the airport."

"Who?"

"Sophia Ackerman. Are you asleep or something?"

"I was."

"I didn't get a chance to call in earlier. We land in Tokyo in forty-five minutes and I'm going to need backup."

"Okay. I'll call you back."

It was a wild night. We couldn't arrange backup in time. Luckily, Andy kept up with her as she got on the Mag-Lev to Osaka. When the train arrived he had all the help he needed.

She took him on a merry chase, from Osaka to Shanghai, to Singapore, to Hong Kong and finally Manila. At each stop she changed her appearance. And at each stop from Osaka on, a female operative followed her into the bathroom. Otherwise we might have lost her entirely: each time, she had a new identity to go with each disguise.

She ended up in a condo in a high-security walled and gated village.

Andy sent us a picture of the happy couple by the condo pool.

"My god," said Joe, "I'd never have recognized him. But it has to be him."

Murdock had a goatee and mustache, had changed his hair and eye color (contacts, I figured), and had picked up a new nose somewhere along the line.

"Right," I said. "If she was going to meet anyone else, why the merry chase?"

"Manila, hmmm," Joe murmured. "No mountains, no beaches, no snow. Clever." Among the useless information we'd piled up about Murdock was that he loved skiing, hiking, mountaineering, boats and deep-sea fishing.

"All you have to do now," he said to me, "is go to Manila and pick him up."

The only nonstop service to Manila was an aging SuperJumbo. I didn't fancy a twelve-hour flight, so I took the rocket to Hong Kong and connected. Hong Kong–Manila took longer than San Francisco–Hong Kong.

As a kid, I loved hearing my granddad's stories about the tax revolt—but I never knew until after he died that he was one of its heroes.

He'd sit on the swinging chair on the porch at night, set me on his knee and tell me how people hated the government, but were afraid. Some arm of the government called the "HSS" was rounding up terrorists, and nobody ever knew where they'd strike next. I'd wake up sweating from nightmares of giants, dressed in black, storming into my room in the middle of the night. Even so, I could never resist another of his stories.

He told me about Amanda Green, a teacher in a small town near San Francisco. When she didn't show up at school one morning, someone went to see if she was hurt—and found her house trashed, all her files and computer gone, but no sign of her.

And her valuables untouched. No ordinary burglars.

Her neighbors had nothing. But they'd heard the familiar sounds of the sirens and car doors slamming and thumping feet in the middle of the night . . . and closed their houses up tight.

A terrorist, claimed the HSS, inciting her students to rebel against the state.

A homely grandmother, a dedicated teacher, loved by her students, and respected by the community a terrorist? For teaching her students the meaning of life, liberty and the pursuit of happiness?

Amanda Green was the spark that lit the fire. It started quietly, like a burning ember, as groups held sporadic protests here and there. Only to be brutally repressed by the HSS police.

The TV coverage inflamed the nation. Within days millions of people across the country were parading with signs saying "Liberty or Death," "Don't Tread on Me" and even "Taxation is Theft."

One night an IRS office was burned down and somebody calling himself Tom Paine appeared on the web, urging people to strangle the government *peacefully* by refusing to pay taxes. As the idea caught on, the government called out the army to help the police help the tax collectors to "do their duty." Despite widespread support for the revolt, the government was winning until a couple of big corporations announced they were joining in.

The way my grandad told me as a kid, the people united against the hated government and brought it tumbling down.

Of course, it wasn't that simple or that easy, as I later found out. And I also learnt how granddad had persuaded some of his fellow policemen to do their *real* duty: protect the public. The sight of police standing *between* the army and the people inspired thousands of other policemen to do the same. When soldiers started joining them, the government had no choice but to cave in.

When the government collapsed the oil-rich states of the Middle East spotted an opportunity and hired a remnant of the US army to "liberate" the Muslims of the Philippines. They had no trouble at all gathering a seasoned force of veterans who were highly skilled in killing people.

That generated an enormous controversy. The soldiers were severely criticized for working for a government. Some pointed out it's a free country—at least now it is, with government gone—so anyone's free to work for anyone . . . including mercenaries. Others said that, right or wrong, it's better for us that these people are somewhere on the other side of the world.

The oil sheiks started a trend: pretty soon American mercenaries were fighting other people's wars for them all round the world. As they still are.

The Philippines—which used to be pretty much all the islands between Taiwan and Borneo—disintegrated. The Philippine Army was no match for the Americans, who threw them out of Mindanao in a couple of weeks. Once Mindanao declared its independence other islands followed suit. Local elites grabbed control, often with the help of a few hundred American mercenaries, and the country disintegrated into a patchwork of competing warlords. What's called the Philippines today is the island of Luzon and not much more.

The ride from the airport to the hotel—a slow crawl through an almost continuous traffic jam on what was labeled an "expressway," interrupted only by detours around numerous potholes—did nothing to convince me that much had improved in three generations. Beggars in rags cadged pennies from millionaires riding in chauffer-driven air-conditioned limousines. Here, a glitzy apartment building that wouldn't have been out of place in San Francisco stood opposite a pile of garbage blocking the sidewalk and spilling out onto the street; there, a wall topped by razor-sharp barbed wire prevented the wealthy occupants of a village from seeing the teeming slums across the street.

My guess was that Murdock was merely waiting for the heat to die down before moving on.

Andy had set up twenty-four-hour surveillance on Murdock. Two of our operatives had moved into one of the condos as a "couple," and had even become vaguely friendly with Murdock and Sophia Ackerman. Murdock's story, they were told, was that he and his "wife" were retired and were taking a slow, multi-year trip around the world. His next stop? "Well, when we've finished here we'll decide. Maybe flip a coin. Who can say?"

Andy introduced me to our local contact, José Guzman, known to everyone as "Boyet," who I'd called on to help Andy "meet" Sophia Ackerman off the plane.

"We've got one of our people in the condo security force, and three or four others discreetly patrolling the streets around the building."

"Is that enough?" I asked.

"You have to understand that in the Philippines most

everything is the opposite to what you're used to. For example, in America, you have law but no government; here we have government but no law."

"Maybe it's jetlag, but I don't get it."

"The system here works on grease. Bribery and corruption. Of course there are laws—the government makes new ones every day. But whether they're enforced, or how, depends on who pays what to whom. Going to court here is like going to an auction.

"What that means is everything and everyone is for sale. So you've got to know who you can really trust. *That's* why I've put so few people onto Murdock. Once somebody talks, inevitably it will get back to Murdock or the people *he's* paid off, and your bird will fly away."

"So what do we do? And there's no extradition agreement we can use."

"Andy and I have talked about that. Here's what I suggest we do. . . ."

It took another week of long days and sleepless nights, intense negotiations, not to mention considerable expense, before we were ready to spring the trap on Murdock. Speed, Boyet stressed, was the essence— a difficult proposition in a country where the local equivalent of the Mexican word *mañana* didn't have quite the same sense of urgency—to make sure Murdock didn't get wind of what we were up to.

As every day passed, more and more people were involved. We did our best to ensure secrecy by paying officials—up to and including the President—bribes we were pretty sure Murdock couldn't match; and one condition of the payments was that 80 percent of the money only got paid when Murdock was on a plane out of the country in handcuffs.

That didn't mean someone who got wind of things couldn't extract a healthy "reward" from Murdock for tipping him off. In my nightmares I was part of a gun battle between two groups of rent-a-cops on the streets of Manila.

On the appointed day, Tim—one of our two operatives who'd befriended Murdock—knocked on the door of his apartment. I, Andy, Boyet, the local chief of police and a couple of cops stood well back from the door. Other police, teamed up with Boyet's people, stood guard on the apartment's rear entrance, and took control of the lobby to guard the elevators as well as prevent the security guards from giving any warning.

"Hey, Tim, come in," said Murdock as he opened the door. Tim took a step forward and then pushed Murdock hard in the chest so he fell backward, landing in a heap on the floor. We rushed in, guns drawn.

"You bastards. And *you*," he screamed, pointing at Tim, "are a low-down, lying, shit-faced scum of the earth."

Two of the cops pulled him up and handcuffed his wrists behind his back. I heard a crash as Andy put his foot through one of the bedroom doors. In a moment a chastened Sophia Ackerman was led into the living room.

"You bitch," said Murdock, his face reddening with his fury. "*You* brought them here." Forgetting the handcuffs, he struggled to hit her. Realizing he couldn't, he spat in her face instead.

"Yes," said Andy, smiling, "she led me a merry chase.

Almost lost her a couple of times. And it looks like we got here just in time: she was packing for a trip."

"And I never saw you, damn your eyes," she said.

"Another hour, we'd have been outta here," said Murdock. "You bastards." I managed to pirouette out of the way as he spat again in my direction.

"Anyway," he said, pulling himself up and trying to look officious and innocent at the same time, "you have no right to be here. I've committed no crime. What's this all about?"

The chief of police pulled out a thick file of papers. Waving them in Murdock's direction he explained: "I have here an order of extradition, signed by the President of the Philippines, for the apprehension of Gerald Murdock and Sophia—"

"Gerald *who*?" said Murdock.

"You," I said. "The goatee and the nose job are certainly a good disguise. Even if you've changed your fingerprints all we have to do is pull off those contact lenses and a retina scan will be conclusive."

Murdock's shoulders slumped.

Sophia Ackerman turned to the chief of police: "You have a warrant for *my* arrest? On what grounds?"

"Embezzlement, false pretenses, defrauding an insurance company," he replied.

"I've not been convicted of any such thing," she said adamantly.

"True and not true. At the same time," I said.

A puzzled look crossed her face. "What bullshit!"

"This gentleman here," I said, indicating the chief of police, "has a presidential order to extradite you from the country. So you *must* have been convicted. Here, at least. By the time we land in San Francisco, All-Risks will have presented its case before an adjudicator. In your absence there's a chance the hearing will find, *prima facie,* against you. The best you can hope for is a new date for the hearing, since All-Risks won't have given the proper notice."

"Anyway," said Murdock, "what's this about extradition? The Philippines has no extradition treaty with America."

"It does now. Here," I said, pulling out a sheaf of papers, "is a treaty between All-Risks and the government of the Philippines, signed by the President. Something for you to read . . . on the plane."

"That can't be legal," said Murdock. "Don't you need an act of Congress or something? Presidential order ain't enough. I want to talk to my lawyer."

"That won't be possible," said the chief of police. Pulling out another sheet of paper which he offered to Murdock, grinning when he remembered the handcuffs, he continued: "This is an order for your immediate deportation. It seems that your visa, as well as Miss Ackerman's, has expired."

Murdock looked like he was about to explode. Then his body relaxed and he turned to me with a glint of admiration in his eyes. "You really pulled out all the stops, eh?"

"Well, Berkshire Re did."

"Oh, that I didn't know."

"You know, you'd have done better to stay at home," I told him. "Not in San Francisco, of course. Some other American city. With your money, your disguise and new fingerprints, just by avoiding retina scans we might never have found you. In a place where government is for sale, you can always be outbid."

"Maybe you're right," he said.

"Look on the bright side. Here, the penalty for murder is death. Back home, all you have to do is pay back all the money and you're a free man." The prospect didn't seem to be all that appealing to Murdock. I could sympathize: from wealth to poverty in matter of moments.

"And what about me?" asked Sophia Ackerman.

"Same thing. The presumption is you're an accessory to murder. That was your plan, right?" I said, looking from one to the other. "You were after Ackerman's insurance—the 110,115 gold ounces Sophia got for your murder of hubbie."

They stared at me blankly, neither agreeing nor disagreeing.

I looked at Sophia admiringly—an easy thing to do.

"You're a good actress," I said. "I saw the holo."

She spat at me, this time connecting.

"Time to go," said Andy, looking at his watch.

"Right," I agreed, wiping the spittle off my face. "Let's move—we all have a plane to catch."

The Colonizing of Tharle

by James P. Hogan

Records from the colony's founding years stated that the town of Ferrydock had grown from an early base established near the river mouth, where a motorized pontoon raft had provided the crossing to the peninsula. With its rocky prominences, dunes, and beaches, the peninsula—later named Strandside—was an attractive place for walks and swims or just lazing around to get away from the routine of the settlement for a while. Later, it acquired some stores, a bar, restaurant, and a small hotel to become one of the more popular recreation spots. Although Ferrydock was now a fair-size town, and a low, sleek bridge of concrete spans with a raisable center section—sitting on incongruously ornate steel piers reminiscent of nineteenth-century ideas of aesthetics—crossed the river, a ferry still ran alongside. Not everybody was in enough of a hurry to need the road, one of the locals had explained to Duggan and another official with the mission sent from Earth to reestablish relations with Tharle. And besides, the kids liked the water ride. Notions of cost effectiveness didn't seem to count for much here—and that fitted with the other bizarre notions of economics that had taken root here, which the theorists up in the orbiting mother ship *Barnet* had already decided were probably the major factor responsible for the planet's evident regression in many ways from the levels of technological and political capability possessed by the founders.

Duggan stood in the square at the heart of Ferrydock's central district—an open space really too irregular to justify its name geometrically, bordered by narrow, erratic streets and buildings of the peculiarly curved architectural style reveling in orange-brick walls and green- or blue-tiled roofs that brought back childhood memories of an illustrated edition of Oz. The Tharleans seemed to delight in turrets and towers too, which was also odd, since there was no history of militancy or defense needs to have inspired them. Simply another of their odd whims and fancies expressing itself, Duggan supposed.

It was apparently market day. The stalls around the square were heaped with assortments of unfamiliar fruits, vegetable-like offerings, and other plant forms that grew under the purple-tinted sky. There were refrigerated racks of strange fish, joints of meat, tanks of live fish, and cages containing furry and feathered animals of various kinds, whether intended for food or as pets, Duggan didn't know. And there were tables displaying tools and other hardware, ornaments, art works, kitchenware, haberdashery, household goods, and clothing—much the same as market places anywhere, anytime. Duggan watched a tall, weathered-looking man in a gray shirt and loose blue jacket examining a pair of ceramic sculptures in the form of elongated feminine heads with a suggestion of styled Oriental features.

"How much for these?" he asked the graying-haired lady in charge of the stall. She was sitting in a folding alloy-frame chair, a many-colored, open-weave blanket pulled around her shoulders. A shaggy, yellow-haired creature with a huge-eyed, owl-like face studied the man alertly from the top of an upturned box next to her.

"Ten draks," the woman replied.

The dialect had drifted to a degree that now sounded quaint; or was it that English as spoken on Earth had progressed? Schooling in Tharlean pronunciations, usage, and idioms had been required of all the delegates on the contact mission, and after a few days on the surface Duggan found he was experiencing few problems.

The man turned one of the sculptures over in his hands again and pursed his lips. "I'll give you fifteen."

The woman smiled in the kind of way that said it was a good try. "What do you think I am, destitute or dysfunctional or something? They're not worth that."

"Hey, come on, gimme a break and let me help you out a little. We've all got our pride."

"Eleven, then."

The man shook his head. "I can manage more than that. How about fourteen?"

They eventually settled on twelve. Duggan turned away, mystified, and shook his head. The two armed troopers that regulations required escort him when away from the surface lander at Base 1 beyond the far edge of the town looked back at him unhelpfully. "A strange way of playing poker," Duggan commented.

"They're all crazy," one of the troopers offered.

Then Duggan noticed the woman in a shirt of leafy design on white and bright red shorts, standing a few yards away in front of a mixed, chattering group of people but apparently not with them. Farther back, others among the crowd had stopped and were staring at Duggan and his escorts unabashedly. The woman was perhaps in her mid thirties if Earth standards were anything to judge by, with wiry, shoulder-length hair that varied between being auburn and orange depending how it caught the light, and the bronzed skin with a hint of metallic sheen that the blue-shifted light from Xylon-B evoked among Tharleans generally. Her body was slim and lithe, her face tapering to a pointy chin, with a straight nose, dimpled cheeks, and a mouth that was hovering on the edge of wanting to smile but at the same time hesitant, as if she were unsure how it might be taken. Instead, she let her eyes interrogate him silently. They were deep, brown, intelligent, and mirthful, the kind that could arouse immediate interest in possibilities and prospects—especially in a new and strange, yet-to-be-explored place, after an excruciatingly uneventful voyage dominated by routine and officiousness. Duggan's features softened. He let his mouth pucker in the way of one of two people unsure of their ground offering to meet halfway.

"I didn't mean to gape," the woman said. "But I haven't seen anyone from the Earth ship this close before. I was just curious."

"Oh, I wouldn't worry about it," Duggan answered. "I've seen plenty of people from Tharle. The only trouble is, I haven't managed to talk to too many of them."

"They're curious too, but trying to mind their own business. It's considered good manners. . . . Some of them are worried about what the soldiers are doing here, too."

"So what makes you different?"

She shrugged. "I just wanted to see for myself what you were like—try to talk to some of you. I hear what other people say, but I never know whether to believe it."

"What do they say?" Duggan asked.

The woman thought for a few seconds, her mouth twisting wryly in the way of someone searching for a safe answer. "They call you Pinkies," she said finally.

He stared at her, then laughed. The barrier of tension they had both been reacting to revealed itself as an illusion and came tumbling down. "Paul Duggan," he said.

"My name's Tawna."

"So . . . hi."

"Hi."

The feelings coming back at him were good. She was looking at him directly and openly with an expectant expression, fears allayed, eager to learn more. Duggan turned his head and lowered his tone to mouth at the escorts. "Why don't you guys get lost for a half hour? Take a walk around; get yourselves a coffee or something."

"Can't. Orders," one of the troopers replied woodenly.

Duggan sighed and turned back to Tawna. "I'm with what the mission calls its Office of Exorelations. That means we're the ones who are supposed to deal with whoever's in charge of things here. But we're not having much luck finding anyone. That's why I decided to come out and walk around the town. Nothing we got over the communications channels made any sense."

Tawna looked puzzled. "I can't see why that should be a problem. There are people in charge of things everywhere."

"How do you mean?"

"Well, it depends what you're looking for. In charge of what, specifically? The Waterfront Agency looks after the harbor installations and the docks. The Power Company produces power. The highway companies consolidated into the Road Services League because tolls got to be such a hassle. . . ."

Duggan waved a hand. "But above those—the works, all of it. Who runs the whole system?" Tawna seemed to want to be helpful, but she appeared honestly not to know what he meant. "The laws," he said. "Who makes the laws here?"

"Laws?" she repeated, as if hearing a new word in the language for the first time.

"What you can do, what you can't. How you're allowed to treat each other. Who tells you the rules?"

"Tells us? . . . Nobody. . . . Why would they?"

"Then where do they come from?"

Tawna showed a hand helplessly. "They don't come from anywhere. They're just . . . there. Who tells you rules for how to breathe air or how to grow older? Nobody needs to. You already know. You just do it."

Duggan glanced again at the two troopers. Trying to pursue the subject further in a place like this, and under these circumstances, would be impossible. But he felt that at last he'd made some rapport and found a line that could lead somewhere eventually—and conceivably in more senses than one. "So what do you do here?" he asked Tawna, abandoning the tack for the time being.

She seemed relieved. "Me? Oh, I'm a dance teacher most of the time—keeps me fit. And I'm also a musician and help organize shows. I've tried writing a couple of plays too, but they weren't very good. I probably let myself get paid too much for them."

It was the same illogic that Duggan had been hearing all over the place. He didn't want to go any further into it now, he decided, anymore than trying to find out who ran the system. "Is Ferrydock where you're from originally?" he asked instead.

They chatted for a while. She had grown up in a farming area on the far side of the mountains standing distantly in the purplish haze to the northeast, and moved here to be with friends. She was curious about

Earth and would maybe have kept them both there
for the rest of the day with her questions, but her
knowledge of its affairs was dated, reflecting the
politics and geography of the period around a century ago, before the colony world of Tharle had
become isolated.

"We need to talk some more," Duggan said when
he spotted the scout car from Base 1 coming to collect him. "Somewhere different from this—where it's
quieter, more private."

"I'd like that," Tawna said.

"How can I get in touch with you?"

She gave him the call codes for her personal phone,
which turned out to consist of the blue-jeweled ear
rings with silver mountings and matching pendant that
she was wearing. Duggan would never have guessed.
He gave her one of his official departmental calling
cards with contact details. Communications engineers
aboard the *Barnet* had already programmed the ship's
system to interface with the planetary net. Tawna waved
brightly after them as people parted to let him and his
two escorts through to the waiting car.

Duggan stared out at the town's busy sidewalks and
pedestrian precincts as they began the short drive back.
The last problem anyone had anticipated the mission
would come up against in reestablishing contact with
the colony's government when it got to Tharle was
finding a government. He looked down at the compak
that he was still holding in his hand, where he'd stored
Tawna's call codes. Electronics so advanced that he
hadn't even recognized it; technology to put satellites
aloft; sophisticated air travel available when the need

arose. And yet, at the same time, the deep-space-going capability that the founders brought had gone into decline; people spent much more time getting around than they needed to, sailing in ships or plain walking; and the supposedly fundamental laws of market trading somehow worked backwards.

Nothing made sense.

Nobody knew who the "Barnet" was or had been, whom the ship was named after. Typically, it would have been some long-forgotten bureaucrat from an extinct department. Duggan sometimes wondered if it might have been the one responsible for the blunder that had resulted in Tharle's disappearing from the records for almost a hundred years. Two rival sections of the Colonial Affairs Administration had each recorded that the other was responsible for handling Tharle, out at Xylon-B, and a hundred years was how long it had taken for the realization to dawn that nobody was. Contact was established, and the *Barnet* and its mission hastily despatched to reintroduce formal diplomatic relations. In the furious exchanges of messages and memoranda, accusations and denials, evasions of blame and attempts to direct it elsewhere that followed discovery of the fiasco, it apparently escaped everyone as significant that in all that time nobody on Tharle had chosen to draw Earth's attention to its omission.

Back aboard the orbiting *Barnet*, Pearson Brose, head of the mission's Office of Exorelations and Earth's designated ambassador-to-be if a government could be found that wanted one, was getting impatient for results. "Of *course* they have to exist," he fumed at the review meeting of his staff, including Duggan, gathered in the conference room of his unit's offices in the Planetary Department section of the Administrations deck. He had a florid face with long, wispy white hair that flailed like a stormy sea when he jerked his head about—which he did a lot at times like this. "They're probably paranoid and gone underground for reasons best know to themselves. Why? What reason have we given them to do that? Have we made threats? Are their cities quavering under weapons that we have deployed? I see no weapons. We've shown nothing but reasonableness and a desire to advance our common interests. So what have I missed? Where am I going wrong? Somebody tell me."

Everybody knew that Brose hadn't gone wrong anywhere. The melodramatic flourishes were his way of reminding the world of how much his responsibilities required him to endure and suffer. Zeebron Stell, with his hefty build, swarthy skin, short-cropped black hair and shaggy mustache, almost an inverse of Brose, brought them back on track. He was supposed to be Duggan's colleague and virtual opposite number, but they seemed to end up at odds over everything. "Well, I did get to talk with that scientific group up north. They're into a new line on catalyzed nuclear processes that will need a high-energy installation and big bucks."

Brose forgot his lamentations and became interested. "Ah yes, the research institute. So where does the funding come from. Did we find out?" He always said "we" if the prospective news was good. It was taken for granted that such a source would be some branch or other of government, the uncovering of which would hopefully lead to the rest.

"Not really," Stell answered. "That is, nothing that you'd be interested in. The bread comes from all kinds of places: a bunch of corporations, as you'd expect; an amazing number of individuals; even a school science club. But none of it was like what we were looking for." Brose looked at him sourly, as if asking why he had bothered bringing it up if that were the case. Stell went on, "But the way they were going about it says to me that they don't deal with anyone in the government anyway."

"How do you mean?" Brose asked.

Stell showed his hands and turned from side to side in an appeal to the others that he wasn't making this up. "When we asked them about procedures, they started telling us that their biggest problem is arguing grants *down* to *less* than the sources want to give them—as if that was obviously what anyone would do. They thought that accepting too much would make them look incompetent. Who ever heard of a government funding agency that would have problems dealing with people like that?" A baffled silence engulfed the room. Then Milford Grimes from Research Resources pronounced what was going through all their minds.

"That's insane."

Amelia Jonkin, another of the Exorelations staff, looked from one to another as if inviting any better ideas before voicing the only one she could come up with. "Maybe they're a second-rate outfit. It could be an indication of lack of self-esteem there, or that they have an inferior image of themselves." She didn't sound as if she really believed it.

"The stuff they were doing looked right-on to me," Stell said. "And Dransel Howess who was with us thought so too. Nuc-cat is his line, and he was big-time impressed."

Duggan shifted in his seat. He had been quiet for a long time. "I saw the same thing when I was down in Ferrydock," he told the room. "They've got a marketplace there in the town, and people haggle. Except they try to sell lower and buy higher. I tried getting some of them to explain it, but nobody could. They couldn't understand what was so strange that needed explaining."

"It just shows that they're all simpletons," somebody from the Planning Group said. "We can't let people like that get the better of us, surely." The tone was facetious.

"Perhaps we should look for the big houses," Amelia mused. "The real rulers in any society always live in the biggest houses."

And that seemed to exhaust the suggestions. Brose looked around for further comment. After a second or two of more silence, it came from the commander of the mission's military contingent, General Rhinde, who was sitting in and so far had maintained silence with visibly rising impatience.

"This nonsense has gone on long enough. You're not going to get anywhere creeping around like tourists frightened of giving offence, and asking polite questions." He glowered around, challenging anyone to disagree. Nobody dared. "The people you're talking about will be all office clerks, anyway, even if you find them. The true government of a country, planet, whatever, is whoever defends it. The way you find them is make them come to you. Just march in, say you're taking over, and wait to see who appears. If nobody does, then you know who the government is anyway. It's you."

Nobody was prepared to argue. But at the same time, it was clear to everyone except Rhinde that nothing that drastic was a candidate for the time being. Ever the able and resourceful organization man, Brose tabled the proposal for further consideration and appointed someone to form a subcommittee to look into it.

After the meeting adjourned, Duggan approached Brose privately in his office at the Executive Suites end of the Planetary Department. "I'd like approval to roam around freely down there, without escorts," he said. "There isn't any threat, and the presence of weapons inhibits the Tharleans. It's a barrier to further progress in getting through to them."

"You really think it's likely to make much difference?" Brose queried. His conviction seemed distinctly far short of total. "I mean, what progress at all is there to take further? Have *you*, for instance, met anyone who looks even remotely capable of being gotten through to?"

"I think so, maybe. Yes."

"Hm." Brose sniffed. "And what if we have to scrape you up out of an alley one morning, and it gets back that I waived regulations. How would I be supposed to explain it?"

"Well, we'd better come up with something before Rhinde gets his way and ends up starting a war," Duggan said. "Would you rather have to explain that?"

Duggan got his request approved—on signing a disclaimer that it was at his own instigation, and against the advice of his superior. "I'm doing it to give you a chance to rack up some points for promotion to subsection supervisor when we get back," Brose murmured confidentially as he signed the paper. "I think you'd be more suited to it, Paul." Duggan had little doubt that Brose was saying similar things to Stell too, who was also a candidate for the slot. Fostering a healthy competitive spirit between rivals was encouraged as part of the Department's management style. It was considered the astute way to develop human resources. They were what at one time had been called "people."

"I'll be coming back down tomorrow," Duggan told Tawna when he called her a half hour later. "No guards to get in the way this time, so we can have that talk. Tell me a good place to meet."

The bronzed, orangey-haired face on the screen looked genuinely pleased. "That's wonderful! Then you can tell me all about Earth." She must have caught a hint of a reaction in his face. "And talk about other things too, naturally. What did you want to do down here?"

Duggan frowned, realizing that he had been unprepared. He thought rapidly. "I want to find out who lives in the biggest houses," he told her.

They met and had breakfast in a cafe by the river, on a terrace at the rear, overlooking the water. It was a fair, sunny day, and there were a lot of small boats about—some sporty and powered, others curvy and delicate with strange-shaped sails, reminiscent in ways of Arab dhows. It was the same incongruous blend of ancient and new existing happily side-by-side that Duggan had been noticing everywhere. A large blimp passed overhead, heading south, maybe following the coast. Tawna explained that on days when the weather permitted, those who could afford it often preferred them to regular jets. By this time, Duggan was surprised to hear that for once the price of something should actually reflect how it was valued. It turned out that what Tawna meant was those who could afford the time.

As he listened, Duggan found himself being captivated by her openness. She played none of the mind games that he was accustomed to in this kind of situation, no jockeying for one-up points to decide who had a controlling advantage. And in a way that he realized was a new concept to him, her absence of deviousness absolved him from any need to reciprocate. He could actually be himself and say what he thought, without having to calculate implications and consequences. It felt liberating and refreshing. Yes, there had been a man that she'd lived with for a while when she moved to Ferrydock. His name had been Lukki. But in the end it hadn't worked out. No, there was no one in particular at present.

The people they were going to meet were called Jazeb and Maybel Wintey, and kept what Tawna described as a "huge" house in a foothill region of the mountains northeast of Ferrydock. She didn't know them personally but had known of them for a long time, and contacted them through an agent in town who provided their domestic staff. Hardly surprisingly, a mention that somebody from the Earth ship wanted to meet them was all it had taken. In her non-questioning, accepting way, Tawna hadn't asked Duggan why he wanted to know who lived in the big houses. When Duggan inquired casually what Wintey did, Tawna replied in an uncharacteristically vague kind of way, that he "collected things." It didn't sound much like what Duggan had been hoping for. But he could hardly change his mind now.

Back outside the front of the cafe, Tawna stopped to run her eye over the assortment of vehicles in the parking area. Tharlean ground autos were generally simpler and less ostentatious than Terran designs, though with the same proclivity for curviness that was evident in the architecture and the boats; a couple looked almost like Aladdin slippers on wheels. She led the way across to a pale blue, middle-of-the-range model, unpretentious but comfortably roomy for two. As they got in, Duggan commented that he'd thought she wasn't sure which car was hers. It wasn't hers, he discovered, but belonged to a common pool that anyone could use, rather like a public comlink booth back home. She started it by inserting a plastic tag that seemed to combine the functions of pay card and driver's license. People who needed to owned their own, but most didn't bother, Tawna said—adding that it was the kind of thing Jazeb Wintey would do. She seemed to find it humorous. Duggan wasn't sure why.

They drove out of the town to an airport that

Duggan knew of from the *Barnet*'s reconnaissance views, where large commercial planes came and went from all over, and parked outside a building serving an area to one side used by smaller craft. Tawna just took her card from the slot in the car's dash panel and walked away. Inside the building, they rented a personal six-seat flymobile that she had reserved, and soon, with the vehicle practically flying itself, were skimming low along the river valley, toward the mountains outlined in the distant purplish haze.

Tawna hadn't been exaggerating when she described the Wintey house as "huge." It would have qualified as a mansion by Terran standards, with a healthy profusion of Tharlean towers and turrets, and stood amid an estate of outbuildings and grounds enclosed by high walls and wire fences. The flymo landed on a gravel courtyard in front of the house and was met by a retinue of household staff who conducted Duggan and Tawna to the portico-framed entrance. Duggan noticed as they crossed the court that the main gate and the fence were protected by armed guards.

His first impression as they threaded their way through the hall inside between barricades of furniture was of being in a cross between a museum and a home goods warehouse. Enormous, glass-fronted cabinets standing from floor to ceiling, jammed with porcelains, chinaware, glassware, and figurines, lined the walls, while the ceiling was all but invisible behind rows of hanging buckets, pots, pans, basins, metalware, and jugs. The room beyond had tiers of shelves carrying all manner of ornaments, decorated boxes, and bric-a-brac, and furnishings wedged, sometimes inaccessibly, between pedestals laden with pottery and vases, ponderous columns and other carvings, and padlocked cubicles of indeterminate nature. Jazeb Wintey received them in an inner redoubt at the center of more wooden and upholstered fortifications overlooked by walls tiled with pictures and prints. He was small and gnomish, with a ruddy bald head, cantankerous expression, and a fringe of whiskers girding his chin like a sunflower. His dress of frock coat and gaitered britches was impossibly stuffy and formal for a Tharlean, and would have been eccentrically antiquated even on Earth. He shook Tawna's hand stiffly and rapidly as if it were a pump handle and repeated the process with Duggan, the sternness of his features remaining unchanged.

"From Earth! About time! It took you long enough! Maybe we'll see some sense and sanity restored to this place then, before much longer."

So much for social pleasantries. If plunging straight in was the way here, Duggan would follow suit. "Why? What's wrong with things here?" he asked.

Wintey looked at him as if he might have just woken up after a thousand-year sleep. "Pah! No ethics, no standards. Things like that all got lost after the colonists stopped building space-goers. Everything's degenerated. Why do you think we have to live walled up in a fortress like this? Envy and malice all around. It's because I'm the only one around here who's got a notion of business." He cast an arm about to indicate the surroundings. For the first time, a hint of a satisfied smile crossed the berrylike countenance. "See what I mean?" He tapped his temple meaningfully.

"Takes acumen to accumulate that kind of worth, young fella. Brains and acumen. People here wouldn't even know what that means."

As Wintey stumped his way ahead of them, between display cases filled with silverware, gold plate, and jewelry, Tawna caught Duggan's eye and sent him an apologetic shrug that seemed to say, well, it was what he'd wanted.

"They don't like us, you know," Wintey went on, as if Tawna were not present. "Try to conspire to drag me down. Outside, among themselves, they do each other favors. But no staff willing to work for reasonable pay ever get sent here. They send me all the beggars and ne'er-do-wells. . . . Thieves, too, if they had half the chance, I'd be bound. Can't even find reliable guards."

They met Maybel Wintey in a sitting area off the dining room draped with silks, cushions, and rugs like movie depictions of a sultan's bridal chamber. One corner constituted a bar, stocked high with racks and shelves of bottles that no longer came as a surprise. Jazeb introduced his wife perfunctorily. She was withered and austere, but glittering with jewels from fingers and chest to a filigreed tiara, worn with a pale green gown suggesting, with a mild touch of absurdity, the robe of a classical goddess.

"What do they want?" she asked frostily, when Jazeb let up on his harangue long enough for a steward to take orders for drinks. "Everyone who comes here wants something."

"Mr. Duggan is from Earth," Jazeb reminded her. "Perhaps we'll see things being put back in order now."

"Well, that's something. At least we won't have to be buying people off to get some peace."

Lunch was a lavish affair, naturally, over which Jazeb continued in much the same vein. Finding peers to develop a satisfying social life with wasn't easy. Tharleans who had something to show for themselves, the ones you'd think would qualify, inevitably proved to be fools when it came to trade, and annoyed him—but he wasn't going to turn them down if they insisted on being gypped. The ones who knew how to bargain were from the bottom of the pile, and fraternizing with them would be out of the question too, of course—which was a shame because if they'd only learn to do something with what they had, Jazeb admitted, he could have had some time for them. It was all beyond him. He only hoped that the administration Earth was presumably going to set up would get things straightened out soon.

Afterward, they toured an entertainments room that reminded Duggan of the command deck aboard the *Barnet*, a gymnasium that could have kept a regiment of space assault troops in good shape, a games room, and a workshop equipped with every form of gadget, widget, and power tool imaginable, none of which showed much sign of having been used. And sure enough, as Tawna had guessed jokingly, there was a shed at the rear housing a collection of polished and gleaming ground autos, along with several flyers. Throughout it all, the domestic staff remained easygoing and cheerful, despite Jazeb and Maybel's constant grumbles and criticisms. Duggan found himself harboring the uneasy suspicion of watching inmates of an asylum being humored. When he and Tawna finally left, the thought of getting back among the people of Ferrydock seemed like a breath of sanity and fresh air.

"I warned you it would be a bit strange, but it was what you asked for," Tawna said as they flew back above the valley's deepening shadows. She waited a few seconds, then looked across the cabin when Duggan didn't answer. "What's up?"

Duggan returned from his realm of distant brooding. "Those two back there. It was just going through my mind . . . Back where I come from, that would be close to most people's ideal. That's how they want to be."

Tawna paused long enough to be polite. "Yes," she said hesitantly. "I thought it might be something like that."

Duggan could have added that now, perhaps, he thought he knew why the Tharleans had looked askance at the guards who had accompanied him around Ferrydock. He decided he didn't want to go into it.

Zeebron Stell had come down from the mother ship when Duggan got back to Base 1 late that evening. They had coffee in the mess room at the back of the gate guard hut, and then Stell suggested a walk in the night air around the perimeter fence. He waited until they were out of earshot of anybody, then switched from casual chat to a lowered, conspiratorial tone.

"Dug, these people are clueless here. They're set up to be taken. Ask 'em for anything you want; they hand over. Tell 'em what you want done; they do it.

If you were ever looking for the place to make out like you never imagined, man, this has to be it.

Duggan paused to look out through the wire at the colored lights over Ferrydock's center. The blimp—or another—was making the return trip, lit up like a Christmas tree gliding silently through the night. "I'm not sure I know what you mean," he said.

Stell edged a pace closer. "Think about it. . . ." he breathed. "Wealth and power: that's what it's all about, eh? What else do we bust our asses year in, year out for, thinking we're gonna get a bigger share of—and put up with jerks like Brose? Well, here you're not talking about waiting years and then maybe watching some operator steal it all from under you anyway. It's already made, right now. All you gotta do is have the balls to take it."

"Take what? How?" Duggan asked guardedly.

"All of it."

"Zeeb, what, exactly, are you proposing?"

"This is were we stay and get rich; get a chance to *be* somebodies."

"You mean jump ship? Stay behind when the mission leaves. Is that it?"

"Why not, Dug? I'm starting to believe what we've been seeing here—or not seeing. There's nobody to stop you." Stell gestured to indicate both of them. "You and me—" The amused look on Duggan's face checked him. "Hey, all that was another time and place, okay? We can leave it behind. There's a planet full of enough of everything to keep both of us happy."

"Well, that's an abrupt change of tune for you, Zeeb,"

Duggan said. "I thought you were going for the sub-supervisor slot when we get back. Brose seems to think so. He'll be disappointed. Who will he have to play carrot and stick games with now and boost himself up the ladder?"

Stell snorted. "Oh, don't tell me you're not as tired of all that crap as I am. . . . Look, I'll let you in on a secret. I've rented a place in town to use as a kind of startup base, and already in one afternoon I've got enough stuff in there to fit out a penthouse. I'm telling you it's a steal, man. But you need someone of your own kind too, know what I mean? We could live like a couple of kings. What do you say, huh?"

"I'm not sure. Have you really figured it through as to how things are here?"

"What's there to figure, Dug? I'm telling you, you don't hit on a deal like this more than once in a lifetime." Stell's eyes were insistent in the light from the town, his expression intense. He clearly wasn't prepared to accept no as an answer.

"Okay, I'll think about it," Duggan promised.

Several days passed by, during which more expeditions returned unsuccessful from different parts of Tharle. A flurry of impatient demands for reports on progress, and replies that the situation was more complicated than expected sizzled back and forth between the *Barnet*'s higher echelons and the supervisory directorate on Earth. Duggan filed a report on his visit to the Winteys, which was absorbed into Pearson Brose's growing collection without significant reaction or comment. Duggan took this to mean that those who knew best were too preoccupied with affairs more befitting of their rank and calling to be distracted by lower-echelon menials and their trivia. Being a conscientious department man, he did his best to help by staying out of their way and making the most of the opportunity that Brose's dispensation had opened up for him to follow up informally on possible local leads. Since Tawna had already shown herself to be a willing and capable guide, this coincidentally meant their spending more time with each other.

Through the early part of the evening, Duggan had watched a rehearsal for one of Tawna's shows. The Tharleans handled their personal affairs in the same way as their financial ones, he noticed: when asked for help, they gave more; when offered a favor, they settled for less. Afterward, he and Tawna joined a group from the cast and supporting staff for a dinner of salad and a taco-like dish of bread, meats, and spicy fillings at a cellar bar along the street. Then the company gradually broke up in ones and twos. After staying to finish a bottle of one of the locality's wines—vaguely Rhônish, but with the ubiquitous Tharlean purple touch—Duggan and Tawna found themselves leaning on a parapet of the downtown riverbank among the nighttime strollers, staring out across the water toward the distant lights of the Strandside bridge. "I can't imagine it," Tawna said. "You mean they just try to keep on accumulating more and more, like the Winteys?" She searched for an analogy. "That would be like eating all day. Obviously, you need to have enough to keep you going. But once that's satisfied, other things in life become more important. You make it sound as if how much people own is the only measure of what they're worth. . . . Why, that would be as ridiculous as everybody being judged solely by weight and competing to be the heaviest!"

Financial obesity, Duggan thought to himself. Not a bad way to put it. It was hardly the first time in history for such an observation to be made; but the trouble with giving handouts to the ones inevitably left behind in the race had always been that it produced more and more free riders who eventually brought down the system. Somehow the Tharleans seemed to have solved the problem of restraining excess without perpetrating injustices or undermining initiative. How, then, did it work with power?

"So who makes judgments and decisions?" he asked. "You have to have disputes, the same as anyone else. Who has the final say when nobody involved can agree?"

"It's true. Somebody has to do it." Tawna made it sound like cleaning the sewers or defusing bombs. "They have a kind of lottery, and the losers get appointed. It's only for a year—and people are sympathetic, so they try to be supportive."

"You mean it's a lousy job. Nobody wants it?"

"Well, of course. Why would anyone . . ." Tawna stopped as she registered the astonishment in Duggan's voice. "You mean that on Earth . . ."

He nodded. "Having power over people is considered a big thing. They fight each other for it. Okay, now go ahead and tell me: you thought maybe it would be something like that."

Then he realized that she was giving him a long, contemplative look that held little real interest in such things just at the moment. He forgot about the subject and held her eye quizzically. "You're different from Lukki," she said. "He was like a child, never questioning anything. You do. You see things, and you think about them. It makes you . . . interesting." She slid closer along the rail of the parapet. Her fingertip traced over his arm. Duggan turned toward her. Her hair and skin shone softly golden in the light from the embankment lamps . . .

Beep . . . Beep . . . Beep . . . Beep . . .

Duggan cursed under his breath and tugged the compak from his shirt pocket. The caller was Brose's assistant aloft in the *Barnet*. All ship's personnel were recalled to base immediately. General Rhinde had finally gotten his way and announced plans to take over Ferrydock as a military demonstration. The occupation force had begun mobilizing aboard the *Barnet* and would descend from orbit at dawn.

Four flights of assault shuttles made synchronized landings at key points and deployed with alacrity to seize and secure the prime means of access and communications. Two task forces sealed the main highway and rail links north and south, another commandeered the airport, while the last took the Strandside bridge and sent a column into Ferrydock to occupy the broadcasting stations and news bureaus. Meanwhile, special details sped through the town to install military administrators and technicians in the offices responsible for transportation, power generation and distribution, and communications. By midday the operation was completed as per the timetable. At noon precisely, General Rhinde went on the air to inform the inhabitants of Ferrydock that their town was now under Terran military jurisdiction and subject to the laws of its governing council. Communications and public services were under control of a colonial administration reporting to an appointed governor, and regulations concerning the conduct of business and finance would be announced shortly.

The townspeople seemed to think it was a great idea. An enthusiastic crowd in the central square greeted the news, relayed through their personal phones or from loudspeakers set up for the occasion, and by early afternoon representatives from the sanitation, harbor facilities, and water supply services were appearing at the governor's downtown headquarters offering their organizations for takeover too. Meanwhile, the management at places the Terrans had declared themselves to be in control of were resigning or taking a holiday to disappear to the beaches at Strandside, visit with grandchildren, or spend time on their hobbies. By next morning, the town was in chaos. Half the communications were down, the airport was barely functioning, and services languished as employees took breaks to line up enthusiastically in hundreds to be issued newly introduced permits and licenses. In the end, Rhinde's officers were forced to send out squads to track down essential professionals and bring them back at gunpoint to carry out tasks which until yesterday they had performed readily and willingly. That was when Duggan began getting his first strong intuition that this wasn't going to work out in the way that had been envisaged.

When all-out war failed to materialize, the restrictions confining non-occupation personnel to base were eased. Duggan was standing on a street corner with Tawna, watching two troopers shouldering assault rifles and clad in riot gear, posted to protect the Municipal Services Building from a gaggle of curious onlookers, when Zeebron Stell called from the office suite he'd rented as a trading base. He sounded agitated.

"Dug, where are you?"

"A few blocks away from you on Johannes Street. You know, Zeeb, I think Gilbert and Sullivan could have done a lot with this."

"Is Tawna with you?"

"Yes, she is. What's up?"

"I've got problems. People here don't seem to understand that I'm running a business, not a thrift store. Can you get over? Maybe she'd be able to do a better job of getting the message across."

"It's Zeeb, from his emporium," Duggan murmured to Tawna. "He's having some kind of trouble with the locals. Wants us over there to see if you can maybe talk to them. Is that okay with you?"

"Sure."

"We're on our way, Zeeb."

A miscellany of vehicles was parked outside the building in which Stell had his premises, including a beat-up truck. Inside, they found him remonstrating with a dowdily dressed woman who seemed interested in some toilet preparations that he had amassed a stack of in one of the rooms. Elsewhere, a couple with two small children were examining a shelf of electronics appliances, while a small, bespectacled, bearded man, wearing a tweed jacket with deerstalker-like hat and waving a list of some kind, hopped about, trying to get Stell's attention. "*No!* You're outta your mind," Stell told the woman. "How is that supposed to be doing me a favor? It's not even what I paid." Then, to the man, "Look, I told you I'm not interested. I don't even know who any of those people are. How in hell do you figure you're helping *me*?" Another man appeared in a doorway at the rear, smiling and holding an elaborate wrist unit of some kind that had a miniature screen. Stell groaned, then caught sight of Duggan and Tawna and steered them gratefully back into the entrance hallway.

"There's some kind of victimization conspiracy," he told them. "With each other, they're real generous. I know. I watched 'em. But when they come here, they try and rip me off with pennies and buttons. It's almost like they think I *owe* them. And Sherlock Holmes's brother back there keeps pestering me with every hard-luck story in town. One guy's house got flattened in a mudslide. Somebody else's baby needs surgery. I even had a lady in earlier, asking if I wanted to put something into an education fund. What's going on?"

Tawna nodded. "Of course. These are people who really do *need* help . . ."

"But they're talking about helping *me!*" Stell protested.

"Well, yes . . . that too." Tawna obviously still couldn't see anything strange.

"How do they figure that?" Stell demanded.

"Well . . ." Tawna hesitated in the way of somebody reluctant to spell out what should have been clear. "To enjoy pride and self-esteem, the way everyone wants to," she said. "The more wealth and material things you acquire, the more you can make things easier for those going through hard times. Once you're reasonably comfortable yourself, it starts to mean more, right?" She glanced at Duggan. "It's like what we were saying the other day about eating all day. Beyond a certain point, any more doesn't make sense."

Stell's eyes bulged. "You mean they'll hassle me like this forever here?"

"Oh, no. Only until you learn to judge for yourself what share to put back in, like everyone else. Since you don't know how it works yet, they're probably just trying to help. It might take a little time."

"Well, suppose I don't want them telling me. What if I put my own guards on the place and keep 'em away?"

"That would be up to you, of course. . . . But why would anyone want to?" She looked at Duggan again and caught the resigned expression on his face. "Okay, don't tell me, Paul. Back home they're all like that. Yes?"

General Rhinde's measures weren't having the intended effect. In a closed-door meeting of the political and military chiefs aboard the *Barnet*, it was agreed that the citizens of Ferrydock were undergoing too little violation of their freedoms and rights to provoke whoever was supposed to defend them into coming out and doing so. Accordingly, since there was no set precedent at Tharle to say how far these things should be taken, the governor was instructed to issue a declaration stating that to facilitate improved control and efficiency, the Terran administration now owned everything in the name of everybody and was taking charge of manufacture, distribution, employment, and other services directly.

But the populace seemed happy to let them take it. A mood of festivity spread as virtually the whole of Ferrydock shut up stores and offices and took to the boulevards or sat back in the sun to await decisions and directions. Very soon, surface landers were shuttling frantically between the *Barnet* and Base 1, bringing extra details of planners and controllers to relieve the harried supervisory offices, now working around the clock. Meanwhile, ostensibly to bolster the security of all by setting up a centrally managed disaster relief agency—in reality, to get faster results through imposed austerity—huge stocks of food, fuel, clothing, materials, and other supplies were impounded and locked up in a large warehouse near the airport requisitioned for the purpose and officially renamed the "Federal Emergency Relief Repository." (Use of the word "federal" was a bit premature since as of yet there were no political entities other than Ferrydock to federate with it, but the planners were already shaping up grand schemes and visions of the future.) The repository was duly furnished with a ten-foot wire fence, traffic barrier and checkpoint at the gate, and a billet of armed guards.

However, the harassed Terran administrators were

like innocents in a Casbah bazaar before the demands of Tharleans taking them at their word that they were now responsible for everything, and in a short space of time just about everything of utility or value had vanished from the stores and the streets. By the terms under which the Repository had been established, the circumstances qualified as a disaster deserving of relief, and the officer in charge dutifully commenced handing back to the town, at enormous cost in overhead and added effort, the goods that had been confiscated at comparable cost in the first place. Eager to help Terran officialdom find satisfaction and self-esteem by the terms of their own morality, the Tharleans didn't take long to exhaust the stocks completely. Since there was nothing in the regulations that said otherwise, the guards continued, befuddled but doggedly, patrolling outside to protect the contents of the empty warehouse. The only threatening incident they had to deal with, however, was when a small procession of trucks from some outlying farms arrived full of vegetables and other produce that the growers didn't know what else to do with—only to be turned away again because there were no orders for dealing with anyone trying to bring things *in*.

By this time, the political opponents of the mission's incumbent regime, seeing ammunition here to unseat their rivals, formed a dissident faction to fire off a joint protest to Earth, giving all the facts and details. A directive from Colonial Affairs Administration terminating the *Barnet*'s mission and recalling the ship forthwith arrived within forty-eight hours.

❖   ❖   ❖

Base 1 was an abandoned shell, unsightly with the litter left by departing military anywhere. Children in makeshift helmets and carrying roughly fashioned imitation rifles marched each other to stations at the main gate guard posts. Duggan stood with his arm around Tawna's waist among a crowd watching the last shuttle out climb at the top of a pillar of light through scattered, purple-edged clouds. If the figure he'd heard was correct, he was one of forty-six who would have been unaccounted for when the muster lists were checked, and whose compaks hadn't answered calls or returned a location fix.

"No reservations or second thoughts, Dug?" she asked him. "No last-minute changes about everything, like Zeeb? I hope not. It would be a bit late now." Stell hadn't been among them at the end, after all. Driven to distraction under the pressures of trying to give things away, he had turned a complete about-face and stormed back up to the ship, berating anyone who would listen that he couldn't get back to Earth fast enough.

Duggan shook his head. "Not me." He gave her a squeeze, savoring the touch of her body through the light dress she was wearing. "My future's cut out right here. Everything I want."

"So Zeeb will probably get that promotion you told me about. I hope he'll be pleased."

"Oh, I'm sure he'll fit right back in," Duggan said. Brose had as good as come out and said that he favored Duggan for the subsection supervisor position and would back him. Duggan had seen it as a pretty transparent ploy to recruit support in the political maelstrom that Brose knew they'd be heading back to, and had no doubt that Brose had told Zeeb the same thing, and for the same reason. It felt like a reprieve from a life sentence to know he was out of all that. "In any case," Duggan added, "I wouldn't have gotten the job. The screening application that Brose made me put through was turned down." Brose had been as stunned as Duggan was pleased when the assessment back from Earth read: *Doesn't display the competitiveness and aggressiveness that success in this appointment would require.* It meant that Duggan had done something right.

"I'm surprised," Tawna said, sounding defensive on his behalf. "I'd have thought that even if you decided . . ." She caught the amused twist of his mouth. "Dug, what happened? What did you do?"

"I filled it in the Tharlean way," he told her.

"What way's that?"

"*I* have to tell *you*?" Duggan frowned in mock reproach. "I said I didn't need as much pay as they were offering, and I told them I could do more than they were stipulating. I guess they couldn't hack it." He shrugged. "But Zeeb will do okay. He, Brose, and the System are made for each other."

Tawna pulled close and nuzzled the side of her face against his shoulder. "And you'll do just fine here too," she promised.

For that was the simple principle that underlay the entire Tharlean worldview and way of life: *Give a little more; take a little less.* At least, with those who reciprocated. Anyone who didn't play by the rules wasn't treated by the rules. That was how they curbed excess.

But how did a Tharlean *know* when enough was enough? By being a part of the culture they had evolved and absorbing its ways and its values from the time they first learned to look at the world, walk around in it, listen and talk.

Every one of them.

That was why nobody from Earth had had any success finding lawmakers—at least, if what they were looking for was a few making rules to be forcibly imposed on the many. The government had been there all along, everywhere, staring them in the face. For on Tharle, *all* made the law, and all enforced it. Every one of them, therefore, was government.

Now Duggan would learn to become a member of a planetary government too. And that sounded a much better promotion to him than anything the Colonial Affairs Administration was likely to come up with, even if he were to carry on fighting and clawing his way up the ladder for the next hundred years.

About the Authors

Dr. Lloyd Biggle, Jr., Ph.D., (1923–2002) was a musician, author, and internationally known oral historian. He began writing professionally in 1955, and became a full-time writer with the publication of his novel, *All the Colors of Darkness*, in 1963, a profession that he followed until his death. Both Dr. Biggle's science fiction and mystery stories have received international acclaim. He was celebrated in science fiction circles as the author who introduced aesthetics into a literature known for its scientific and technological complications. He published two dozen books as well as magazine stories and articles beyond count. His most recent novel was *The Chronicide Mission*. He was writing almost to the moment of his death. "I can write them faster than the magazines can publish them," he once said, with the result that even though his writing has been stilled, his publications will continue until his backlog of stories is exhausted.

Robert J. Sawyer won the Nebula Award for best novel of 1995 for *The Terminal Experiment*; he's also been nominated six times for the Hugo Award. He has twice won Japan's top SF award, the Seiun, and twice won Spain's top SF award, the Premio UPC de Ciencia Ficción. His twelfth novel, *Calculating God*, hit number one on the bestsellers' list published by *Locus: The Newspaper of the Science Fiction Field*, and was also a top-ten national mainstream bestseller in Sawyer's native Canada. His latest novel, *Hominids*, a June 2002 hardcover, was the third of Sawyer's novels to be serialized in *Analog*, the world's number-one best-selling SF magazine. Visit Rob's website at sfwriter.com.

Mike Resnick worked anonymously from 1964 through 1976, selling more than 200 novels, 300 short stories and 2,000 articles, almost all of them under pseudonyms. After a more than ten-year hiatus to pursue a career in dog breeding and exhibiting, he returned to fiction writing. His first novel in this "second career" was *The Soul Eater*. His breakthrough novel was the international bestseller *Santiago*, published by Tor in 1986. Tor has since published eleven more of Mike's novels and the collection *Will the Last Person to Leave the Planet Please Shut Off the Sun?* Mike's most recent novel is *The Return of Santiago* for Tor Books. His work has garnered fans around the world, and has been translated into twenty-two languages. Since 1989, Mike has won four Hugo Awards, a Nebula Award, a Seiun-sho, a Prix Tour Eiffel (French), two Prix Ozones (French), 10 Homer Awards, an Alexander Award, a Golden Pagoda Award, a Hayakawa SF Award (Japanese), a Locus Award, an Ignotus Award (Spanish), a Futura Award (Croatian), an El Melocoton Mechanico (Spanish), two Sfinks Awards (Polish), and a Fantastyka Award (Polish). In 1993 he was awarded the Skylark Award for Lifetime Achievement in Science Fiction.

Tobias S. Buckell is a Caribbean born speculative fiction writer who now lives (through many odd twists of fate and strangely enough to him) in Ohio with his wife Emily. He has published in various magazines and anthologies. He is a Clarion graduate, Writers of the Future winner, and Campbell Award for Best New SF Writer Finalist. His work has received Honorable Mentions in the Year's Best Fantasy and Horror. His first novel, Crystal Rain, will be out from Tor Books in July of 2005. You can visit www.TobiasBuckell.com for more information.

Brad Linaweaver has worked frequently in the alternate history subgenre, producing stories such as "Destination: Indies," an alternate telling of Christopher Columbus's journey across the Atlantic, and "Unmerited Favor" which takes a more militant approach to the story of Jesus Christ's life. He is also the author of the books Moon of Ice, Clownface, The Land Beyond Summer, and Sliders: The Novel; and was a co-editor of Free Space, a collection of original libertarian SF short stories. Winner of the Prometheus Award in 1989, he lives and works in Los Angeles, California.

Michael A. Stackpole is the author of eight *New York Times* bestselling *Star Wars* novels. He's the author of thirty-seven novels, including *Fortress Draconis*, the second novel in the *DragonCrown War Cycle* of fantasy novels. "According to Their Need" is the fifth story set in his *Purgatory Station* universe.

New Zealand has held a special place in **Jane Lindskold**'s heart since she visited there some years ago. The opportunity to celebrate that lush green land along with its interesting and varied people gave her the setting of this story. Currently, Lindskold resides in New Mexico, a place unlike New Zealand in every way except in its variety. She is the author of a dozen or so novels, including The Firekeeper's saga, beginning with *Through Wolf's Eyes* and *The Buried Pyramid*, along with fifty-some short stories. She is at work on another novel.

Jack Williamson has been writing science fiction since 1928, with more than fifty novels published. The most recent is *Terraforming Earth*. One section of it, "The Ultimate Earth," received the 2000 Hugo Award as the best novella. He lives in New Mexico, where he arrived with his parents and siblings in a covered wagon when he was seven years old. He is still writing, as well as teaching occasional courses at Eastern New Mexico University, his hometown school. His new novel, *The Stonehenge Gate*, will be published in the spring of 2005.

Mark Tier is an Australian who lives in Hong Kong partly because, as he puts it, "paying taxes is against my religion." A long-time SF fan and hard-core libertarian, he was a co-founder of the Australian equivalent of the Libertarian Party. He published and edited the investment newsletter *World Money Analyst* from 1974 to 1991.

James P. Hogan began writing science fiction as a hobby in the mid 1970s, and his works have been well received within the professional scientific community as well as among regular science fiction readers. In 1979 he left DEC to become a full-time writer, and in 1988 moved to the Republic of Ireland. Currently he maintains a residence in Pensacola, Florida, and spends part of each year in the United States. To date, he has published twenty-one novels, including the libertarian classic *Voyage From Yesteryear*, a nonfiction work on artificial intelligence, and two mixed collections of short fiction, nonfiction, and biographical anecdotes entitled *Minds, Machines & Evolution* and *Rockets, Redheads & Revolution*. A new nonfiction work, *Kicking the Sacred Cow*, will be released by Baen Books in June 2004. He has also published some articles and short fiction. Further details of Hogan and his work are available from his web site at www.jamesphogan.com.

MORE...
ERIC FLINT

Got questions? We've got answers at

BAEN'S BAR!

Here's what some of our members have to say:

"Ever wanted to get involved in a newsgroup but were frightened off by rude know-it-alls? Stop by Baen's Bar. Our know-it-alls are the friendly, helpful type—and some write the hottest SF around."
            —**Melody L** *melodyl@ccnmail.com*

"Baen's Bar . . . where you just might find people who understand what you are talking about!"
            —**Tom Perry** *perry@airswitch.net*

"Lots of gentle teasing and numerous puns, mixed with various recipes for food and fun."
            —**Ginger Tansey** *makautz@prodigy.net*

"Join the fun at Baen's Bar, where you can discuss the latest in books, Treecat Sign Language, ramifications of cloning, how military uniforms have changed, help an author do research, fuss about differences between American and European measurements—and top it off with being able to talk to the people who write and publish what you love."
            —**Sun Shadow** *sun2shadow@hotmail.com*

"Thanks for a lovely first year at the Bar, where the only thing that's been intoxicating is conversation."
            —**Al Jorgensen** *awjorgen@wolf.co.net*

Join BAEN'S BAR at
WWW.BAEN.COM
"Bring your brain!"